PRAISE FOR THE N

Over 2 Million ̲ ̲ ̲ ̲ pies Sold.
Over 80,000 Five Star Reviews.

"Soon to be a critically acclaimed masterpiece."

AMAZON REVIEW

"This series has replaced Vince Flynn's Mitch Rapp as my favorite read."

AMAZON REVIEW

"No remorse. No guilt. No inner conflict. The perfect assassin."

AMAZON REVIEW

"I would highly recommend it to everyone that likes Lee Child, Brad Thor, David Baldacci, etc."

AMAZON REVIEW

"Camelot is going to rank up there with Dirk Pitt and Jack Reacher."

AMAZON REVIEW

NOAH WOLF THRILLERS
Code Name Camelot (Book 1)
Lone Wolf (Book 2)
In Sheep's Clothing (Book 3)
Hit for Hire (Book 4)
The Wolf's Bite (Book 5)
Black Sheep (Book 6)
Balance of Power (Book 7)
Time to Hunt (Book 8)
Red Square (Book 9)
Highest Order (Book 10)
Edge of Anarchy (Book 11)
Unknown Evil (Book 12)
Black Harvest (Book 13)
World Order (Book 14)
Caged Animal (Book 15)
Deep Allegiance (Book 16)
Pack Leader (Book 17)
High Treason (Book 18)
A Wolf Among Men (Book 19)

SHADOWS
OF
ALLEGIANCE

ISBN-13: 978-1-63696-191-0

ISBN-10: 1-63696-191-6

Cover design by: Damonza

Printed in the United States of America

www.righthouse.com

www.instagram.com/righthousebooks

www.facebook.com/righthousebooks

twitter.com/righthousebooks

USA TODAY BESTSELLING AUTHOR

DAVID ARCHER

& VINCE VOGEL

SHADOWS OF ALLEGIANCE

A
NOAH WOLF
THRILLER

RIGHTHOUSE

PROLOGUE

THE PRIVATE JET GLIDED SMOOTHLY OVER THE Atlantic, its cabin filled with a deceptive calm. Noah Wolf, Marco, Renée, Jenny, and several other team members were seated in plush chairs, their attention riveted on the man in the middle, Dr. Morozov. The Russian scientist's revelation, given just seconds ago, had cast a heavy cloud over the team, leaving them grappling with its dreadful implications.

Noah, his sharp eyes reflecting the turmoil inside, broke the silence. "The one at the facility. Is it the only one?" he asked, his voice steady but loaded with urgency.

Dr. Morozov, a trace of fear flickering in his eyes, opened his mouth to respond. But before a word could escape him, the unthinkable happened.

With no warning, the cabin's electronics flickered and died, plunging the space into semi-darkness. A thin stream of smoke began seeping from beneath the cockpit door, and the steady hum of the engines ceased abruptly.

Noah exchanged a quick, knowing glance with Marco

and Renée. Renée checked the screen of the satellite phone before looking back at Noah and shaking her head. It wasn't working. The sudden lack of communication, the dead electronics—it all pointed to one horrifying possibility: an EMP attack.

"Everyone, stay calm! We need to assess our situation," Noah commanded, his voice cutting through the mounting crisis. He knew the stakes; without engines, their jet was nothing more than a gliding metal coffin. Every second mattered. As the team scrambled into action, the reality of their situation dawned with chilling clarity—they were thousands of feet in the air in a plane that was now a ghost.

In the darkness, Noah took charge. "Marco, check the backup communications. They work off a separate battery. They might still be working. Jenny, Renée, secure everything that's loose. We can't afford flying debris."

Marco got on the plane's emergency phone, but it was no good. Every attempt to call for help was met with the same unresponsive void.

"It's dead, too," he announced grimly.

With each passing second, the ocean loomed closer, its vast expanse a menacing sight through the windows.

Jenny's voice cut through the chaos. "We need to get inside the cockpit."

Noah's eyes fixed on the door. Tendrils of smoke curled and twisted into the air from beneath it. Without a word, they moved as one, determination steeling their steps.

Inside, they were met with the sight of destruction. Sparks danced like malevolent fireflies around the cockpit, the aftermath of the electrical panel's violent eruption. The pilot and copilot slumped in their seats, knocked uncon-scious by the exploding panels.

"Get them out of their seats, quickly!" Jenny yelled.

As the plane hurtled toward the rough water, Noah grappled with the pilot's seatbelt. Beside him, Jenny worked to free the copilot.

They dragged the men clear, then took their places. The ocean loomed large in the windshield, a vast expanse of angry waves rushing up to meet them.

Jenny's hands flew over the controls, guided by memo-ries of her father's lessons in their old Cessna. Beside her, Noah, driven by sheer will, scanned the instrument panel, looking for anything that might help.

Together, they fought to wrestle the aircraft away from the clutches of the sea, every second an eternity, every heart-beat a promise of survival.

ONE

ONE WEEK BEFORE NOAH WOLF WAS DUE A HARSH
meeting with the cold waters of the Atlantic Ocean, it was
just another day of subterfuge and obfuscation in the world
of espionage. In the shadows of the world's most influential
cities, where secrecy is currency and misinformation wields a
power all its own, the clandestine organization known only
as the Council cast its long, ominous shadow. Unseen by the
masses, their malevolent influence reached far and wide,
stretched across continents, and pulled the strings of
disorder with calculated precision. As Noah and his
colleagues at E & E followed every lead they could, the web
of deception spun by the Council tightened, engulfing entire
nations in a maelstrom of fear, panic, and distrust. The
consequences of their orchestrated misinformation
campaigns rippled through the lives of ordinary people,
leaving a trail of devastation in their wake. In this world of

cunning and intrigue, the Council's sinister machinations remained hidden, their true motives obscured by a fog of deception, setting the stage for the gripping and harrowing events that were unfolding on a daily basis all over the world.

———

WITHIN THE CONFINES OF A SLEEK, high-tech trading office nestled in the heart of London's Financial District, the bustle of commerce continued unabated. Traders, their faces illuminated by the glow of multiple screens, were deeply engrossed in their work when the tranquility of the room was abruptly disrupted.

News alerts began to cascade across their screens, each one flashing a dire message of sudden financial collapse. Initially, disbelief washed over their faces as they struggled to process the gravity of the situation. But the atmosphere in the room quickly shifted from one of casual routine to obvious concern.

Furrowed brows and worried expressions rippled across the faces. The frenzied tapping of keyboards and the rapid movement of stock graphs on their screens set the tone for the mounting crisis. The once-efficient trading floor now crackled with a sense of impending disaster as traders scrambled to verify the shocking information that had upended their world.

———

AT THE SAME TIME, in a dimly lit basement somewhere in Ohio, Don Sanderson, patriot, sat hunched over, his face a portrait of intense concentration. He was absorbed in a podcast, one that was busy spewing a barrage of conspiracy theories. The voice from the speakers was fervent, proclaiming that liberals were forcing puberty blockers on six-year-olds and that there is a supposed satanic cabal within the Democratic Party. "They're coming for your children, people!" the announcer bellowed, feeding into Don's growing paranoia.

Around him, the room was a chaotic shrine to conspiracy theories. Walls plastered with news clippings and paranoid scribbles created a disturbing tableau. This was a space marred by misinformation, where each piece of paper, each distorted voice from the speakers added to a growing sense of unease and delusion. This man, isolated in his beliefs, was a ticking time bomb of misguided fear and fury.

––––––

DON WAS NOT ALONE in his misinformed paranoia. In the dappled light of early morning, on the other side of the world, a small Burmese village stirred to life. Among its narrow streets, a group of men gathered, their focus intensely drawn to the screens of their smartphones. They passed around the devices, each video and message they viewed seemingly more inflammatory than the last, claiming to depict atrocities committed by Rohingya Muslims against local Buddhist girls.

As they watched and read, their faces were bent and twisted by anger and fear, emotions that were bubbling over in the close-knit circle. Each video, each shared message, added fuel to the simmering unrest within them. The murmurs that rose from their mouths were a mixture of disbelief and rising fury, reflecting the tense and charged atmosphere that hung over the group.

———

THE NEWS in London began to spread like wildfire within the trading office—the disconcerting word was that people were starting to pull their deposits from banks. Panic coursed through the room as traders received frantic calls from worried clients, their voices a cacophony of anxiety and distress.

The once-organized office descended into bedlam, its background noise intensifying with the rising panic. Traders shouted urgent instructions into their phones. The normally controlled atmosphere was interspersed by the frenetic tapping of keyboards and the anxious undertone of traders as they attempted to navigate the rapidly deteriorating situation.

Outside the office, the scene mirrored the growing turmoil. All across the country, crowded banks became epicenters of unease. Long lines of anxious customers stretched down the streets. ATMs ran out of cash in a matter of minutes, leaving people frustrated and desperate. Bank staff, overwhelmed and struggling to maintain order, were caught in the maelstrom of a financial crisis that was sweeping through the nation with relentless force.

Even if none of it was actually true.

———

BACK IN THE OHIO BASEMENT, Don Sanderson turned his attention to a rifle lying on the table. His hands moved with precision, each bullet sliding into the magazine with an unsettling sense of purpose. The meticulousness of his actions, the careful handling of the weapon, revealed a grim determination.

His weapon ready, he began to dress in tactical gear. The transformation was methodical; each piece of armor, each strap and buckle, was secured with a sense of finality. His face showed no doubt, only a disturbing determination as Don mentally prepared for the act he was about to commit.

IN THE HEART of the Burmese village, a transformation unfolded as the mood shifted from anger to action. The men, their faces still filled with fury, began to arm themselves with machetes and homemade weapons. It was a somber scene, marked by a sense of macabre determination as they prepared for what lay ahead.

Stirred up by the false claims of Rohingya Muslim gangs raping Buddhist girls, a chilling transformation had taken place: fury to action. Blades were sharpened meticulously, each stroke of the whetstone honing the weapons to a lethal edge. Hands gripped the handles of machetes and clubs with a white-knuckled resolve, fingers digging into the wood and metal. Their expressions were set in stone, a blend of determination and readiness that set the tone for impending violence.

The group of men then began their ominous march from the village toward the nearby Rohingya settlement.

Each step they took only intensified the growing agitation that was thickening the very air around them.

————

Amid the chaos of the London trading floor, a cacophony of voices rose to a deafening crescendo. Traders, their faces contorted with shock and disbelief, shouted over one another in a frenzied attempt to make deals within the rapidly deteriorating situation.

The sea of red on their screens served as a chilling visual backdrop, a grim reflection of the devastating plunge in stock prices. Faces, once marked by confidence and composure, now registered sheer shock and despair. Some traders were on the brink of tears, their voices trembling with the weight of the unfolding crisis, while others unleashed panicked shouts that pierced the tumultuous air.

The noise level was overwhelming, an unrelenting onslaught of sound. Phones rang incessantly, adding to the bedlam as traders frantically answered calls. Orders were screamed across the floor. In this tumultuous moment, the trading floor became a battlefield of shattered expectations and frantic efforts to navigate the financial wreckage.

————

Don Sanderson drove through Cleveland, his expression set with intensity. His hands gripped the steering wheel tightly, the only sound in the car being the low hum of the engine and his breathing, steady but laced with an unmistakable tremor.

He approached the heart of the city, where a political rally was taking place. Flags and banners fluttered in the breeze, and the air was filled with the sound of passionate speeches and cheering crowds. The downtown area was vibrant, alive with people of all ages gathered to support their cause.

However, this lively scene only served to intensify Don's frustration and rage. His face twisted into a snarl—especially when he passed a large poster of the candidate currently speaking. Spotting the barricade cordoning off the rally, he made up his mind.

With a sudden, violent acceleration, he propelled the car forward, smashing through the barrier. The vehicle lurched onto the sidewalk. Pedestrians, caught off guard, screamed and scattered in all directions, trying desperately to evade the oncoming threat. The scene was one of utter mayhem, terror, and confusion. The sound of crashing barricades, panicked shouts, and the revving engine filled the air.

———

THE MEN, fueled by anger, purpose, and indoctrinated hatred, finally arrived at the Rohingya village. An edgy, foreboding silence hung in the air as they stood at the border of the settlement, eyes fixed on the thatched roofs and clay walls of the humble homes belonging to their unsuspecting targets.

In this brief, charged moment, time seemed to stand still. The men's faces reflected a chilling mix of determination and anticipation, breaths held in readiness. The village, bathed in the soft light of day, remained unaware of the impending threat that loomed at its doorstep.

Then, like a sudden storm, the silence shattered. A collective roar erupted from the men's throats, a chilling battle cry that announced their descent upon the village. With an explosive surge of violence, they rushed forward, charging at the houses with a terrifying fervor that left no room for escape or mercy.

———

THE LONDON TRADING floor reached a fever pitch as market indicators nosedived. Traders watched in horror as the numbers on their screens plummeted relentlessly, an unforgiving descent into financial turmoil.

Then, as if in slow motion, a hush fell over the room—a collective, breathless silence—as a major index hit rock bottom. The weight of the crash, the implications of the catastrophic market collapse, hung so heavily in the air that some of the traders fell into chairs or simply onto the floor.

The stunned silence was a haunting stillness that belied the turmoil that had preceded it. In the midst of this eerie quietude, a lone trader broke down, the harsh reality of the crash finally setting in. His anguished cries pierced the silence, a visceral manifestation of the despair and devastation that had gripped the trading floor.

———

THE CAR, battered and barely holding together, sped relentlessly toward the bustling heart of the rally. Seconds ago, the space had been alive with the energy of passionate speeches and the crowd's enthusiastic cheers. Now it transformed into a scene of horror as Don Sanderson's car barreled into the unsuspecting crowd. People were thrown aside in a chaotic, desperate scramble to escape the destructive path as it came to a stop.

Emerging from the wreck, the patriot's movements were deliberate and terrifying. Rifle in hand, his eyes were unyielding, his resolve chilling. The crowd, now fully aware of the imminent danger, scattered in a frenzy—their faces, once bright with fervor, now expressed fear and disbelief.

As he raised the rifle, aligning it with the panic-stricken crowd, a horrifying suspense filled the air. The terror of the moment was stark, the impending violence almost tangible. With deliberate hatred, Don placed his eye to the scope and began shooting.

———

IN A WORLD increasingly governed by the flow of information, the power to manipulate this stream becomes the ultimate tool of influence. Those who hold this power, capable of weaving intricate webs of falsehoods, have the ability to shape reality itself, bending perceptions to their will. Like puppet masters, they pull the strings of public consciousness, sowing seeds of confusion and discord.

In such a landscape, truth becomes malleable, and facts are no longer absolutes but variables in the hands of the influential. This distortion of reality doesn't just mislead; it breeds chaos, stirring unrest and division. The repercussions of these deceptions ripple through societies, eroding the foundations of trust and understanding.

As the Council crafted their many narratives, they did more than just spread lies; they created new worlds—alternate realities that aligned with their interests, always at the cost of the greater good. In this age, where the line between fact and fiction is blurred, the battle isn't just for the truth, but for the very fabric of everything we perceive as real and just.

TWO

THE ROCKY MOUNTAINS STOOD AS SILENT
sentinels, casting their long shadows over the serene ceme-
tery. Noah Wolf, his wife, Sarah, and their five-year-old
daughter Norah strolled quietly along the pathways. It was a
peaceful yet somber morning, the gentle rustle of leaves in
the mountain breeze the only sound breaking the stillness.

They walked hand in hand, each lost in their own
thoughts, until they arrived at their destination. Before them
lay the grave of Allison Peterson. The headstone was a
simple, dignified piece, much like Allison herself. It was a
reminder of the life she had lived and the sacrifice she had
made. The inscription was brief, but it spoke volumes about
the woman who had once been a part of their lives.

A Leader in Shadows, A Light in Our Hearts.
Her Legacy Is Our Guiding Star.

Noah knelt down, tracing the letters of her name with a
quiet reverence. Sarah stood by his side, little Norah
clutching her hand. Here, in this tranquil place, surrounded

by the majesty of the mountains, they paid their respects to a fallen comrade, a friend, and a part of their past that would forever be etched in their memories.

Noah stood motionless, his gaze fixed on the headstone. In his eyes, a complex mix of emotions was evident—respect for the fallen, a profound sadness for what had been lost, and perhaps a lingering sense of unresolved business that still clung to his heart. He seemed to be both there and far away, lost in memories only he could see.

Beside him, his family offered their silent support. Their presence was a comforting touchstone for Noah, a reminder that while the past could not be changed, the future still held warmth and love. Together, they stood, a family united in their remembrance and in the shared impact of Allison's loss, which reverberated through their lives like a quiet, persistent echo.

Sarah watched as Norah ran off, the little girl's laughter trailing behind her as she chased a butterfly.

"I should have been there to protect her," Noah said in an undertone, practically speaking to himself. "I should have known Schultz was coming."

"You can't know everything, Noah," Sarah gently reminded him.

Noah turned to her, his face a mask of regret. "But I should have," he insisted. "Allison... she saved both our lives when it mattered. If it weren't for her, we would have never met." He paused, glancing sideways to watch Norah chasing butterflies. "She brought us together," he went on. "Without her, we wouldn't have Norah." Turning back to his wife, he added, "But where was I when it mattered? When Allison needed me?"

Sarah reached out, touching his arm softly. "You can't blame yourself for what happened," she said.

Noah's gaze returned to the grave. "Henrik Schultz took her from us. Burned down her house... and all he left us..." His voice faltered. "All we had to bury was a fistful of ash."

Sarah stood beside him, a bastion of comfort. "*We* remember her, Noah. *We* keep her memory alive. That's all we can do."

Noah nodded slowly, the weight of his guilt and the burden of his loss evident in his eyes. He knew Sarah was right, but the thought that he could have prevented Allison's death, that he should have seen through Schultz's deception, haunted him.

The family's drive home was more lighthearted. As they sang along to "Let It Go" from the film *Frozen*, there was an unmistakable sense of joy permeating the air of the car. Yet the mood was layered with an undercurrent of apprehension. Noah, while joining in the chorus, kept one eye on his phone, betraying the fact that part of his mind remained anchored to his work and the looming threats they faced.

As though his constant looks had willed it, Noah's phone rang, slicing through the singalong. It was Jenny, her tone urgent yet composed. "Noah, Neil's found something," she said the second he answered, her words sharp and quick. "It could be big. We're at R&D, better to speak when you get here. Jenny out."

Noah's demeanor shifted instantaneously. The family man singing a moment ago was replaced by the sharp, focused operative. This call, this potential breakthrough, reawakened his professional persona, and he was immediately absorbed, his mind already racing with possibilities and strategies. The drive home was no longer just a return to normalcy but a gateway back into the intricate and dangerous world of espionage.

Back at the farmhouse, Noah helped Sarah and Norah out of the car before returning to the driver's seat. "I have to go," he said, his voice tinged with the promise of return. "Neil's discovery... it sounds important."

Sarah nodded, understanding the gravity of the situation. Norah clung to her father for a brief moment, a silent plea for his safe return, and then he left.

As Noah drove away, the farmhouse receded into the background, leaving Sarah and Norah standing there.

THREE

NOAH ARRIVED AT THE BUILDINGS OF E & E'S
Research & Development (R&D) department. Inside, the
atmosphere was electric, a blend of focused intensity and
groundbreaking energy. Staff in lab coats bustled about high-
tech workstations with purpose, the lighting flickering intermittently from the high-energy discharges caused by many
of their experiments.

Inside one of the main labs, Neil, Jenny, and Wally were
deeply engrossed in their work, surrounded by a constella-
tion of screens that flickered with real-time data and satellite
surveillance footage. This high-security chamber, known as
the War Room, served as the nerve center for their covert
operations against the Council.

The War Room was a marvel of technology and strategy,
equipped with the latest advancements in cybersecurity, data
analysis, and digital forensics. Walls lined with monitors
displayed live feeds from various hotspots around the world,
tracking the digital footprints left by the Council. A large

central table was laden with interactive maps and holographic projections, allowing the team to visualize the spread of misinformation in real-time and strategize their counter-measures.

As Noah entered, the trio paused their work.

"Glad you're here," Neil said. "We've stumbled upon something... something big."

Neil Blessing was the lanky and seemingly unassuming CEO of The Hive, the world's largest Council-independent social media company. A company he was currently leaving to someone else to run while he helped Noah here at E & E. Because despite his dorky appearance, Neil was a formidable force, trained in both physical and armed combat as well as every espionage tactic known to man.

Jenny stepped forward, her tone serious. "It could be the breakthrough we've been waiting for."

Jenny was Neil's wife. She was also an intimidating special ops assassin, her skills honed from childhood by her Green Beret father. Jenny was a survivor in the truest sense. Since Allison Peterson's death, she had shifted her focus from corporate security to the mission at Kirtland and here, in their war against the Council.

Wally Lawson simply nodded in agreement, his eyes returning to the screens, his glasses reflecting the garish blue light. Wally was the genius at the head of R&D, a man of high IQ and minimal social skills. His inventions were as brilliant as his conversations were often longwinded. He had the type of look you'd expect to see in a middle-aged man who has never exercised regularly and whose fashion sense is more utilitarian than aesthetic.

Noah's own eyes swept over the room, taking in the flurry of activity. "All right, let's hear it. What have you got?"

"It's everywhere, Noah," Neil said gravely. "Just today we've found at least two examples of the Council's misinformation campaign. There was an attack at a political rally in Cleveland. The man responsible left a video manifesto. I got a copy off the FBI. He was babbling about several Council-sponsored conspiracies. Then there was a massacre at a village in Myanmar this morning between Buddhists and Muslims after false reports were spread."

"The Council's lies are like a virus," Wally suddenly pronounced, his eyes never leaving the screen he watched. "They infect the minds and hearts of people. Turning the world against itself."

"Philosophical, Wally," Noah commented.

The genius merely nodded.

Jenny turned from her screen. "It's like fighting a hydra," she complained. "We take down one operation, and two more spring up. Still, we're making some headway, slowly but surely."

A sense of dissatisfaction crept over Noah. "So is this your something big, then?" he put to them.

He felt instantly better when Neil looked over at him, grinning like the kid who knows what you've got for Christmas.

"No," Neil said through the smirk.

"Then what have you got?"

"Are you ready for this?"

"Just get on with it, Blessing."

"Earlier today, we successfully pinpointed the physical location of one of the Council's hacking farms. And not just any. From what we've picked up in chatter, it's one of the main sites for their entire misinformation campaign."

He brought up satellite images on the main screen, capturing everyone's attention. "Here," he said, pointing to a structure that poked out of an ocean on four legs. "This research platform standing in international waters off the coast of North Carolina is what we believe to be a key hacking hub for the Council."

Noah gazed hard at the screen, analyzing the footage. The platform, isolated and fortified in the middle of the Atlantic Ocean, represented a significant challenge. "This could be our chance to get a step ahead of them," he mused. "We need to figure some way of shutting it down."

"No," Neil countered. "Not shut it down. I was thinking. If we can get inside the place, maybe we can set something up."

"Something? Like what?"

"Like something to monitor their activity."

FOUR

It was night when Noah finally left R&D, the chill mountain air wrapping around the building and forcing him to raise the collar of his jacket as he stepped outside. Under the intermittent glow of a flickering street-lamp, his Dodge Charger stood waiting, its dark silhouette merging with the night, save for the faint ember glow of a lit cigarette atop its hood.

There, seated as if he were part of the Charger's own mystique, was Doc Parker, the acting head of E & E: Noah's boss. An ex-CIA shrink with a formidable background in espionage, Parker sat with his arms folded across his chest and the cigarette sticking out of the corner of his mouth, its smoke curling into the night.

His voice, smooth yet edged with a hint of jest, broke the silence. "Evening, Noah. Coming from the War Room, are you?"

Noah's response was curt. "Yeah. Busy night."

"Would be nice to get an invite sometime. I hear it's

quite the setup in there." The lightness in Parker's tone belied the depth of his words.

"You don't need an invite to walk into your own agency, Parker" was Noah's flat reply.

The air hung heavy between them, laden with unspoken truths and the ghost of Allison Peterson's legacy. With the loss of E & E's former leader and architect, Doc Parker had been thrust into very big shoes.

"As you know," he began, "I had a lot of respect for Allison. She was... one of a kind. I'm not trying to replace her, Noah. I just want to carry the torch she left behind." His gaze drifted, lost to memories and what-ifs, his voice barely a whisper against the night. "And to do that, Noah, I'm gonna need the full support of my best agent."

Doc Parker fell silent, and the two men gazed at one another. There was nothing but the sound of the insects for several seconds.

"You have it," Noah eventually told him.

"I hope so," Parker responded. "I really do." There was a softness to his voice, a vulnerability rare and raw. "You know," he added after a moment or two, "they told me they offered you the job first and you turned it down. Why?"

"This—isn't about titles for me."

In that moment, a silent acknowledgment passed between them, a mutual recognition of the burdens they bore.

"Well," Parker said, getting up off the hood and flicking his cigarette to the gutter, "I'm due to meet the president at the Pentagon in a day or two. Big meeting about our efforts against the Council. Apparently, he's got something to show me."

Interest piqued, Noah's response was measured, a guarded curiosity. "And?"

Parker approached him, stopping when they were level. When he spoke, his voice carried a sincerity that resonated in the still night. "I'll let you know what happens," he said. "Because despite the way you appear to feel about me, Noah, I trust you. You're the best agent we have, and I would never jeopardize that by keeping you out of the loop."

With those final words, Parker stepped away, leaving Noah to the silence of his thoughts and the endless night.

FIVE

It took Team Camelot just 24 hours to come up with a plan. Now they were reconvened in the War Room. Amidst the low hum of machines, a large, sleek table stood central, illuminated by the soft glow of monitors.

Having helped with the planning, Neil and Jenny would be sitting the actual mission out. Marco and Renée would be taking their places.

As Noah entered the War Room, Marco gave a curt nod. "Boss man," he said.

Standing tall with a sinewy build that spoke of years of disciplined training, this well-muscled Cajun assassin from Louisiana carried the lethal grace of a swamp panther, his deep-set eyes smoldering beneath a tangle of dark, unruly hair, evidence of his fierce and untamed spirit.

Renée, his equally formidable wife and Team Camelot's tech sorceress, glided into the room beside him. Her fingers, adept and swift, wove magic across keyboards, commanding the digital realm with the same ease and finesse as she wielded weapons and explosives. She was, it had to be said, a seamless blend of cyber mastery and in-field tactical prowess.

At the front of the room stood Noah, his easy gaze surveying his team as they took their seats. Wally Lawson and Molly Hanson were standing beside him. Molly was Noah's oldest friend. She was also E & E's best strategist. With an intelligence as sharp as a razor, her insights often cut through the complexity of their missions, offering clarity and direction.

With Marco and Renée settled in, Molly initiated the briefing with a flourish, her fingers gliding over a control panel. A large holographic model of the Atlantic Ocean platform gradually materialized in the center of the War Room. The hologram, a spectral array of blues and greens, cast a ghostly glow across the faces of Team Camelot. Intricate details of the structure were meticulously rendered—from the angular jut of newly added levels to the subtle hints of advanced satellite dishes and antennae—transforming the room into a dynamic, three-dimensional representation of their target.

"This structure," Molly explained, gesturing toward the hovering model, "was originally a US Navy research platform. But as you're about to see, it has transformed significantly over the years." The room's screens lit up with a series of historical photos. "These images," she added, "captured over years, chronicle the platform's transformation."

The earliest photos depicted a basic structure with the stark, utilitarian lines of a marine research facility. Over time, however, additional levels emerged, each more sophisticated than the last. The photos showed workers adding complex arrays of equipment and reinforced structures, hinting at the facility's new purpose. All the way up to the final images. These revealed a modern, fortified complex, bristling with advanced technology and gun towers, a complete contrast to its humble beginnings.

Marco leaned forward, his eyes scanning the model. "When did the Council take over?" he asked, his voice low but clear.

"We're not exactly sure," Molly replied. "The Council hides behind so many shell companies and other entities that it's hard to know when they got anywhere. But the US government sold the original structure back in the seventies."

"What about their Internet access?" Renée asked.

"The platform is positioned directly over an underwater cable," Molly answered. "So it's direct."

"Strategic," Renée chimed in, pointing to a photo. "Its location and direct Internet access make it invaluable."

Marco nodded, his brow furrowed. "So it's more than just a hacking hub."

"That's right," Molly said. "We think it could be housing one of the Council's main servers. Where they store their own information, and where internal communications are relayed. It could be a doorway into the rest of their operations."

Wally took control of the screen, displaying a series of satellite and thermal images. "Look here," he said, zooming in on a section glowing with the colors of intense heat. "This pattern of energy consumption is typical of heavy server use."

Marco nodded, his eyes fixed on the screen. "So we're looking at a server farm, essentially?"

"Exactly," Wally replied. "And based on these heat signatures, we can start to guess the layout inside."

The team leaned closer.

"These external changes"—Wally pointed at several spots of white—"they must correlate with internal modifications. Server rooms, cooling systems..."

Marco whistled softly. "That's a lot of power for a platform. They're running something big there. So what's the plan?"

Wally held up a rectangular module, approximately the size of a standard smartphone, with a matte black finish and subtle blue LED indicators along one edge. "The plan," he began, "is to access the platform's server room and get *this* device connected to their main router."

Marco spoke next. "So this is gonna be one of those don't get seen kinda deals, then?"

"That would be the idea," Wally replied.

Molly took over the presentation. "Now let's talk security," she began, pulling up a detailed schematic of the platform's defenses. "First, there's a contingent of armed mercenaries—at least twenty men present at all times. These aren't your average guards, either; they're well-trained and lethal."

She flicked to the next image: video footage showing patrol boats circling the platform. "Then we have spotlights and patrol boats, ensuring no approach goes unnoticed."

Marco whistled low. "And air support?" he asked.

"They have helicopters, equipped for both surveillance and combat," Molly confirmed. "The Council isn't taking any chances. The platform is heavily fortified."

She advanced to images displaying the platform's underwater defenses. "There are mines around the perimeter, motion sensors, and advanced surveillance systems covering every possible angle."

Renée gently shook her head. "Breaking into Fort Knox would be easier."

Wally shifted the discussion, addressing the team. "A direct assault is out of the question," he said, bringing up an image on the large telescreen. "This is our alternative." The image was of a sleek two-man mini-submarine, its design sharp and angular.

"This is Shadow Fin," Wally explained. "The shape of the submarine is key to deflecting sonar waves, making it nearly invisible acoustically."

Marco and Renée examined the submarine's design, noting its predatory-like angles and compact frame. They also studied the design of the plating that coated it, recognizing it from other technology. "It's equipped with quantum cloak technology," Renée commented.

"Good eye," Wally replied. "It is indeed, making it invisible to both radar and digital cameras. It's our best shot at getting close to the platform undetected."

The team leaned in, studying the submarine, its design a tribute to advanced engineering and stealth. Wally began explaining the intricacies of the technology. "Over the past month, R&D has been enhancing quantum cloaking for underwater use," he said. "Shadow Fin is plated with a new generation of quantum metamaterial. It's tough, designed to withstand the harsh underwater environment."

Marco, intrigued, leaned in closer. "And heat?"

"The sub's engines and internal machinery emit minimal heat," Wally explained. "This is thanks to advanced cooling systems involving circulating coolant and heat exchangers that disperse heat more evenly. Meaning you'll be practically invisible when you reach your destination."

Next Molly spoke, pointing to a spot on the hologram. "Two of you will be inside the sub. You'll have to anchor on the ocean floor about thirty meters from the legs of the platform and swim from there. It's the only way to avoid detection on the surface."

"However," Noah chimed in, "that presents its own challenges." He switched the screen to a disturbing set of footage that captured the peril faced by whoever was unlucky enough to end up in that submarine. The video, taken from the platform, showed men dangling beef carcasses on large hooks over the edge, an eerie ritual against the backdrop of the open ocean. As they watched, a great white shark, drawn by the scent, breached the surface, surging from the water with primal ferocity, its massive body launching into the air to rip the meat from the hook in a display of raw power. As the giant shark fell back into the water with the carcass in its jaws, the ocean around the platform churned violently, resembling a cauldron boiling over, as shark after shark competed for the offered feast.

"The platform," Noah pointed out, though it was by now obvious, "is surrounded by sharks. At least one large great white in the vicinity and several other species, including tiger sharks. And as if that wasn't bad enough, it appears the people on the platform enjoy feeding them."

"Oh, great," Marco commented dryly, watching the footage. "And which sucker has been chosen to be shark food?"

"Me," Noah responded without hesitation.

"Unlucky," Marco said under his breath.

"And you," Noah added, looking right at him.

Marco could only groan. "Great. Wish I'd never asked."

"Nevertheless," Wally interjected, anxious to address his concerns, "you won't be on your own in this. You'll be equipped with a range of deterrents such as specialized wetsuits covered in unique patterns that confuse a shark's visual perception, making you look less like prey. You'll also have electronic shark repellents that emit a field of electro-magnetism which messes with the sharks' electroreceptors, creating a sensation they'd rather avoid."

Noah added, "We also have advanced sonar that special-izes in tracking shark movements. That's where Renée comes in." His eyes met hers. "You'll be monitoring the sonar from several miles away aboard a command relay craft."

Wally stepped forward, his tone turning serious. "How-ever, remember, none of these measures are foolproof. You might still need to fend off an attack physically."

With this warning ringing in their ears, Noah took over, detailing the next phase of their mission. "Once we leave the sub," he began, "Marco and I will make our way to the plat-form's base."

"Through all the sharks," Marco whispered sideways to Renée, making her smile.

"Our wetsuits," Noah continued explaining, "will employ the same quantum cloaking as the sub, giving us an added layer of stealth to evade being spotted by the plat-form's underwater cameras. Upon reaching one of the plat-form's legs, we'll use specialized climbing gear to scale up the less guarded northern section of the platform. Then, once

Marco and I are on top, we'll quietly enter the inside of it through a rear maintenance hatch, moving to the main server room." He used a laser pen to highlight their route on the holographic model, tracing a discreet path to their target.

Wally took over to explain their objective in the server room. "Here at R&D, we've designed this device for a very special purpose." He once again held up the rectangular module. "It's a quantum computing-based interceptor cuff."

Marco furrowed his brow. "And what is one of those?"

"It's designed to tap into the platform's network undetected and relay the data back to us here in Kirtland. It needs to be attached to the main network router. Then, once it's in place, it will give us remote access to the platform's network. We'll be able to monitor communications, access data, and trace other hacking farms belonging to the Council. In other words, it'll give us the upper hand we so desperately need."

The team contemplated this for a moment before Noah focused on exfiltration. "After we plant the device," he emphasized to Marco, "we'll need to exit without leaving any evidence we were ever there. We'll have to retrace our steps, climbing down the platform and swimming back to the submarine as stealthily as we arrived."

"I get it, boss," Marco said. "A clean exit."

As the meeting drew to a close, the team sat in a moment of contemplative silence, each member mentally preparing for the daunting task ahead. Noah stood up, his eyes sweeping across the room. "This mission will redefine our fight against the Council," he stated. "It's risky, but the stakes have never been higher." He paused, his gaze lingering on each member of his team. "We've always been one step behind. Not anymore. This is where we turn the tide."

SIX

NOAH ARRIVED HOME AROUND NOON, HIS STEPS heavy as he left the Charger. The sound of laughter and splashes was coming from the lake. Rounding the house, he saw that Norah and Sarah were swimming. Upon spotting his arrival, Norah climbed out and dashed along the jetty, her small feet pounding on the wood. "Daddy!" she exclaimed, leaping into his arms for a big, wet hug when she reached him on the bank.

Sarah, following behind, smiled warmly at her husband. "Come swim with us?" she invited.

He forced a smile, shaking his head. "I'm all good. I'll just hang out in the house," he replied, his voice lacking its usual warmth.

Sarah's smile faltered. "Are you okay, Noah?" she asked, concern coloring her tone.

He nodded, offering a reassurance that didn't quite reach his eyes. "Yeah, I'm fine."

But as he stood a short while later in front of the bay

window, gazing out at the lake, his body was there, but his mind was far away, tangled in thoughts and plans. The peacefulness of the lake, with its gentle ripples and the laughter of his family as they swam, was very different than the turmoil churning inside him.

Unable to stay still, the restlessness growing within him, Noah found himself in the backyard, an axe in hand, methodically chopping wood. The sun blazed down, intensifying the harshness of his labor, but he paid it no mind. Each swing of the axe was precise, powerful, adding to an already substantial pile of wood. It certainly wasn't the need for firewood that drove him; it was a desperate need to stay busy, to keep his mind away from the gnawing thoughts that refused to settle.

A little later, having finished swimming, Sarah quietly stepped outside to check on him. She stood for a moment, observing his intense focus on chopping wood. Then, approaching slowly, she placed a hand on his shoulder. It was a small yet profound gesture, full of understanding and concern, a silent offer of support and an acknowledgment of his pain without the need for words.

Noah turned to her, and under Sarah's empathetic gaze, his composure began to waver. "I can't stop thinking about her," he confessed, his voice strained. "She wasn't just my leader. She was my mentor, my guiding light in the darkest times. She gave me a reason to fight, a reason to be better."

Sarah listened, her hand still resting on his shoulder. "You keep blaming yourself, but you shouldn't," she said.

Noah nodded, his eyes distant. "But I do. More than I thought possible. She was more than a boss; she was the one who pulled me out of darkness. And when she needed me most, I wasn't there."

"Is that why you refused to take her place?" Sarah asked.

Noah didn't speak, confirming Sarah's intuition.

So she did what any loving partner would do. She threw her arms around him. In this embrace, their deep connection was something solid that grew between them, a shared understanding of the heavy legacy Noah bore and the daunting path that lay ahead. He was about to once again venture into the darkness. And he wondered what he would find there this time.

SEVEN

Squashed together in Shadow Fin, the quantum-cloaked submarine, Noah and Marco navigated the gloomy oceanic waters under a brewing storm. The rough weather above had created a turbulent underwater environment, reducing visibility to just a few meters at best. The shadows of sharks loomed in the murky depths around them, adding a very real sense of danger as they brought the sub to a stop on the Atlantic seabed about thirty meters from the platform.

Prepared for the perilous swim in their shark deterrent wetsuits, they began to get ready. They rubbed shark repellent chemicals containing necromones into the wetsuits, enhancing their defense. "Gosh, this stuff stinks," Marco commented as he lathered it over the suit.

"It's supposed to smell like dead shark," Noah told him. "Sharks don't like dead sharks, apparently."

"Neither do I," Marco complained.

Additionally, they activated the electromagnetic shark repellent devices that were attached to their belts.

Equipping earpieces, Noah checked in with Renée, who was stationed on a surveillance boat several miles away. "You getting us, Renée?" he asked as they donned their masks.

Despite the storm rocking the surveillance boat, Renée was focused on her sonar screen. "Loud and clear," she responded.

"How we looking for sharks, baby?" Marco inquired, a hint of stress in his voice.

Renée's screen showed numerous moving shapes around their position. "Eh? Well, you've got your shark repellent devices, right?" she replied.

"That's not really the answer I wanted," Marco commented.

Fully geared up, Noah and Marco placed regulators in their mouths and armed themselves with stun harpoons, ready to face the dangers as they prepared to leave the submarine and enter the cold embrace of the open ocean.

Exiting Shadow Fin, Noah and Marco found themselves in an eerie, shadow-filled underwater world. The cloudy water was disorienting, and above them, the storm churned the surface into a frothy tumult, distorting the little light that penetrated the depths.

It was in these conditions that they began their treacherous swim toward the platform, every one of their senses heightened. As they moved, the gloomy water around them teemed with the menacing shadows of sharks, silent threats lurking in every direction.

Suddenly, the water beside Noah stirred. A tiger shark, its stripes barely visible in the dim light, emerged from the gloom, its sleek body cutting through the water with terrifying grace. In a heartbeat, Noah pushed it away by its nose, his movements fueled by both fear and reflexes, the shark moving out of there with a flick of its tail fin.

From their earpieces, Renée's voice came, "Marco, your heart rate's spiking. You need to calm down, baby."

Marco fought to calm his racing heart. He took slow, controlled breaths, trying to reduce his presence in the water, to become just another shadow among many. The threat of the sharks, coupled with the need for absolute stealth, made their swim not just a physical challenge, but a mental battle against their own instincts.

As Noah and Marco continued, Renée's voice came through, tinged with urgency. "Hey, guys. Something big is heading your way, and it's moving fast."

"Great white?" Marco's voice was a mix of alertness and dread.

"Could be. Stay sharp," Renée replied.

Marco scanned the foggy waters around him, but the visibility was too poor to see anything in any detail beyond the innumerable moving shadows. His heart pounded in his chest at the return of Renée's voice. "It's making a beeline straight for you, Marco. You need to stop and cut it off."

He turned, searching the gloom, but saw nothing. His breathing was becoming erratic, the tension in his chest unbearably tight. He felt himself hunted, his stun harpoon feeling useless in his hands. Ahead of him, Noah was slowly fading into the endless milky blue.

"Marco!" Renée came back, her voice frantic now. "It's close, Marco, really close!"

He searched the water in a frenzy, pushing his eyes to see

something, anything, in the gloom. Renée was almost shouting now. "Marco, it's right there!"

A massive great white emerged right beside him, its sudden appearance sending his heartrate into overdrive. Reacting on pure instinct, Marco fired up his stun harpoon, driving it into the side of the shark. The impact startled the great white, which quickly turned and disappeared back into the depths, becoming just another shadow. Marco's heart raced, and he took a moment to still himself before continuing.

Reaching the base of the platform, Noah and Marco swam upward, breaking the surface into a world where the storm's fury was all-powerful. Rain pelted them, and the tall waves made it a dangerous and awkward job getting onto the legs, the rough water throwing them at the barnacle-clad framework with a mighty force.

They eventually managed it, but even after they left the water, the two men weren't free from the storm's wrath. Gusts of wind tugged at their gear as they began their climb up the slippery, algae-covered legs, the sea's spray mixing with the rain, creating a slick, treacherous surface. Above them, the storm's force caused the massive structure to creak and groan, adding an eerie soundtrack to their precarious ascent. Each hand- and foothold was a battle against the elements, their fingers grappling for secure grips on the cold, wet metal.

As they climbed higher, the sound of footsteps and muffled voices from the platform's watchmen drifted down to them. Some of them sounded very close.

Silently cresting the top of the platform, Noah and Marco slipped through a maintenance hatch, finding themselves in a dimly lit corridor of the main structure. They moved covertly, making no more sound than a shadow, their every step calculated to avoid detection.

As they navigated the maze of hallways, they came upon two armed guards stationed in a stairwell. Tucked around a corner with Marco, Noah pulled out a parametric speaker, a compact device capable of directing sound to a specific target area. He adjusted the settings, and a moment later, the sound of a loud crash resounded, seemingly coming from above the guards. Startled, the two men exchanged a quick look before hurrying up the stairs to investigate the source of the noise, leaving the path clear for Noah and Marco.

Continuing to the server room, they found it unguarded. Inside, the room hummed with the sound of servers and blinking lights. Noah carefully planted Wally's hacking device, hiding it among the tangle of wires and equipment. Marco watched the door, his body tense, ready to signal any approaching danger.

With the device in place, they exchanged a brief, satisfied glance and exited the server room the same way they had entered, proceeding until they reached the maintenance hatch. That was where they hit their first snag. Around it stood five men, Marco and Noah observing them from a distant corner of the corridor. Marco was about to use his parametric speaker, but Noah stopped him. Using hand signals, Noah conveyed that finding an alternative route would be wiser.

It didn't take them long to find one. In less than a minute, they were stealthily moving out of the main structure and onto the platform, where the rain swept across in gusts. The path appeared clear, the absence of personnel allowing them to reach the platform's edge without any incidents.

However, the lack of incidents did not mean danger was far behind. As Noah and Marco readied themselves to descend from the platform, a sudden movement caught Noah's eye. Across the platform, a group of people had just left the structure and were advancing toward an opposite corner. They were led by an imposing figure. The man was a giant, towering over seven feet tall, with a chest as broad as a truck. Trailing behind him were two armed men, their assault rifles slung casually over their shoulders, escorting a fourth, disheveled individual, who was being dragged with rough indifference.

"Noah?" Marco's whisper was urgent in the nervous air. "We gotta go."

But Noah was immobile, his gaze fixed on the unfolding scene. The group stopped at the edge of the platform. The giant lifted the battered person by the neck, holding them over the churning sea below. That was when Noah's blood ran cold. He recognized the person in the giant's grasp.

It was Allison Peterson, alive but in grave danger.

That was when Noah's heart briefly stopped. Because the giant released his hold, dropping Allison into the tumultuous waters below. Noah's training and self-preservation vanished in the face of loyalty and desperation. Without a moment's hesitation, he leapt from the platform, diving into the stormy sea below in a daring attempt to save Allison—his fate and hers hanging in the balance.

EIGHT

Noah's plunge into the ocean was a headlong race against time. As he hit the water, the cold was an immediate jolt, but he pushed through, propelling himself deeper. The murky waters around him were disorienting, each shadow a potential lurking danger. His eyes strained for any sign of Allison in the gloom. He swam fiercely, muscles burning, heart pounding in his ears. The storm above made the waters below churn unpredictably. Then, in the dim, shifting light, he saw her—Allison, her form sinking, her movements slow and weakening. She was barely struggling now, a fading silhouette in the deep.

Noah surged forward, every second critical. His mind raced—he had to get her to safety, away from the ever-present threat of the sharks and back to the sub. As he reached her, he quickly steadied her flailing limbs, and with quick precision, brought the regulator to her mouth, ensuring she could breathe. Their eyes met, his gaze steady and reassuring. Recognition dawned in her eyes, and she gave in to his will.

Gripping her securely, Noah began the swim back to the submarine. Their vulnerability in the open water was obvious, each stroke through the murky depths a race against unseen threats. The tension was a living thing, coiling around them as they moved, fear and determination driving them forward. Noah's every muscle strained, pushing through the water with Allison in tow, her life in his hands, the two sharing the regulator to breathe.

Then the last thing that Noah wanted to happen happened. The stillness of the water was shattered by the sudden emergence of a great white shark. Its massive form cut through the gloom, a silent, deadly predator. Noah's heart raced as he tried to maneuver both himself and Allison away while simultaneously extracting the stun harpoon from the harness on his back. But in the tumult, he lost his grip on the harpoon, and it trickled down to the ocean floor.

The shark circled back, its massive form cutting through the water with turbulent force. On its next approach, it ventured alarmingly close, prompting Noah to thrust it away with determined hands. Feeling the sheer mass of the shark, he realized the futility of his own mass against it. As its giant length passed, the shark's rough skin grazed Noah's wetsuit, a harsh rasp that felt purposeful, direct. Noah understood the unspoken threat: this was the shark's final warning. The next pass would be more serious.

The shark's attack, when it came, was terrifying. It turned suddenly in the water, its gaping jaws opening wide, the water rushing into its maw creating a powerful current. Then, with a whip of its massive tail, it burst forward at them, its rows of teeth a nightmarish sight, promising immediate destruction. Noah took the hunting knife attached to his belt. It was all he had.

But just as the great white's massive jaws were about to ensnare them, the shark suddenly convulsed and twisted in the water, its attention abruptly pulled away from them.

The beast swam off, revealing Marco and his harpoon, its end covered in a cloud of blood. It had taken him all that time to find them in the shadows, but luckily he had. With a marksman's accuracy and a rush of adrenaline, he had fired the harpoon at the shark and struck it squarely, the impact sending the colossal predator recoiling in pain, its attack ended.

With Marco's assistance, Noah quickly maneuvered Allison into the safety of the submarine. Once inside, the toll of the ordeal overwhelmed her, and she collapsed into unconsciousness, her body succumbing to exhaustion. Noah and Marco didn't waste a moment. They rapidly navigated the submarine away from the platform, keenly aware that every second they remained in the water multiplied their risks.

Back on the platform, the men that had dragged Allison out were huddled around security monitors in the control room, scrutinizing the footage of the churning, murky waters. The resolution was poor, the details of the rescue lost in the shadows and swirls.

One of them, a technician, finally broke the silence. "It's no use. She's gone. The sharks must've already got her."

The large man, the one who had dropped Allison into the sea, leaned forward, his face a mask of disappointment.

"A shame we didn't get to see it," he remarked coldly, his voice devoid of emotion.

With the submarine moving away from the danger zone, Noah and Marco found themselves grappling with a whirlwind of emotions. Relief at their escape was mixed with confusion over Allison's unexpected presence. Her phoenix-like reemergence raised a myriad of questions about where she had been all this time. Obviously with the Council, but doing what?

"What the hell is this, boss?" Marco asked as they navigated through the bleak water.

"I don't know," Noah replied, glancing at Allison.

The quiet hum of Shadow Fin's engine couldn't be further from the storm of questions in their minds. Allison, unconscious and enigmatic, lay before them—a living puzzle whose presence upended all their expectations.

NINE

WHILE NOAH AND HIS TEAM GRAPPLED WITH THE shocking revelation of Allison's return from the dead, Doc Parker and Molly Hanson made their way to the Pentagon, their journey shrouded in the secrecy of pre-dawn darkness. Their car glided to a stop at a checkpoint bristling with security measures. The air was thick with anticipation, the kind that precedes events destined to alter the course of history. Today, they were not merely guests but key players in a clandestine dance of power, poised on the precipice of decisions that would shape the nation's destiny.

The security procedures were exhaustive, a meticulously choreographed routine that left no stone unturned. Every credential was scrutinized, every piece of equipment examined with an intensity that bordered on invasive. Yet Parker and Hanson endured it with the patience of those accustomed to the burdens of secrecy.

Once cleared, they were escorted to a nondescript elevator, its doors sliding open to swallow them into the bowels of the earth. The descent was silent save for the hum of the elevator, a descent into the heart of American defense strategy.

The underground base that unfolded before them was a revelation, a sprawling complex of technology and military might carved into the bedrock. They were led through corridors that reverberated with the soft steps of their escort, past doors that concealed operations too secret to name, until they reached a large conference room.

It was no ordinary conference room. It was a fortress of strategy, lined with screens displaying encrypted data streams and maps dotted with the movements of unseen players. The room was populated by a veritable who's who of military and intelligence leadership. Four-star generals mingled with admirals and chiefs of staff, each bearing the insignia of their rank. Their faces were etched with the gravity of their purpose, united in their focus against a common enemy: the Council.

President Jackson T. Whitmore stood at the front, a commanding presence amidst the sea of uniforms. His gaze fell on Parker and Hanson as they entered, a nod of acknowledgment that bridged the gap between civilian and military realms. They were ushered to seats at the front, the room's attention subtly shifting to acknowledge their arrival.

The meeting commenced with the president's introduction, his voice resonating with authority. "Ladies and gentlemen," he began, "we gather today in the shadows to light a beacon of hope. In the face of adversaries that lurk in the darkest corners of the globe, our resolve has been unyielding, our spirit indomitable."

He paused, allowing his words to sink in, then continued, "Our enemies, the Council, believe they can operate from the shadows, undermining our way of life. But they forget: America thrives in adversity. We innovate. We overcome. And most importantly, we unite."

A murmur of agreement rippled through the room.

"As we stand on the brink of a new dawn in warfare and intelligence, remember this—our cause is just, our mission noble, and our victory inevitable."

The president nodded to a uniformed figure waiting in the wings—a four-star general with wide shoulders. As President Whitmore took his seat next to Doc Parker, the general stepped forward, the room falling silent in anticipation.

"Thank you, Mr. President," he began, his voice gravelly but commanding. "The courage of our operatives in the field and the brilliance of our strategists have brought us to the cusp of a breakthrough."

He gestured, and the screens around the room lit up, displaying schematics and data streams that hinted at technological marvels.

"Our adversaries have been busy, but so have we. The advancements in surveillance, drone technology, and cyber warfare you're familiar with are just the tip of the iceberg." The room's attention was captive, each person leaning in as the general continued, "Which brings us to the reason we're all here."

At that moment, the lights dimmed further, and the main screen transitioned to a high-definition video. The imagery was cryptic, showcasing components and mechanisms that defied easy explanation, the promise of a leap forward in military capability.

"Ladies and gentlemen, I give you," the general announced, pausing for effect, "the Chicago Project."

As the attendees watched, spellbound, the video culminated in a visual demonstration so revolutionary it felt like witnessing the future being born. The general's voice filled the room once more. "This is the dawn of a new era in warfare, one where the battlefield is everywhere and nowhere, and our enemies will find no shadow to hide in."

In that moment of revelation, Parker felt a nudge at his side. Turning, he met the president's gaze, a spark of determination alive in Whitmore's eyes.

"See, Parker. Didn't I tell you that our boys wouldn't be sitting on their hands this whole time?"

Parker's response was a nod, his eyes wide not just with the spectacle before him but with the realization of the stakes they were playing for.

TEN

THEIR ARRIVAL AT KIRTLAND WAS SHROUDED IN the secrecy of night. During the flight, Noah had spoken with the head of Kirtland's airport security to ensure minimal staff presence so that when they finally touched down, everything went largely unnoticed.

Allison was currently anything but the Dragon Lady. Instead, she was a portrait of vulnerability. Her consciousness ebbed and flowed like the waves of the ocean they'd left behind. On a stretcher and wrapped in a thermal blanket, she was placed straight into the back of a Dodge Caravan and driven out of there.

Evading the usual entry points, they navigated the streets of Kirtland with a singular focus, heading straight to the R&D building.

Once there, Allison was taken straight to the building's infirmary. A team of medical experts were waiting there, swarming around her the second she arrived. With clinical efficiency, they worked to stabilize her critical condition.

Noah, Marco, and Renée stood at the window to her room, watching intently as nurses attended to her. The poor woman, visibly shaking, looked terribly frail under their careful attention.

Noah's voice broke the heavy silence. "They played my own trick back on me."

Marco glanced at him, a little confused. "What's that, boss?"

Locking eyes with Marco, Noah reiterated, his voice barely above a whisper, "My own trick... they turned it back on me."

Marco exchanged a puzzled look with Renée, who offered a helpless shrug in response, Noah's cryptic words hanging in the air.

Marco sought clarity. "I'm lost here, boss. What trick are you talking about?"

"Protocol 9," Noah finally offered.

Recognition flickered in Marco's eyes. "You're talking about that mean trick you played on us all where you faked Molly and the boss lady's deaths, right?"

"Yes," Noah confirmed.

Renée's brow furrowed. "So you're saying this is a repeat of that scenario?"

Noah offered a grim smile, meeting her gaze squarely. "No, this isn't my doing. This is all them—Schultz and the Council. Even in death, Henrik Schultz is playing his games. I tricked him into believing she was dead once. And he went and did it back on me. Made me think that she'd burned to ashes in that house along with everyone else. But all along" —he paused, his gaze drifting back to the window, to Allison's fragile form being settled into a bed—"they had her."

Team Camelot fell back into silent contemplation, their eyes fixing once more on the miracle before them.

A few minutes later, one of the doctors, a small man wearing large glasses and possessing a calm demeanor, came to speak with them. "She's suffering from mild hypothermia," he said, his voice steady. "And there are signs of physical trauma. From our early analysis, there are broken bones, contusions, and general... indications of torture."

"Understandable," Noah replied, his voice dead calm. "The Council has had her for more than six months. They would have taken their time with her."

"We've also done some quick blood analysis," the doctor went on. "Though we'll have to wait for the remainder of tests, early analysis is showing that there are traces of various chemicals in her system. The types used in psychological torture."

The disclosure of these grim details regarding Allison's ordeal was met with a heavy silence from those outside the room, their eyes pinned to her as the medical team worked around her diligently.

"Poor Allison," Renée murmured.

The doctor quickly offered his excuses before making a swift departure, leaving Noah, Marco, and Renée in a charged silence that hung in the air between them. However, their moment of contemplation was abruptly broken by the arrival of Jenny.

Moving with her usual purposeful stride, her eyes wide with disbelief, she approached the window. "It's really her," she whispered, almost to herself as much as to the others, her gaze fastening on to the figure in the hospital bed. "The Dragon Lady."

The air thickened with the weight of those three words; the nickname that carried stories of legend within their ranks.

Noah broke the silence that followed. "It's why Schultz burned down the house," he said. "To hide the fact that there wouldn't be a body."

Jenny, her eyes not leaving Allison's bruised face, added softly, "They've had her all this time."

"From the extent of her injuries," Noah said, "it's clear what the Council have been doing with her. Trying to get her to turn."

Jenny nodded in agreement. "Looks like she put up one hell of a fight," she murmured, her gaze not leaving Allison's bruised face.

Marco clenched his fists. "This is what we are up against," he said grimly. "They enjoy breaking people."

Renée, usually composed, looked shaken. "And when they don't need them," she added, "they toss them to the sharks."

"We can't rule out that they might have gotten what they wanted," Noah said.

Jenny nodded gravely. "That means they could know as much about E & E as she does. The Council might be several steps ahead by now. That's why I had security at Kirtland increased while you were away. The town is in lockdown. We can't take any chances, not with what Allison knows."

As the team grappled with the gravity of this, Esmeralda's voice suddenly cut through their apprehension, broadcasting over the PA system. "Noah and Team, I am informing you that Mr. Blessing has just found something important," she announced. "He requires your immediate presence in the War Room."

WHEN THEY GOT THERE, the team was met with an alarming sight. A large monitor displayed a graphic of the Earth—and it was covered in a sprawling web of red dots.

Noah's reaction was a mix of disbelief and concern. "What am I seeing, Neil?" he asked, trying to comprehend the scale of what was before him.

"Nothing good," Neil responded grimly. "The first communications have come in from the platform, and they've revealed the extent of their network. Each dot on that map represents one of the Council's hacking farms."

Renée asked, "How many are there?"

Neil turned to their AI for the answer. "Esmeralda, how many hacking farms have we found?"

The AI's reply was chilling: "There are seven hundred and eighty nine hacking farms in total."

"And in the United States alone?" Noah prompted further.

"One hundred eight" came the response.

Neil summarized the dire situation. "They're everywhere."

Approaching the map, Noah's realization was striking. "It's even bigger than we thought."

The scope of the Council's influence and reach was becoming a daunting reality for the team. They stood around the monitor, each member processing the intimidating revelation.

Marco broke the silence. "This is... it's like they've got their fingers in every corner of the planet."

Jenny added, "It's not just about hacking anymore. This is a full-scale information war."

Noah, his eyes still fixed on the map of red dots, voiced the team's shared sentiment. "We knew they were a threat, but this... it's even bigger than we thought. We're not just up against a group; we're up against an empire."

Neil then laid out the staggering implications of the Council's network. "There's not a nation on Earth with as much scope as them," he remarked. "We're gonna need more than the US government behind us. This is a global issue."

As the team grappled with the vastness of the Council's reach, their intense discussion was suddenly interrupted. A member of the medical team burst into the room with news that cut through the nervous atmosphere. "She's coherent," the woman said, visibly out of breath. "And she's asking for Noah."

———

RETURNING TO THE R&D infirmary, Noah and the team stood around Allison's bed. She was sitting up, her expression one of disorientation, a thermal blanket wrapped around her shoulders, the strip lighting reflecting off it in streaks. Slowly, as she recognized the faces around her, a glimmer flickered in her eyes.

The team members were in a state of shock and disbelief, still struggling to comprehend the reality of Allison being alive. As her gaze moved from one familiar face to another, a wave of emotion washed over her. When her eyes met

Noah's, she broke down, whispering his name with a mixture of pain and relief. "Noah..."

Noah immediately stepped forward and enveloped her in a comforting embrace, offering a silent promise of safety and understanding. Sensing the need for privacy, he gently asked everyone to step outside. "We need a moment," he said.

The team exited the room with respectful, albeit hesitant steps, leaving Noah and Allison alone.

In the quiet of the infirmary, Allison's voice was fragile but determined. "Noah, the torture was... it was endless," she began, her hands fidgeting with the blanket. "Since Schultz took me, they've been moving me around, but the one thing that was always the same was the torture. They kept asking the same things, over and over, about E & E— about you."

Noah's expression was pained, anger and guilt swirling in his eyes. "Allison, you don't have to..."

She interrupted. "I didn't tell them anything. It took every bit of self-control, but I never uttered a single secret to them. Still, the things they did..." Her voice trailed off.

Noah reached for her hand. "I'm so sorry, Allison. This... it must have been hell what they put you through. If I'd known you were alive, I would have done everything to find you."

Allison looked at him, her eyes reflecting a deep, enduring trauma. "It's not your fault, Noah. But we have to stop them. What they're capable of..."

She trailed off a second time, her eyes glazing over, mind drifting away with the things she'd seen, the things she'd felt —the pain and horror. "They're bigger than we ever imagined," she suddenly said. "They've been around longer, are more connected, and have greater capabilities than we ever thought."

Noah's own assessment was grave. "I have to agree with that," he said. "I've spent the past six months hunting a monster that gets bigger every time I think I've got it by the tail."

Her eyes still glazed, Allison said, "They have monsters, too. Real ones. How much did you see before I went into the water?"

"I saw the big guy lift you up and drop you."

"Then you saw one of their monsters."

"The giant?"

"Yes. His name is Gruber," she told him, her tone deadly serious. "He's the product of the Council's genetic engineering experiments. Gruber was made in a lab in Munich, part of a program to create elite soldiers unlike any other," she explained. "Out of forty-four test subjects, all genetically modified, only Gruber survived into adulthood. The others suffered from a range of catastrophic genetic failures. Most were just children when they died, their bodies unable to handle the enhancements. This program... it wasn't just about creating people with superior physical strength. It involved neurological and psychological modifications as well, making Gruber an unparalleled strategic and combat asset," Allison added gravely. "I heard all of this from his own mouth. I was with him most of the six months, being dragged from one place to another."

As Noah listened, his brow furrowed. "A super-soldier?" he said, trying to grasp the full implication. "Made in a lab?"

Allison nodded slowly. "Yes, and he's fixated on you,

Noah. Gruber is one of the Council's deadliest weapons. He's not just physically formidable; he's a strategic threat, too."

It was revelation stacked upon revelation, each one adding a new, ominous layer to the threat they all faced. Noah felt a chill at the prospect of a direct confrontation with this mammoth known as Gruber, a being created for destruction and honed for strategic warfare.

"What about leadership?" Noah asked her. "Were you ever introduced to any of the major players?"

"No," Allison replied. "I never saw the true members. Just their intermediaries, torturers, henchmen, monsters like Gruber," she added, a distant look in her eyes. "I was confined to cells, shuffled between bases, always blindfolded when they moved me."

"So you have no idea where you might have been?" Noah asked.

"No," she admitted. "I didn't even know I was in the middle of the ocean until they dragged me out of my cell and flung me into it."

As she spoke, her eyes shone at him with the horror of the last six months. Noah reached for her hand. "Then we'll start from what we know and bring them down together. Gruber, the Council, all of them."

Allison squeezed his hand back. "With everything I've seen, everything I've learned... they underestimated one thing—our resolve to fight back."

ELEVEN

The next day, Noah drove Allison to her home at the edge of Kirtland, the interior of the Dodge Charger steeped in a reflective silence. Allison seemed lost in thought, her gaze distant, as if she was mentally bracing herself to return to a home that, while familiar, now represented a life irrevocably altered by recent experience.

Noah, meanwhile, wrestled with his own complex mix of emotions. Guilt gnawed at him for having accepted her presumed death without question, for not searching harder. Yet, beneath this, there was an undercurrent of what felt like destiny—a sense that their unexpected reunion was somehow meant to be. This thought offered him a quiet resolve, a renewed vigor for the challenges ahead. With Allison's return, it wasn't just about fighting the Council anymore; it was about reclaiming what they had lost and standing together as a united front.

Arriving at Allison's home, a sense of desolation hung in the air. The three-story house, perched up a mountain road, stood in stark isolation, surrounded by an expanse of nature with no neighbors visible for miles. Allison stepped out of the car, her eyes scanning the quiet surroundings. The silence was overwhelming, almost solid enough to touch.

She stood at her front door, a hand hovering over the handle, but couldn't bring herself to turn it. The house, once a sanctuary, now felt like an echo chamber of her recent traumas. She turned over her shoulder, looking back at Noah in the car.

Walking back to the Charger, she leaned down to Noah's open window. "I, eh, I... the loneliness here is too much," she confessed. "Can I stay with you at the lake? I don't think I can face this alone."

Understanding, Noah opened the passenger door and waited for her to get in before taking her back to his home. There, Sarah and Norah waited for them, their faces a blend of joy and concern. Earlier, Norah, her childlike curiosity evident, had started to voice her confusion about Allison after Sarah had told her who was coming.

"But I thought Aunty Ali was..." The little girl hadn't been able to finish her sentence, the unspoken word hanging in the air.

Sarah had stepped in with gentle reassurance. "Sweetheart, sometimes miracles happen," she had said.

As Allison stepped out of the car, Sarah and Norah came to meet her. Norah, with the unfiltered joy of a child, ran to her. "Aunty Ali!" she exclaimed, her arms wide open.

Allison, overwhelmed by the welcome, knelt down to hug her. "I've missed you so much, little one," she whispered, her voice thick with emotion.

Inside the farmhouse, Allison moved through the rooms

with a quiet unease; the warmth and vibrancy of the home was very different than her inner turmoil. Sarah and Noah, attuned to her discomfort, showed her to a spare room. "We want you to feel at home here, Allison," Sarah said softly, crossing a rug to a chest of drawers and pulling out some fresh sheets for the bed.

Allison offered a small, grateful smile. "Thank you, Sarah, Noah. This means a lot."

As the night settled over Temple Lake, the house filled with the comforting sounds of a family brought together by fate and circumstance. Allison, though still haunted by shadows, found in their company a flicker of hope, a sense that maybe, just maybe, she could start to heal.

TWELVE

In the soft embrace of next morning, Doc Parker and Molly Hanson made their way to Noah Wolf's lakeside farmhouse. The mountain air was crisp when they got out of their car, sweeping across the driveway as they approached the front door.

Their knock was soon answered. As the door swung open, revealing Allison Peterson, time seemed to stand still. Molly, overwhelmed by a surge of emotions, rushed forward, closing the distance in a heartbeat and throwing her arms around her former boss. Allison's own arms then found their way around Molly. Their embrace was a silent testament to the fact that since the last time they'd seen each other, they'd been sure that the other was dead. This hug was for the losses mourned and the miraculous threads of fate that had woven their paths back together.

Gathering themselves, they all moved to the veranda, where the tranquil beauty of Temple Lake and the mountains offered a serene backdrop to the unfolding conversation.

Doc Parker spoke first. "Allison, it's beyond words to have you back with us. When you're ready, your place at E & E is waiting for you."

Allison didn't hesitate. "I'm ready now, Doc."

Molly exchanged a glance with Parker. "Let's not rush," Molly interjected softly. "After all you've been through, it's important to take a moment, to heal."

Allison's gaze swept over the idyllic view before them, her voice firm yet reflective. "The Council isn't going to wait for me to heal. You need all the help you can get to stop them."

Parker nodded, understanding her urgency but prioritizing her recovery. "We want you back, Allison, but only at your best—when you're truly at one hundred percent. Your well-being is our top priority."

"I'm at one hundred percent *now*, Doc," Allison insisted.

Doc Parker gave her a look that mingled concern with sincerity. "Can you at least give it a week?" he asked gently. "Trust the advice of an old friend and shrink who's known you for over two decades?"

"A whole week?"

"Yes, a week."

After a moment's hesitation, Allison nodded. "Okay, I'll wait."

"Good," Parker said, visibly relieved. He then shifted in his seat, signaling a change in topic. "There's someone else who's eager to say hello. Someone who couldn't be here in person."

Turning to Molly, Parker received a tablet from her and then handed it to Allison. "Touch the screen," he instructed, standing up. "It'll activate the call."

Allison did so, and the screen flickered to life, revealing the familiar face of President Jackson T. Whitmore. Doc Parker and Molly discreetly wandered off toward the lake, leaving Allison to her conversation.

"Allison Peterson," the president began, his voice carrying a mix of respect and relief, "seeing you alive and well makes me feel that our nation sleeps a little sounder tonight. We are all incredibly grateful that luck appeared on our side this time."

Allison, taken aback by the direct acknowledgment from the president himself, found her voice. "Mr. President, it's an honor. I'm just glad to be back, ready to continue our fight."

The president's smile was both warm and somber. "Your dedication is invaluable, Allison. Rest assured, the nation stands with you as we brace against the shadows. Your survival sparks hope—not just for us but for the principles we're fighting to protect."

"Our enemies are strong, sir," Allison said gravely.

"I know. But rest assured we're doing everything we can on our end to build a force powerful enough to take it to them. Allison"—his tone darkened and his expression also— "tell me, you were with them. What are their capabilities?"

Allison took a deep breath. He wasn't going to like the answer. "They have bases everywhere, sir. And they are building things…"

"What things?"

"Weapons of mass destruction."

Their conversation continued, a private exchange of cautionary portent, gratitude, determination, and the shared commitment to a cause greater than themselves. At the lake's edge, Doc Parker and Molly looked on, a silent pledge between them to support Allison through the challenges ahead, knowing the road was long but not insurmountable with her back by their side.

THIRTEEN

Two days later, the early morning routine at the farmhouse was in its usual rhythm. The sound of running water filled the ensuite bathroom as Noah, standing under the shower, was interrupted by his phone's urgent ring. It was Neil. "Blessing, what've you got?"

"You need to come to R&D. See for yourself," Neil replied cryptically.

"Give me ten."

The call ended, and Noah quickly wrapped up his shower, understanding the gravity of Neil's call. He dressed quickly, strapping his SIG Sauer M17 to his hip, checking his hair, then leaving the room.

Downstairs, a scene of familial bliss was unfolding. Allison was in the kitchen with Norah, making pancakes, her laughter mingling with the child's. Unnoticed, Noah stood in the doorway watching them. It was a moment of normalcy, of peace and family. However, he didn't go unnoticed for long.

With her back to him, Allison broke off the conversation with Norah to say, "You gonna stand there watching us or are you gonna come in?"

Norah turned sharply at Allison's words, her eyes lighting up as she spotted Noah. "Daddy!" she exclaimed, running over to greet him.

"Good morning, sunshine," Noah said, bending down to kiss her on the cheek.

He straightened up and moved to the coffee maker, pouring himself a cup. The homey sound of coffee brewing filled the kitchen, blending with the comforting aroma.

Allison watched him for a moment before speaking up. "Your phone was pretty insistent a moment ago. Hard not to hear it with the shower right above the kitchen," she said, her tone casual but probing.

Noah glanced over at her, the coffee pot pausing mid-pour. "Yeah, it was Neil. He's got something he wants me to see at R&D. Says it's urgent," he explained, trying to maintain a nonchalant demeanor.

Allison leaned against the counter. "Anything you can share? Or is it top-secret Neil stuff?" she teased lightly, though her eyes searched his for more information.

Noah chuckled, resuming his coffee pouring. "You know how it is with Neil. Could be groundbreaking, or he could've just found a new way to automate his coffee machine. I'll find out more when I get there."

Allison nodded. "Well, just so long as you're back before dinner. Norah and I were planning on trying a cake recipe we found online, weren't we, Norah?"

Norah, who had been quietly listening, nodded vigorously. "Yeah! You and Mommy have to help us taste-test, Daddy!"

"I wouldn't miss it for the world," Noah promised, smiling at them both.

Grabbing his coffee and a slice of toast to go, Noah headed out. He got into his '69 Dodge Charger, and less than five minutes later, he was inside the bustling War Room.

Neil's excitement was obvious as he presented his findings to Noah. "Check this out," he said. "Esmeralda has just finished deciphering the Council's encrypted messaging service." He gestured to a complex network of data displayed on the screen in front of them. "Not only do they have their own Internet, they have their own communication channels. This here is how they speak to each other without the rest of the world knowing. They've created a completely closed system using their own unique Internet cables, making it virtually inaccessible to outsiders. Until now," he added with a sly wink. "Look at this, Noah," he went on, bringing up an image on the screen of a stern-faced man with piercing eyes. "This is Dr. Alexei Morozov. His work in electromagnetics and quantum technologies was on the cutting edge. He was a pioneer in fields that could reshape the world. And he was supposed to have died in a plane crash over Siberia five years ago."

Neil brought up a series of messages onto the screen. "This is a communication between two high-ranking members of the Council. Look," he said, pointing at a particular message. "They are discussing a meeting with Morozov at an undisclosed installation."

"And you're sure it's *this* Morozov they're talking about?"

"The messages mention Dr. Morozov giving a demonstration of electromagnetic energy production. They talk about a giant machine that was able to disable a target satellite they'd placed in the earth's atmosphere. In other words, Morozov's theories in practice. It has to be him."

Noah leaned in. "But where was he?" he asked. "Where was this demonstration?"

Neil gave him a coy smile. "Now that's where my smarts really come into play."

Noah lifted an eyebrow at him. "Smarts?"

"Yes, smarts. See, through a little detective work, your man Neil here has managed to piece together the location using nothing more than what I read in the messages. There it is." He pointed to some satellite images on a separate screen: a collection of nondescript buildings, almost camouflaged against a vast snowy landscape.

Noah stepped closer to the screen, intrigued. "Where is it?"

"Siberia."

"How'd you figure it?"

Neil smiled. "One message mentioned a flight from Singapore to an undisclosed city, then a six-hour private plane ride through heavy snow, followed by a journey in a large Sno-Cat. Another was an inventory list. Cold weather clothing was a priority. I checked weather patterns and flight times for that day. Then worked out where he'd gone through a series of eliminations."

"That's some serious detective work," Noah remarked, impressed. Before adding, "It doesn't look like much."

"No it doesn't," Neil said, pointing to the satellite images of the remote scattering of buildings in the Siberian tundra. "Just a few sheds and compounds on the surface, but look at this thermal image." He pressed a button on his keyboard, and the screen displayed imagery of massive heat signatures sprawling underground from the site. "On the surface," Neil went on, "it seems like nothing more than a series of basic structures, but the thermal images reveal a different story. Beneath the unremarkable exterior lies a sprawling, heavily fortified underground complex."

The heat signature spread out for at least a square mile.

"It's huge," Noah couldn't help commenting.

"They're definitely up to no good," Neil concluded. "This must be where they're hiding whatever they're building with Morozov."

Noah's resolve hardened as he considered their next move. "We need to go there ourselves," he declared. "If they're building some type of weapon there, it's our job to make sure it's destroyed. It's about time someone showed these assholes who's boss."

FOURTEEN

In the main briefing room at Kirtland, the combined members of Teams Camelot and Cinderella huddled around a table, looking down at the screens of tablets. Their focus was riveted on the latest satellite imagery and intelligence reports on the Siberian facility, all of it collected within the last 24 hours.

Molly Hanson stood at the end of the room, a large screen behind her. Around the table representing Camelot were Noah, Marco, and Renée. From Cinderella were Jenny Blessing, her tech guy, Jim Marino, and her driver, Dave Lange. Jim Marino was sharp-minded with a knack for deciphering complex data. As for Dave Lange, he was a tall, solidly built specimen known for his calmness under pressure, especially when behind the wheel.

Molly, pointing to the map of the facility on the large screen, immediately highlighted the unique challenges they would face. "First thing to mention is the location. It isn't just remote; it's in one of the harshest environments on Earth. You'll be dealing with extreme cold, unpredictable snowstorms, and potential whiteouts. Every move you make out there has to account for these conditions. It's not just the security you're up against; it's the environment itself."

Renée asked, "What's the weather going to be like on the day of the mission?"

Molly replied, "Not good. We're expecting heavy winds and snowfall. Remember, it is the Arctic Circle."

They now concentrated on the detailed map of the facility as Molly began to describe it. "Situated in Siberia's vast, desolate north, the facility is well-hidden. From above, it looks like nothing more than a few storage depots and abandoned buildings. But underground," she continued, "it's a sprawling research and development center."

"And what is it they're developing?" asked Jim Marino.

"We think they're focusing on electromagnetics, quantum computing, advanced weaponry—all exclusively for the Council." She then highlighted its self-sufficiency. "The facility is equipped with its own power generation, a mini nuclear reactor, and has reserves for food and water. There are also living quarters for scientists and security."

Marco shuffled in his chair. "How the hell did they build it out there without the Russians knowing?"

Molly gave a brief history. "Originally it was a Soviet secret research program. They enriched uranium and built nuclear warheads there. Post-Union, it was abandoned. The Council saw its potential and bought it. They now operate it without the Russian Federation's full knowledge."

"What do the Russians think it is?" Dave Lange asked.

Meeting his eyes, Molly replied, "They don't really care. So long as the one billion US dollars per year comes into the president's own private bank account."

"That'd do it," Lange remarked, grinning at his pal Jim Marino beside him.

"Staffed by a private army," Molly went on, "international scientists and Council loyalists, they are pretty much free to do as they want out there. The Siberian location was clearly chosen for its remoteness and the difficulty it presents for any assault or espionage."

Noah took over. "If you look at the next images on your tablets," he began as they flicked their fingers across the screens, "you can see that it's heavily fortified with state-of-the-art security. We're talking advanced anti-surveillance systems designed to detect and jam electronic spying efforts. Armed guards patrolling the area at all times. And we shouldn't be surprised to encounter automated defense systems—drones, motion sensors, maybe even automated turrets. This place is built like a fortress, designed to withstand any conventional assault."

Molly pointed to the schematic that had suddenly filled the screen behind her. "We've got a few potential entry points. This service entrance here seems less guarded. There are also underground tunnels and a series of air vents that circumvent much of the more well-guarded areas."

Jenny considered the options. "Service entrance might offer the least resistance," she analyzed. "Tunnels could be risky, and vents offer limited access but could get us close to key areas."

"Access is gonna be a thing," Jim Marino pointed out.

"Surely that service entrance is mechanically locked. How do we get inside?"

Renée chimed in, "We'll need to set up a remote support, something to hack into the place's security system from the outside."

"Wally's already on it," Molly told her. "He should have something ready for when the mission is a go."

The team nodded.

"Once inside the facility," Molly continued, "you'll split up. Dr. Morozov will be essential to understanding the capabilities of the Council's forces. Therefore, we need to extract him. Team Cinderella, that's your primary focus."

"What if he won't come?" Jenny put to her. "What if Morozov was in on faking his death and joined the Council willingly?"

"If Morozov happens to be unwilling," Molly explained, "then you'll each be armed with a syringe gun. If necessary, you'll use a rapid working sedative to facilitate a safe extraction."

"You mean one of us will have to carry him?" Dave Lange observed.

"If it comes to that," Molly said. "Nevertheless, I trust your skills of persuasion will suffice in getting Dr. Morozov into our hands."

"I guess they'll have to," Dave Lange muttered.

"Now," Molly continued, outlining the next part of the mission, "while Team Cinderella is handling Morozov, Team Camelot will focus on the giant machine described in the messages. Their goal will be to locate it and then destroy it by planting explosives. We're hoping the force may also cause a cave-in at the base."

Noah added, "We have to make sure the destruction is complete, leaving no chance for them to rebuild or replicate it. The mission we're about to embark on is crucial. We're up against one of the biggest threats yet. Let's stay sharp and coordinated. Because if we come out of this with both Morozov and this machine destroyed, we may just be on our way to turning this thing around."

FIFTEEN

Noah returned home to a scene of domestic tranquility. In the living room, Allison was on the floor, playing dolls with Norah. Their laughter and chatter filled the room.

In the kitchen, Noah found Sarah. "How's she doing?" he asked in a low voice, meaning Allison.

Sarah sighed, stirring her tea. "She's been a little distant. But I've noticed she's showing a keen interest in E & E's affairs. It's like she's trying to find her way back."

Noah leaned against the kitchen counter. "It's a lot for her to take in, coming back to... the way things are with the Council," he said, glancing toward the living room where Allison and Norah were playing.

Sarah nodded. "She's trying, Noah. But it's clear she's still processing everything. Maybe being more involved with E & E will give her a sense of control, something familiar."

Noah exhaled slowly, his gaze thoughtful. "Yeah, it might. But Doc Parker is adamant she needs another week."

He looked back at Allison and Norah, a soft smile forming. "At least she's not alone through this."

Later that evening, Noah's basement operations room was a hive of focused activity. Maps and monitors illuminated the space, each displaying crucial details of the Siberian mission. Absorbed in his work, he reviewed every aspect of the plan, ensuring no detail was overlooked.

The sound of footsteps creaking on the stairs announced Allison's arrival. She emerged at the bottom carrying a tray, bringing Noah a piece of the cake she'd baked earlier with Norah. As she stepped into the room, a soft glow from the laptop lit Noah's concentrated face.

"Working late again?" Allison asked gently, setting the tray down.

Noah glanced up. "Just going over some last-minute details," he replied, instinctively reaching out to close his laptop. The screen, which displayed satellite images of the Siberian base, snapped shut.

Allison noticed the swift motion. "I don't need to know the details. Just... stay safe out there," she said.

Noah nodded. "I will. Thanks for this, Allison," he said, gesturing to the cake.

"It's red velvet. Norah did the piping all by herself."

Noah took up his fork and began eating the delicious cake. "It's real good," he observed in between bites.

Allison smiled, but she wasn't really concerned about his thoughts on the dessert. There were other things bothering her.

"I want to help, Noah," she said as he chewed. "Maybe there's something I remember that could be useful."

Noah considered her offer before finally cracking. After all, she was the Dragon Lady; he trusted her with his life.

"We've found the location of some type of underground facility," he told her. "We think they're building a weapon there."

Allison's eyes narrowed keenly. "Where is it?"

"Siberia."

Allison's expression turned thoughtful. "One of the places I was at," she recalled, "was deadly cold when they dragged me out of the plane. Even though I was blindfolded, I knew there was snow. I could feel the snowflakes melting against my face. Later, when I was in my cell, I remember the power going out intermittently and feeling vibrations, like tremors. One night, everything went pitch black. All of a sudden, there was running and shouting outside my door. Then the lights burst on, so bright they exploded."

The room fell quiet, the pieces of the puzzle slowly fitting together, bringing them closer to unraveling the Council's sinister plans.

SIXTEEN

OVER THE COURSE OF THE NEXT 48 HOURS, TEAMS Camelot and Cinderella embarked on a meticulously planned journey to Siberia. Disguised as everyday civilians, they departed the United States on separate commercial flights, skillfully maintaining their covers as they traversed across continents to reach Russia from separate directions.

Landing in Moscow, the teams transitioned to flights bound for Yakutsk, with a brief stopover in Irkutsk. Their journey took them deeper into the vast expanse of Russia, the landscape growing more rugged and remote with each mile.

From Yakutsk, they shifted to a more covert mode of travel. Small, unmarked charter planes and helicopters, subtly equipped with basic stealth technology, carried them closer to their target deep in the Sakha Republic, near the frigid waters of the East Siberian Sea. These aircraft, unassuming yet capable, glided through the skies, expertly avoiding radar detection.

As they flew over the extensive Siberian landscape, a sense of anticipation built among the team members. The harsh, icy terrain below was both beautiful and daunting, a reminder of the challenging mission that lay ahead.

The final leg of their journey was to a secluded, predetermined landing spot, safely distanced from the Council's facility, where their equipment had already been placed. The teams then embarked on foot, initially using snowmobiles to traverse the expansive and treacherous Siberian tundra, where the landscape was a canvas of endless snow, framed by a gray, overcast sky.

The transition to cross-country skis for stealthier movement was challenging yet necessary. As they moved, the harsh winds howled around them, and the snow underfoot was a constant adversary, changing from powdery to treacherously icy. This barren and unforgiving environment encapsulated their isolation and the dangers they faced.

Navigating the difficult terrain, the teams pushed forward, their figures mere specks against the vast, white expanse. As they reached the outskirts of the facility, they spread out to survey the compound. Noah, peering through binoculars, whispered, "See those watch towers? Snipers, most likely."

Renée, scanning the area with a thermal scope, added, "There's a heavy guard presence just beyond the entrances. We'll need to be extra cautious."

Jenny noted, "There's a shift change happening soon. Might be our best chance to slip in unnoticed."

Teams Camelot and Cinderella moved into position, each targeting a different entry point to the facility. Team Camelot approached a service door located on the north side, partially concealed by a mound of snow and adjacent to a storage unit. It was a discreet point of entry, offering cover and a less visible approach.

Meanwhile, Team Cinderella headed toward a hatch located on the southern end, camouflaged by the rugged terrain and near a cluster of discarded industrial equipment. This entry point, although more exposed, provided direct access to the underground sections of the facility.

Both teams moved with utmost stealth, using a combination of skill and technology to stay undetected. Team Camelot approached the service door, its outline barely visible against the snow. "Looks clear," Noah whispered, checking the surroundings. "But stay sharp."

Meanwhile, Team Cinderella neared the southern hatch. "This is more exposed than I'd like," Jenny murmured, eyeing the open terrain. "You ready, Jim?"

"Affirmative," Marino confirmed.

Braving the biting wind and swirling snow, he made his way to an access panel close to the door. Then while Dave Lange and Jenny provided cover, Jim skillfully connected another of Wally's devices to the panel's electronics, the snow whipping against his face in fierce gusts as he worked away.

Once he'd secured a line, he contacted Esmeralda. "Esmeralda, confirm if you've made contact and are inside."

"Confirmed," the AI's response crackled through. "I'm in their system and have full control, Jim. You're clear to proceed."

Both teams, poised at their entry points, were a blend of apprehension and readiness. The moment to infiltrate the facility had arrived.

SEVENTEEN

In synchronized precision, Teams Camelot and Cinderella initiated their infiltration. As they breached the perimeter and headed underground, they were immediately engulfed in a world of advanced technology housed within dark, cramped corridors that snaked like a complex web under the frozen Siberian landscape. The facility's interior was a fusion of futuristic innovation and claustrophobic spaces, illuminated by the eerie glow of strip lighting.

With both teams split up, Team Cinderella advanced toward the facility's laboratories, their path illuminated by the soft glow of the tablet strapped to Jenny's right forearm. As they navigated the maze of sterile, metal-lined corridors, the map on the tablet guided them to a secluded section of the facility, marked by reinforced security doors and a noticeable increase in surveillance cameras. It was therefore lucky that their body armor was quantum cloaked.

They found Dr. Morozov in a high-security lab, a sterile, brightly lit room filled with screens displaying complex data and workstations cluttered with instruments. Morozov himself was deeply engrossed in work.

Staying outside the room, Jim Marino whispered into his comms, "Okay, Esmeralda. Time for a diversion."

As Esmeralda initiated a diversionary alarm, an urgent message blared over the facility's tannoy system, alerting the security officers: "Attention, anomaly detected in the western sector. All units respond immediately." This announcement prompted the security guards stationed inside the lab to hastily depart, leaving the room unguarded.

Team Cinderella, taking advantage of the distraction, left their hiding places and moved into the lab. The second Jenny called his name, Morozov looked up in fear and disbelief, his eyes widening at the sight of the team.

"Doctor, will you come with us?" Jenny asked, her hand touching on the syringe gun attached to her belt.

"You're American," Morozov observed.

"Yes."

"US government?"

"Yes."

The scientist relaxed. "Good," he said, stepping toward them. "You won't need that." He nodded toward Jenny's syringe gun. "I'll come willingly."

Jenny touched her comms. "Bossman, we've got Morozov," she communicated back to Camelot. "And just so you know, he's a willing passenger."

The rescue of Morozov was a critical step, but the danger of their mission was far from over.

———

"RECEIVED," Noah whispered back to Jenny. "We're almost there ourselves."

Team Camelot had just reached a formidable set of blast doors blocking their path to a place labelled the 'Main Chamber' on the schematics. Renée quickly contacted Esmeralda. "Got a big set of blast doors we need opened, Ez. Level Five, right before the Main Chamber."

"I'm on it," the AI responded.

Marco and Noah stood guard, their eyes scanning both ends of the corridor. After a moment filled with angst that seemed to drag on for much longer than it actually did, the doors began to groan and slowly opened, revealing the immense chamber beyond. It was an awe-inspiring and unsettling sight. The room was dominated by a gargantuan machine, a complex array of wires, metal, and pulsating energy cores. The air was filled with the sound of machinery and the intense glow of welding torches as technicians and scientists feverishly worked on the colossal structure.

Noah, Marco, and Renée paused before the doorway, taking in the enormity of the device. "What in the..." Marco muttered under his breath.

"No time to admire it," Noah snapped in a hushed voice. "Time to do what we came here for."

Bursting into the room with a surge of adrenaline, Noah, Marco, and Renée quickly assessed the layout, their eyes lined with the scopes of their M4A1 carbines. The three armed guards in there, caught cold by the sudden intrusion, barely had time to reach for their weapons before they were taken out by quick, pin-point bursts.

In a matter of seconds, the trio had gained control of the situation with precision and speed. The sudden violence inside the vast chamber, now quiet except for the echo of their discharged carbines, left the technicians and scientists in shock. It meant they already knew who was boss, allowing themselves to be quickly corralled into a secure group.

A new phase of the mission had begun.

EIGHTEEN

TEAM CINDERELLA, WITH DR. MOROZOV IN TOW, moved rapidly through the dimly lit corridors of the facility. As they made their way toward the exit, Jim Marino kept in constant communication with Esmeralda.

"How many are we talking about?" Jim asked.

Esmeralda had just that second finished warning about incoming personnel moving their way.

"Judging from their heat signatures, I'd say roughly thirty," Esmeralda's voice crackled through their earpieces.

Jenny quickly assessed the situation. "That'll be the cavalry," she pointed out. "So get ready." She turned to Morozov with a decisive look. "Can you shoot?"

Morozov, with a firm nod, affirmed his capability.

"Then take this," Jenny said, handing him her SIG Sauer M17 pistol.

Jim Marino spoke into his comms. "Esmeralda, better warn Camelot."

"I'm trying," the AI replied. "But it appears our communications are being jammed."

That made Team Cinderella all glance at each other. With heightened alertness and weapons at the ready, they continued their uneasy journey through the meandering corridors of the facility, steeling themselves for an impending confrontation.

———

Team Camelot worked briskly to sabotage the colossal machine, the team members climbing all over it, planting explosives at strategic points, the atmosphere thick with urgency as they wired the charges, aware that every second mattered. Their hands moved deftly, methodically securing each explosive in place, ensuring the weapon's complete destruction.

"Wait!" Renée exclaimed abruptly, pausing in her work.

"What?" Marco responded, glancing toward her while his hands fixed another charge in place.

"Do you hear that?" she whispered, straining her ears.

At this, even Noah ceased his work, the trio falling silent to listen intently.

"Sounds like marching feet," Marco observed with a crease of concern on his forehead.

Realization gradually flooded Noah, his heart jumping into his throat. "Quick!" he snapped urgently. "Finish setting the explosives."

The marching got louder, until, suddenly, the nervous atmosphere shattered as a flood of armed men burst into the room. "Halt!" commanded one of the invaders as they rapidly encircled them.

The team froze in their vulnerable positions. These were not ordinary soldiers; their movements were precise, their equipment state of the art. They surrounded Camelot, guns aimed with unerring purpose, effectively sealing off any chance of escape.

The trio, positioned around the machine with hands raised in surrender, faced the intense demand: "Get down or we'll shoot!"

The threat was emphasized when the men cocked their IWI Tavor bullpups. Complying, Noah, Marco, and Renée cautiously descended from the machine, the detonator poking out of Noah's back pocket.

Gathered before the group with arms still raised, they were commanded to stay put. It wasn't long before the guards parted, and into this charged atmosphere stepped the genetically engineered giant, Gruber, his formidable presence like a dark cloud swooping in. Towering and broadshouldered, his every step resonated with controlled power. His face was an impassive mask, but his eyes, cold and calculating, missed nothing. He surveyed the room, his gaze eventually locking on to Noah.

A smile pierced his face. "We meet at last, Herr Wolf," Gruber intoned, his voice deep and resonant, a chilling edge to his words. The air seemed to thicken with anticipation, the encounter between these two formidable adversaries now inevitable.

———

Team Cinderella had lost contact with Esmeralda some time ago, leaving them deaf and blind. As they cautiously plotted their way along another sterile corridor, their journey was suddenly interrupted. Armed guards emerged in front and behind, seemingly out of thin air, their rapid appearance cutting off any route of escape.

Jenny issued a hushed command, "Back to back, stay alert." The team instantly formed a tight circle, facing outward. "Doctor, with me," she told Morozov, placing him between herself and Dave Lange. Their gazes flickered rapidly, taking in every detail of their assailants as they came to a stop on both sides.

———

Standing across the room from Gruber, Noah quickly assessed his situation. His mind raced through options: resist, negotiate, or stall for time. The tension was like a tightly drawn bowstring, the three team members exchanging quick glances, silent signals communicated, subtle shifts in positioning.

Gruber's voice filled the chamber. "It would appear the bear has caught the wolf," he said, his eyes never leaving Noah. "The one purpose I was born for."

"You weren't born," Noah snapped back. "You were *made*."

"Whether inside a lab or a womb," Gruber retorted, "we are all made, Herr Wolf. But not all of us are born with purpose."

"And what purpose were you born with?"

Gruber held Noah's eye. "Hunting," he said.

"Hunting what?"

"Hunting you, Herr Wolf," Gruber concluded.

———

SURROUNDED BY ARMED MEN, Team Cinderella found themselves at an impasse. The tight air of the narrow corridor resounded with the guards' commanding voices, demanding in no uncertain terms, "Dr. Morozov, step forward and come to us. The rest of you, drop your weapons!"

Jenny, standing firm with a steely resolve, held her assault rifle with a confident grip. Her eyes, fiercely determined, met the gaze of the lead guard. With defiance lacing her voice, she responded, "No one's ever gotten me to drop my weapon yet. It'll take me being stiff and dead for anyone to pry this out of my hands."

The situation in the corridor was quickly escalating, every person there keenly aware that things were reaching a critical point.

———

IN THE PULSATING atmosphere of the giant chamber, Noah stepped into the role as a negotiator. "Gruber, let's talk about this. There's no need for bloodshed," he said, trying to find an opening or a way to de-escalate the situation.

Gruber remained unfazed. "Herr Wolf, your reputation

precedes you. But you're in my domain now," he replied, a slight smile playing on his lips.

Noah, maintaining his composure, pressed further. "Okay. So you've got us. What's your endgame?"

Gruber leaned in slightly, his confidence unwavering. "Endgame? We are the endgame. The Council's plans go far beyond you, Herr Wolf. Here in this facility, you've only seen the surface. What we've allowed you to see. After all"—he paused, his gaze piercing—"we have been tracking your moves for quite some time. You should know we're always a step ahead."

Noah's mind raced, analyzing Gruber's words for any hint of leverage, any clue that could turn the tide in their favor. They needed enough time to get away from the machine; they needed some kind of distraction.

And that was when one came.

In that critical moment, Noah's eyes flicked to a tele-screen that stood on the wall behind Gruber. Amidst routine facility updates, a message caught his eye—'Noah, get ready for the lights to go out.' In a split-second, Noah realized that this was a discreet signal from Esmeralda, the AI still hidden somewhere within the facility's systems.

Noah glanced at Marco then Renée, a silent message in his look: Get ready.

The AI enacted her plan, plunging the room into sudden darkness as she cut the lights of the subterranean lair, throwing Gruber's men into disarray. In the ensuing confusion, Noah, Marco, and Renée snapped down the ocular lenses of their night-vision goggles and became shadows within the confusion. Their movements shrouded, they navigated undetected toward the exit, away from the device —and the explosives.

"Get the lights back on!" Gruber shouted at his men.

Reaching a safe point close to the exit, Noah paused, taking a steadying breath. Then, pulling the detonator from his back pocket, he pushed the button.

NINETEEN

THE SECOND NOAH TRIGGERED THE EXPLOSIVES, the underground facility was thrown into pandemonium. The explosion was immense, engulfing the room in a maelstrom of smoke and debris. The initial blast wiped out a line of Gruber's men, caught unaware and too close to the machine. As parts of the giant contraption buckled and collapsed, several more guards were crushed under heavy wreckage.

Amid this, Team Camelot used the darkness, smoke, and disarray as cover to make their escape.

————

WITH EVERYTHING THROWN into darkness and the distant thunder of the explosion reverberating through the entire facility, Team Cinderella seized the opportunity. Jenny, with sudden decisiveness, neutralized the nearest guard, turning him into a makeshift shield. She and the rest of her team then flipped down the ocular lenses of their night vision, the corridor transforming into a surreal landscape of green shadows and silhouettes. The guards, still reeling from the sudden darkness, appeared as disoriented figures in their vision.

Taking advantage of this mayhem, Team Cinderella took out most of the guards, the darkness exploding with gunfire, before moving away from the remaining men with deadly efficiency.

With calm authority, Jenny guided Morozov and her team through the maze of corridors. In the aftermath of the explosion, emergency alarms wailed throughout the facility, creating a cacophony that bounced off the walls.

Within this din, Team Cinderella moved with purpose. The facility, now a labyrinth of confusion and disarray, was something they navigated with practiced accuracy, having spent the last two days going over the schematics until they knew the place as well as their own homes.

———

IN ANOTHER PART of the facility, Team Camelot was also using the disarray as a cloak, slipping through the shadows and avoiding major confrontations as they got out of there. They moved through pre-determined escape routes, familiar with every turn and corner from their meticulous planning.

The two teams, though operating separately, were united in their singular focus to evade and escape. They were ghosts within the disorder, unseen yet ever-moving, turning the facility's state of upheaval to their strategic advantage. The nervousness of the moment creeped over them. It was a real thing, grabbing at them, both teams caught in a thrilling race against time as they edged closer to freedom and safety.

As the alarms continued to blare, Teams Camelot and Cinderella arrived back at their separate entry points, primed for exfiltration. Team Camelot had retraced their steps back to the service door. Team Cinderella, with Dr. Morozov in tow, hurried back toward the hatch they had used earlier.

Their departures were swift. As they emerged into the frigid air, the difference between the facility's interior bedlam and the serene, icy landscape was striking. The night vision goggles, once highlighting the green-hued chaos inside, now guided them through the darkness of the cold, silent Siberian night. Both teams, though departing separately, shared a sense of accomplishment and relief as they left the tumultuous facility behind.

A short way from their exits, they reconvened on their stashed ski equipment. Bracing themselves against the biting Siberian cold, they quickly strapped on the cross-country skis. On the southern edge, Jenny, having already given him coat and gloves, handed Dr. Morozov a pair of ski boots, quipping, "I hope you can ski, Doctor."

"As well as I shoot," the scientist replied, rapidly getting them on, followed by his skis.

"Just stay close to me. Okay?"

Morozov nodded.

Less than a minute later, Team Cinderella set off at a breakneck pace toward their snowmobiles concealed about half a mile away. The facility's forces weren't far behind. Men began pouring out of the building, firing their assault rifles, the snow lighting up with muzzle flashes, bullets whipping the icy air around them as they glided on their skis.

Minutes later, both teams converged on a wide, rocky hill that led down a steep incline toward a pine forest, Cinderella coming from the east and Camelot from the west.

"How's it going, Camelot?" Jenny shouted as she cut through the snow and ice.

"It'll be a lot better once we're home and dry," Noah replied.

The conversation was cut short when more muzzle flash erupted behind them, their pursuers mounting snowmobiles.

Reaching the trees, they burst into the harsh Siberian wilderness, skis cutting through the thick blanket of snow. The blizzard was relentless, whipping around them, reducing visibility to mere meters. They navigated the treacherous terrain at lightning speed, the threat of their pursuers spurring them on into the unknown. Behind them, the facility's forces were mere shadows against the white expanse.

Caught within the howling wind and the blur of the snowstorm, Noah's focus remained unwavering. He steered his team through drifts and over icy patches, his eyes constantly scanning for dangers. The pursuit was a high-stakes chase, a test of skill and endurance against the merciless Siberian elements and the relentless pursuit of their enemies.

In the thick of the Siberian forest, Team Camelot and Team Cinderella made a strategic decision to split up, weaving through the dense trees to evade their pursuers. Jenny, with a protective stance, stayed close to Dr. Morozov, ensuring his safety as they navigated the treacherous terrain within the light of the moon.

Meanwhile, Noah, bringing up the rear, suddenly found himself in the crosshairs of a snowmobile with an armed man on the back, the bark of his assault rifle punctuating the incessant howl of the wind. As it hurtled after him through the trees, Noah's instincts kicked in. He gauged the distance and, with a sudden, calculated move, pushed off his left ski toward a thick pine, swinging around to the other side of it and dropping off a ledge of rock that split the forest floor. He landed heavily on the powdery snow below, his knees taking the brunt of the impact, but he stayed upright, moving forward. As for the snowmobile, it couldn't follow, having to take a short slope on the other side of the rocky drop to get back to him. This allowed Noah to swing right-wards—to effectively cut them off.

As they emerged from the trees, he was right there, coming in from the side. In a flash, he grabbed the gunner from behind, using his momentum to pull him off the snow-mobile and onto the snow-packed ground. The gunner, taken by surprise, was unable to react in time, a single gunshot marking his immediate death.

A second marked the death of the driver, caught out as he tried to pull his assault rifle from his shoulder but unable to do it in time.

Its driver dead, the snowmobile veered out of control and crashed into a snowbank. Noah, without missing a beat, skied off into the blizzard, though now slightly waylaid behind the rest of his team.

One after another, the members of Team Camelot and Team Cinderella reached their snowmobiles, revving the engines before disappearing into the swirling storm, the next leg of their escape just beginning.

Noah was the last to reach his snowmobile. He leapt onto it, ready to disappear into the tundra like the others. But as his hand reached for the ignition, a blur in his periphery caught his attention—something massive moving through the snow. In a split second, a powerful arm burst out, grabbing him. He was yanked off the snowmobile and tossed through the air with terrifying force. Another hand quickly disarmed him, his SIG Sauer M17 flung into the snowy abyss. Noah landed hard, scrambling to his feet, only to find himself face to face with the imposing seven feet figure of Gruber.

He stood ready in the storm, his towering stature looming over Noah. "We meet again, Herr Wolf," he said, his voice shaking the frozen air. He then took his pistol from his belt and tossed it away. "Armed combat isn't my style," he said. "Not when I meet an adversary such as yourself. One whose reputation is of the highest. When I meet someone like that, I wish to pit my body against his, mano a mano."

"Not exactly fair," Noah quipped as he stood in the gigantic shadow Gruber cast.

The giant smiled down at him. It was one of those smiles that tells you he's about to enjoy this—and you're not. Snow swirled around the fighters, their figures barely discernible in the whiteout of the blizzard. Then the smile began to fade, and Noah knew that it was about to happen.

Gruber exploded at him. Fists and feet, huge and deadly, burst out of the snow. The giant's every move was a display of raw power. Noah, agile and determined, met this force the best he could with a fierceness born of years of training. He darted in and out of Gruber's reach, delivering a series of rapid jabs and well-placed kicks, each one aimed with precision.

Their confrontation was like a clash of titans in a world of white. The snow beneath them crunched and shifted with their movements, the storm all around. Noah's face, set in concentration, was the complete opposite of Gruber's, the monster's expression fixed in brute determination.

Noah unleashed a barrage of quick, precise jabs and kicks, each one slicing through the thick snow with intent. The flurry of his movements contrasted Gruber's sheer brute force, a skilled warrior using agility and technique against an overpowering giant.

On the defense, Noah did well at dodging blows that would kill most men. But his luck wouldn't last forever. The inevitable would eventually come. And come it did.

Gruber landed a heavy blow on Noah's side. The force of the strike felt like a sledgehammer against his ribcage, sending him staggering back through the swirling snow. The hit thundered through his body, leaving Noah gasping for breath and struggling to maintain his stance in the face of such overpowering might.

As Gruber's knee came swinging toward his face, threatening to crush his nose into the back of his skull, Noah threw himself down, rolled, and flipped himself back onto his feet, ready for more. And more would most certainly come.

The physicality of the fight was intense and punishing. With each powerful strike from Gruber, Noah felt shockwaves of pain, testing the limits of his endurance. His own attacks, though delivered with accuracy and skill, seemed to only slightly impact the massive figure of Gruber. In a furious storm of action, Noah unleashed a series of rapid strikes, aiming at Gruber's vital points with all the speed and accuracy he could muster. His fists and feet moved in a blur, each hit delivered with the intention of weakening the giant adversary. But Gruber seemed almost unfazed by this onslaught, shrugging off Noah's rapid blows as if they were mere nuisances—flies on a horse.

This display of Gruber's resilience to Noah's well-executed strikes was an almost overwhelming reminder of the extraordinary physical capabilities of his genetically engineered foe.

As the battle raged on, Noah found himself increasingly pushed onto the back foot, absorbing the brunt of Gruber's superior strength. The harsh reality of battling a genetically enhanced adversary was starkly clear. Noah, despite his resilience and combat prowess, was continually reminded in the harshest sense of his human limitations against such overwhelming force.

Exhausted and battered, Noah's resilience was wearing thin. The cold air bit into his lungs, turning each breath into a painful struggle. In a last-ditch effort, he mustered his remaining strength for a Hail Mary attack, a desperate attempt to turn the tide. Channeling years of martial arts schooling, Noah launched into a dynamic assault. He unleashed a flurry of precise kicks and punches, his movements a blend of speed and technique. Drawing from Muay Thai, his kicks aimed for Gruber's vulnerable points, while his punches, influenced by Pencak Silat, sought to penetrate the giant's defenses. Each strike was executed with the hope of finding a chink in the giant's armor, his fists and feet moving in a blur. But Gruber easily repelled this final effort.

His counter was swift and incapacitating. The punch that hit Noah's mouth almost ripped his jaw off.

Noah was knocked to the ground, his consciousness fading. As he lay there, barely hanging on, Gruber towered over him, a dominant figure against the backdrop of the storm, embodying the harsh reality of Noah's physical limits against such a formidable opponent. Incapacitated and vulnerable, he was at Gruber's mercy. Before Noah could get up, Gruber was on top of him, easily containing his resistance. Reveling in his dominance, he held Noah down, his knee pressing into Noah's back. As Noah tried to get him off, Gruber ensnared one of his arms in a vise-like grip. "I want to pull you apart, Herr Wolf, like a child pulling apart a spider," he whispered menacingly into Noah's ear, his voice as cold as the frozen air itself. "Break you apart piece by piece, bone by bone." The searing pain as Gruber began to pull at Noah's arm was unbearable, shooting through Noah's body. The joint began to crack, the ligaments pulling apart, Gruber's knee pressing Noah into the snow.

Leaning into his ear, Gruber growled, "I love the popping sound it makes when it leaves the joint."

With the skill and exactitude of a machine, Gruber twisted the arm a millimeter at a time, bit by bit, the pain screaming in Noah's head, the look of twisted joy on Gruber's face exposing his sharp, little teeth, until—

Gruber's eyes lit up with a sudden light that burst from the snow. As the giant looked up, the blizzard's frenzy was pierced by the bright glare of headlights. Out of the storm, Marco's snowmobile charged at Gruber. With precise timing, he collided with the giant, forcefully knocking him off Noah and breaking the hold he had on him.

Almost immediately, a second snowmobile arrived with Jenny on its back, and together, she and Marco quickly helped the battered Noah onto the vehicle, making a swift and urgent escape.

As they sped away, leaving Gruber and the turmoil of the facility behind, Noah, his arm searing with pain and his breaths coming in ragged gasps, was acutely aware of the narrow escape from death he had just experienced. Thank God, he thought, for his team.

TWENTY

Leaving behind the billowing smoke and pandemonium they had unleashed at the Siberian facility, Team Camelot and Team Cinderella, along with Dr. Morozov, embarked on a rapid and stealthy departure from Russia. After successfully evading their pursuers through the treacherous Siberian wilderness, they finally reached the frozen city of Yakutsk. There, they quickly boarded a waiting Gulfstream G650.

As the plane ascended, leaving behind the vast, snow-covered terrain, a collective sense of relief washed over them. The successful conclusion of their perilous mission in Siberia was marked by the plane soaring away into the skies across western Europe.

Now they were relatively safe, they needed to debrief with Dr. Morozov. The renowned scientist, surrounded by the attentive team members, began to delve into an explanation of the giant machine they'd blown up.

"It was an electromagnetic pulse cannon," he told them

as clouds drifted by the windows. "Far more advanced than anything else in the world. It can disable satellites orbiting the earth, cause citywide blackouts, wipe out entire Internet infrastructure."

"Was it in working order?" Noah asked.

"Oh yes. The scaffolding you saw was for minor alterations. We are always updating it. This type of technology is constantly evolving."

"And how does it work?"

"It uses advanced superconducting materials and magnetic field generators," Morozov explained, his voice tinged with a mix of awe and fear. "Powered by a miniature fusion reactor, it's capable of unleashing a continent-scale EMP."

The team listened intently as Morozov described how the device could be launched into orbit or detonated strategically to disrupt global communications and navigational systems. "Don't you see?" he put to them. "Everything runs on electricity these days. Everything relies on a computer at some point. Even everyday cars have onboard computers which control their brakes, steering, navigation. Think if you had a device that could instantly destroy all electronics in an area, knock out satellite, Internet, all forms of communication and transport. You could immobilize whole cities in a matter of seconds. Then swoop in and take over against an unorganized and chaotic enemy."

After that, he went on to speak about his own involvement, revealing it was against his will. "I refused the Council years ago," Morozov said. "That's why they kidnapped me and faked my death. For the past five years, they've kept me locked underground, forced to work on their projects. I'm not alone, either. There are others, world-class scientists, some coerced like me, others willingly aiding their plans. All of them designing and building weapons of mass destruction."

The revelations were startling, painting a picture of a vast and ominous conspiracy that threatened the world's technological infrastructure. A heavy silence fell over the cabin as they all contemplated the technological supremacy of their enemy.

As they did, Noah turned to Morozov with a crucial question. "The one at the facility. Is it the only one?"

But before Morozov could answer, the plane shuddered violently. In an instant, the unthinkable happened: an EMP strike. The cabin was cast into chaos as lights flickered, sputtered, and died. The hum of electronic systems abruptly ceased. An oppressive silence enveloped them, leaving everyone in darkness. The theoretical discussion they had just been having about EMP technology's potential for destruction had just turned into a harsh, immediate reality—a demonstration jarringly close to the bone. Panic surged through the passengers of the Gulfstream. Noah, maintaining his composure, quickly took charge. "Everyone, stay calm! We need to assess our situation," he commanded.

But the situation was escalating quickly as they faced the harrowing reality: they were in a powerless plane floating over the Atlantic Ocean, rapidly losing altitude and hurtling toward the rough waves.

TWENTY-ONE

IN THE WAKE OF THE EMP BLAST, THE PLANE'S cockpit was a scene of devastation. The controls had exploded, leaving the pilot and copilot critically injured. Amidst the frenzy and the shrill sound of alarms, Noah and Jenny, drawing on their limited flight experience, sprang into action.

"Get them out of their seats, quickly!" Jenny yelled as they entered the smoke-filled cockpit.

The pilot and co-pilot were slumped over the smoldering instrument panel, bloodied and unconscious. Noah and Jenny moved them, taking their places at the now barely responsive controls. "We've got to stabilize the plane for a water landing," Noah shouted, hands grappling with the controls. The ocean loomed menacingly closer as they struggled against the failing system of the plummeting aircraft.

Swiftly assessing their dire situation, Noah remembered the aircraft's emergency protocols. "Jenny," he yelled over the roar of the wind, "I'm deploying the RAT. It might give us enough power to get some control back!"

With a decisive action, he activated the Ram Air Turbine (RAT) system, which is designed to generate electrical and hydraulic power when deployed into the airstream, providing enough energy to power essential flight control systems and some cockpit instruments in a power-out scenario. A slight whirring sound filled the tense atmosphere as the turbine deployed, slicing into the airstream beneath the G650, harnessing the airflow. Moments later, a flicker of life returned to the side stick, offering a glimmer of hope.

Noah felt a surge of resistance from the side stick as the FBW system sputtered to life, drawing minimal power from the RAT. It was far from normal, but it was something. "It's working... somewhat. Hold on!" he shouted to Jenny, his hands wrestling with the newly empowered controls. The side stick responded sluggishly, demanding Noah's utmost effort to wrest control from the clutches of gravity.

With the ocean rapidly approaching, Noah worked feverishly to stabilize the plane. With the primary flight display and other electronic instruments disabled, they relied on the mechanical standby instruments and their instinctive understanding of the aircraft's behavior.

Jenny kept her eyes fixed on the altitude indicator and airspeed while Noah focused on manually controlling the pitch to angle the aircraft for a less catastrophic impact. "Keep the nose up, just enough!" Jenny shouted over the noise. Noah, with a steady hand, fought to maintain a delicate balance, aiming to hit the water at a shallow angle to reduce the force of impact.

Everyone else was in their seats, strapped in and bracing

themselves for what was about to come. Marco and Renée sat side by side, their hands entwined. Renée whispered, "I love you," squeezing Marco's hand tightly as the inside of the cabin shook violently. Dr. Morozov, in a protective posture, had his head tucked between his knees. At the back, Jim Marino and Dave Lange were seated together, stern, almost impassive looks on their faces. Both men had been in similar situations before.

"Hold on!" Noah shouted over his shoulder at them.

Their efforts to land the plane safely were met with a violent reality as the plane hit the rough Atlantic waters. The impact was almost catastrophic, the force instantly tearing off the wings.

Noah's skill at least prevented the fuselage from breaking apart. By managing to strike the ocean at an optimal angle, they were able to skim the surface. The sound of metal rending and rushing water filled their ears. The crash wasn't finished with them yet. The impact intensified, the cabin turning into a maelstrom of havoc as they tore across the waves. All around them, objects unbolted and began flying through the air. The harsh, metallic shrieks of tearing metal filled the cabin.

In a horrific twist, the force of the impact began unbolting the seats at the rear. Jim Marino and Dave Lange were sent hurtling backward, propelled with such force that when they smashed to a stop against the rear wall, the impact was devastating. More seats and debris slammed into them. Jim felt excruciating pain as his legs were crushed under the weight.

As the wrecked plane came to a relative stop, water rapidly began flooding the fuselage.

Noah, amidst the mayhem, shouted, "Everybody get to the emergency exit, now! Move!"

The survivors scrambled toward the exit, battling against the fast-rising water. The plane, now sinking beneath the waves, added a sense of urgency to their escape.

Reaching the back, they found Jim and Dave. "Jim's hurt real bad!" Renée called out, pointing to Marino. He had sustained severe injuries, both legs broken below the knee, his head dripping with blood from a large gash above the right eye. He was barely conscious.

As for Dave Lange, it was too late. He lay crushed beneath the wreckage of the seating. "Dave's... gone," Marco announced, his voice heavy with grief as he held the dead man by the wrist, feeling no pulse through his fingertips.

"Poor Dave," Jenny said sadly, reaching forward and plucking his dog tags from around the dead man's neck. "You were one hell of a driver and a good friend. I'm sorry I didn't get you home this time."

Amid the rising water and growing unease, Noah sprang into action, retrieving a rucksack and an inflatable lifeboat from the back. "Listen up!" he shouted over the noise of the waves swallowing the plane. "We're going to use this dinghy to get out. But first we need to open the door."

"And how are we going to do that underwater?" Jenny put to him, pointing at the windows, where the water was almost all the way to the top.

"You forget. We didn't have time to stash the gear in Russia. We had to bring it onboard," Noah said, holding up the rucksack. "That means we still have some explosives."

"Okay," Jenny replied, nodding, a slight grin lifting the corner of her mouth. "I get it."

"Once we blow the door open," Noah went on, "we'll hold on to the dinghy and let it inflate. It should pull us to the surface."

"Should?" Marco put to him, the Cajun raising a thick black eyebrow at him.

Noah met the look. "Do you trust me?"

"Into hell, bossman," Marco replied without a second's hesitation.

As Noah explained how it would work, Renée and Jenny began placing the plastic explosive around the door. In less than a minute, the fuse was set. They all gathered as far back from the door as they could, each of them taking ahold of the dinghy as the plane sank farther into the ocean, the cold water swirling around their waists.

"Now when this blows," Noah explained, the detonator held firmly in his hand, "the water is gonna rush in, quickly filling the rest of the cabin. That's when I'm going to inflate the dinghy. You all need to hold on. Tight."

Though anxious, everyone prepared to follow Noah's lead.

"On my count," Noah shouted, his voice steady against the impending danger. "Three... Two..." The team gripped the dinghy tightly, their hands slick and trembling. "One... Now!" Noah pressed the detonator, setting off the explosives.

The moment the door burst open, the dinghy inflated rapidly, pulling them with a sudden force out of the plane and into the dark, icy water. As they were dragged upward, they clung on for dear life. Yet the surface seemed so far away. Dr. Morozov, already weakened and disoriented from the crash, struggled to maintain his hold. His fingers, numbed by the icy cold, began to slip despite the desperate attempts of the others to keep him secure. In a moment that seemed to stretch on endlessly, Morozov's grip finally gave way. His figure, a fading silhouette, slipped silently into the abyss, disappearing into the murky depths of the Atlantic.

They finally broke through the surface, gasping for air amidst the stormy sea, rain pelting down mercilessly, trying to drown them from above. One by one, the survivors climbed into the inflated dinghy, their relief obvious yet overshadowed by the grim task of assessing injuries and gathering bearings.

The reality of their losses soon became clear. Jim Marino hardly moved after Marco and Jenny hauled him into the dinghy. With one member of her team dead and the other badly wounded, the emotional impact hit Jenny hard. She didn't cry—that wasn't Jenny. But she did make sure to comfort Jim, holding his arm tightly as Marco and Renée reset his legs and tended to his head.

"Where's Morozov?" Jenny suddenly asked, only just realizing the scientist wasn't there.

"Gone," Noah told her, the images of the Russian fading into the black depths of the Atlantic still replaying in his mind.

As they sat in the dinghy, adrift in the vast ocean, storm clouds gathered around them, the rain intensifying and the waves beginning to rise. Their future was as uncertain as the turbulent waters they found themselves in.

TWENTY-TWO

IT WAS LATE AFTERNOON WHEN DOC PARKER arrived at the farmhouse wearing a solemn expression. Greeted by Sarah and Allison, he acknowledged Allison with a respectful nod before turning to Sarah. "Sarah, I'm afraid I come bearing bad news. As of zero-eight-hundred hours Eastern Standard Time, E & E has lost all contact with Noah Wolf," he said gravely.

They moved inside the house.

"What do you mean, lost contact?" Sarah asked in a voice tinged with anxiety as they sat in the living room.

Parker carefully explained, "There was a plane crash. We received a distress signal as it went down over the Atlantic. However, we've lost all contact since."

Sarah's face drained of color, her hands trembling. "But... he can't be..." she stammered, disbelief and grief washing over her in waves.

Allison stepped closer, gently placing a hand on Sarah's shoulder in a silent offering of support. "Sarah, I know how hard this is," she said softly. "But you have to remember. Noah is strong. We've seen him get through impossible situations before."

Sarah looked into Allison's eyes, finding a flicker of hope. "But what if this time is different, Ali? What if he's...?"

Allison squeezed her shoulder reassuringly. "We can't lose hope. Noah's survived worse. We both know that."

Allison turned to Parker, her expression firm. "They had GPS trackers on them, didn't they?" she asked pointedly. "What about rescue efforts? Are we utilizing every resource to find them?"

Parker hesitated for a moment before responding. "Yes, the team was equipped with trackers, but something must be disrupting the signals, because they've gone cold. It's probably atmospheric. The weather's pretty bad out there at the moment. We've deployed search and rescue teams, and it shouldn't be long before they get a sign of them."

Allison, perceiving hesitation on Parker's part, confronted him directly. "Could their signals have been intentionally jammed? Is that a possibility?" she asked, her tone insistent.

Instead of answering the question directly, Parker merely sought to reassure Sarah. "I understand your concerns, and I assure you, E & E is utilizing every available resource to locate and retrieve Noah and the others," he said earnestly.

After Doc Parker left, Sarah and Allison were left in a state of anxious waiting. Sarah paced the living room, her mind racing with worry. "How long will it take for them to find anything?" she asked, her voice strained.

Allison, looking out the window as Parker's car left,

responded, "E & E won't give up. I can guarantee you Doc was being sincere when he said they're doing everything they can to find them."

Both of them knew that waiting for news would be agonizing, clinging to the promise of E & E's search and rescue efforts. The room filled with an anxious silence, the two women trying to maintain hope in a situation filled with uncertainty.

TWENTY-THREE

ADRIFT IN THE VAST EXPANSE OF THE OCEAN, THE survivors of the crash huddled in the small, overcrowded dinghy, the endless waves spreading out around them. The wind hadn't let up, but at least the sky had cleared and the rain had stopped. Nevertheless, that brought its own problems. Exposed, Noah, Jenny, Marco, Renée, and Jim Marino faced the unforgiving sun and the rough water, the salt clinging to their skin from the spray and the sun burning it into them.

The survivors grappled with the loss of Dr. Morozov and Dave Lange. A heavy silence had fallen over them in the hours since the crash. Their faces bore the marks of shock, grief, and exhaustion.

Resources were critically limited—just a few bottles of water, no food, and minimal survival gear. The reality of their predicament was harsh and unyielding. Signs of dehydration and sun exposure began to show on the first day. Alongside two badly broken legs, Jim Marino was suffering a severe concussion. As night fell over them like a blanket, he suddenly, in his stupor, leaned out of the dinghy and began scooping up handfuls of seawater. He'd managed to swallow several before Jenny caught him, pulling his hand away and trying to reason with him, Marco and Noah helping her settle him.

The first night at sea was awful, marked by a storm that churned the ocean into a violent, restless entity. The dinghy was tossed mercilessly on the rough waves, the night ripped apart by thunder that rumbled in the distance and lightning that exploded, briefly illuminating the vast, dark, writhing sea around them. The relentless assault of wind and rain left them drenched and shivering, clinging to the hope of seeing another day.

Then as the dawn set fire to the horizon and the next day began, the survivors in the dinghy once again faced the relentless and unforgiving sun. With no shade, the physical effects of prolonged exposure began to set in: skin burned, heads throbbed, and bodies weakened.

Marco squinted against the glare, his skin reddened and peeling. "We need to find some way to cover up," he said hoarsely. To protect his wife from the sun, he was holding Renée close to him, her face buried in his chest.

Jenny checked their water supply. "We've barely got enough to last until tonight," she informed them grimly.

Renée looked up from her husband. Usually composed, she looked visibly shaken. "How long can we last like this?" she murmured, more to herself than anyone else.

Jim Marino, injured and concussed, struggled to maintain his composure. "Where's Dave?" he kept asking.

Noah tried to offer words of encouragement. "We've

been through tough situations before. We'll make it through this one."

The psychological impact of their situation was as harsh as the physical. Each survivor grappled with fear, uncertainty, and the daunting prospect of an unknown amount of time lost at sea, possibly forever, their reactions varying as they each fought to keep it together in the face of such overwhelming odds.

The long hours and uncertainty weighed heavily on them. "What if they don't find us?" Renée whispered, her voice laced with exhaustion and fear as she clung to her husband.

Marco, trying to maintain some hope, replied, "They're looking for us, baby. We just need to hold on."

But as the second day progressed, their situation became increasingly hopeless. Physical exhaustion and the mental strain of being lost at sea pushed them to their limits. Jim Marino was completely out of it, babbling away nonsense, hardly even conscious. "We might need to prepare for the worst," Noah finally admitted, the reality of their predicament written clearly on his face. "I don't think Jim's gonna last much longer unless he gets help."

However, just when despair seemed to envelop the survivors, the waters beneath their dinghy began to churn unexpectedly. Confusion and fear gripped them as a dark, massive shadow loomed below. Suddenly, with a great surge, a massive submarine surfaced beneath them, lifting the dinghy out of the water. The survivors all stood up as they rose, stunned by the sheer size of the submarine.

As the submarine settled, all eyes fastened to the hatch.

"What now?" Marco murmured, holding Renée tight to him.

The hatch began opening, the team steeling themselves for what was to come. And come it did. When the hatch was open all the way, a mammoth emerged: Gruber. He rose out of the submarine, followed by several men armed with IWI Tavor bullpup assault rifles, the giant blocking out the sun.

Noah stepped forward, a defiant expression on his face. "Gruber," he said, his voice steady, "is this a rescue?"

Gruber's response was cold and mocking. "Rescue, Herr Wolf? No, consider this a... relocation. Your survival skills are commendable but ultimately futile. Nevertheless, I can leave you all out here, should you wish it."

Noah's fists clenched. "I guess relocation will have to do, for now," he growled.

Gruber merely smiled, a chilling expression that confirmed their worst fears. They were not being saved; they had been captured.

Then, as if that wasn't enough, things turned even darker.

Pulling a pistol from his belt, Gruber, in a voice devoid of empathy, said, "Regrettably, however, I only have room for four." Without ceremony or hesitation, he turned the pistol on the injured Jim Marino.

A single, cold shot rang out, the bullet going through his forehead, ending Jim's life.

Jenny screamed in horror and rage. With all her remaining strength, she threw herself at Gruber. Her sudden movement startled the armed men, who instantly cocked their bullpups.

"Noah, stop her!" Renée shouted. Noah was already

moving. Just meters from Gruber, he caught Jenny, pulling her back with all his might. "Live to fight another day," he said firmly, doing his best to control her movements.

Jenny struggled against him, her eyes wild with desperation. "He killed Jim!" she cried out.

"I know," Noah said. "But we need you alive, Jenny. We need to survive this—for Jim, for all of us."

Jenny's resistance slowly faded as the reality of Noah's words sank in. She collapsed into his arms, her body wracked with a sudden weakness. Noah held her tightly, his eyes never leaving Gruber's, a silent vow passing between them.

TWENTY-FOUR

THE WATERS OF TEMPLE LAKE SHIMMERED UNDER A bright morning sky, casting a deceptive sense of tranquility over the old farmhouse. Inside, Sarah, restless and anxious, paced the living room, each step mirroring her mounting dread. In the background, Norah played quietly with her toys, unaware of the gravity of the situation that surrounded her. The quiet was shattered when the screen of Sarah's cell phone lit up with the name Doc Parker, his call bringing with it a momentary flicker of hope.

"We've located the wreckage of the plane in the south Atlantic," Parker began as soon as she answered the call, his voice low, "but there's no sign of Noah and the others."

Sarah's face, a portrait of hope just moments before, drained of color. She began trembling, clutching at the back of the sofa for support, while Norah, sensing her mother's distress, looked up with a mix of confusion and concern. "No sign at all?" Sarah whispered, her voice barely carrying down the phone.

"I'm sorry, Sarah. We're continuing the search, but the weather and the ocean are unpredictable."

As the call ended, the weight of Doc Parker's news pulled Sarah into a chair, despair wrapping around her like a thick fog. Nevertheless, she wasn't alone. Allison, who had until now been a silent sentinel, stood in an opposite corner with a tenacity that seemed to fill the room. She approached Sarah, her determination clear in her stance and expression.

"Come on," Allison said, her voice firm yet gentle as she helped Sarah to her feet. "We'll find them ourselves."

Sarah looked at her. "You think we can?"

"Yes," Allison replied firmly, while Norah, now by her mother's side, offered a small, comforting hug.

The farmhouse became a frenzy of activity, the two women setting themselves up in the basement, Noah's usual base of operations when at home. Allison, with a strategic mind honed by decades in intelligence, pulled out maps and began plotting potential drift patterns, her fingers tracing the lines of ocean currents and wind conditions. Sarah, initially paralyzed by grief, found herself inspired by Allison's unwavering commitment. She dove into gathering information about rescue operations, her eyes scanning satellite imagery with a newfound purpose.

"If we can narrow down the search area, maybe we can direct the rescue teams more efficiently," Allison said, her eyes never leaving the maps.

Sarah, sparked by an idea, added, "What about local fishermen or cargo ships in the area? They might have seen something. There could be recorded chatter on maritime channels or with local coastguards."

Allison nodded. "Good idea. Any piece of information could lead us to them."

Their work was relentless, driven by a cocktail of hope and desperation. As the day drew on and the sun dipped below the horizon, Sarah and Allison, their faces lit by the soft light of the setting sun, continued searching, sifting through a mountain of information, their determination to find Noah and the others as fierce as ever. Norah, asleep on a makeshift bed in the corner, symbolized the personal stakes involved, reminding them silently of the family waiting for their return.

TWENTY-FIVE

THE COUNCIL'S SUBMARINE CUT A SILENT PATH toward Cuba, its destination. Inside, the vessel's interior was a labyrinth of narrow corridors and hushed compartments.

Since being marched aboard at gunpoint, each of them had been medically checked, treated for exposure, and fed. They were under no illusion, however. The medical checks and meals were preparation for prolonged torture.

They now found themselves in tiny, individual cells. Noah sat in his, a cramped space barely larger than a closet, his mind racing.

Across the corridor, in a cell identical to Noah's, Jenny tried to keep her composure. "Stay sharp, Jenny. Remember your training," she murmured to herself.

Several hours into the journey, Gruber escorted Noah from his cell, his hands bound in front of him as two armed men trailed behind them. They ascended to the submarine's bridge, a room bathed in the soft glow of screens and blinking lights, crew members stationed at their posts, eyes fixed on their tasks.

"He wants you to see this," Gruber announced, guiding Noah to the front of the command center.

"Who's *he*?" Noah asked.

"You'll find out. Now look."

He pointed to a large screen displaying footage of the rocky southern coast of Cuba, zooming in on the mouth of the Rio Cauto river, where it meets the Atlantic in a delta. The images on the screen changed, the footage now submerged, an outside camera on the submarine. It displayed a vast bank of underwater rock.

"What am I seeing here?" Noah inquired.

"Keep watching, Herr Wolf. He wants you to see it" came the reply just as the rocky shelf began to shift, the rock separating in the middle and opening up, revealing a massive underwater hangar.

The submarine approached the now-visible mechanical doors hidden within the rock, which began closing back up once they had admitted the sub into the gargantuan chamber. Inside, the scale of the operation became apparent, with the vast space equipped to house and service multiple vessels.

"Did you think Siberia was all we had?" Gruber remarked as Noah looked in disbelief at the sophisticated setup hidden beneath the waves.

The submarine emerged from the water like a phantom, docking within the cavern. The base, a fortress carved into the bedrock, was a formidable structure, seamlessly blending with its surroundings.

Upon disembarking from the submarine, Noah and the others regrouped, the armed men corralling them together as they stepped from the confinements of the vessel onto a metal walkway.

They proceeded, flanked by armed escorts, through a warren of corridors that showcased cutting-edge technology and surveillance systems.

"This place is a fortress," Noah muttered under his breath as they passed a row of high-tech labs.

Marco, his eyes scanning their surroundings, replied softly, "More than that. I bet there are things here even worse than that EMP we blew up in Siberia."

Each room they passed—labs, armories, command centers—was a hive of activity, meticulously organized and buzzing with the energy of hidden agendas.

As they were led deeper into the heart of the base, Noah and his team could sense the depth of the enemy's reach. The complexity of the challenges they faced, even if they managed to escape this place with their lives intact, was now brutally apparent.

They reached a cellblock, guarded by a substantial contingent of armed personnel. Noah and his team were ushered into their individual cells. Each was a barren, oppressive chamber, a claustrophobic space enclosed by four bare walls that seemed to absorb light and hope alike.

The only features were a set of heavy chains that dangled ominously from the high ceiling, a telescreen mounted on one wall, emitting a low, constant hum, and an aluminum gurney. On this gurney lay an array of items for the sole purpose of causing severe pain to the human body, a macabre mix of the savagely primitive and the chillingly clinical. Baseball bats and pliers lay alongside scalpels and surgical drills, tasers beside watering cans.

One by one, they were subjected to their cells' most menacing feature: the chains. With their wrists shackled, they were hoisted into the air, suspended a few feet above the ground in a torturous position.

Noah grunted in pain, the metal links clinking ominously as he was lifted. "You think you can break me?" he muttered through gritted teeth, his muscles straining against the relentless pull of gravity.

This method of suspension, a cruel nod to medieval dungeons, was a terrible reminder of the Council's willingness to use any means necessary, ancient or modern, to break their enemies.

As Noah hung there, alone in his cell, his body stretched and aching, his mind raced. He knew he needed to find a way out, not just for himself, but for his team. They were up against an enemy that wielded both the brutal simplicity of the past and the complex horrors of the present. In the silence of his cell, the distant sounds of the base humming around him, he began to formulate a plan. The Council might have had the upper hand for now, but Noah was far from defeated.

TWENTY-SIX

As the sun cast a warm glow over the farmhouse, Sarah and Allison, surrounded by maps and satellite images, reached a pivotal conclusion.

"We've gotten as far as we can on our own," Sarah admitted. "But we're missing pieces of the puzzle."

Allison, her gaze fixed on a satellite photo, nodded in agreement. "It's time we bring in Neil and Wally. Wally's tech expertise and Neil's field experience could be exactly what we need. Plus, that War Room of theirs might come in handy."

Sarah picked up her phone. "I'll arrange it. Do you think they'll help?"

Allison's response was firm. "Remember, Jenny's out there, too. I'll be surprised if Neil's not already looking. And Wally cares about Noah just as much as we do. They'll help."

Both women sprang into action. After arranging the meeting with Wally, Sarah rushed to Norah's side, gently coaxing her daughter away from her toys with the promise of an adventure. "We're going on a little trip, sweetie," she said.

Allison, meanwhile, retrieved their coats from the hallway closet. She handed Sarah Norah's tiny jacket, watching as she dressed the child with care. The warmth of the morning sun did little to ease the chill of apprehension that had settled over the household.

With Norah ready, Sarah and Allison grabbed the keys for the Durango. "Let's not waste any time," Allison said.

They moved out of the farmhouse with a sense of purpose. As Sarah secured Norah in the back seat, Allison took one last look at the farmhouse, its tranquility the complete opposite of the storm brewing within each of them. Then, with a deep breath, they set off.

TWENTY-SEVEN

IN THE GRIM CONFINES OF THE COUNCIL'S SECRET base, Noah, Jenny, Marco, and Renée hung suspended in the middle of their sparse cells, vulnerable and exposed.

The torturers entered with a haunting presence. They were men with washed-out looks, their eyes, empty of any empathy, reflecting nothing but the darkness within their souls. Two men came into each cell, one taking a position before the prisoner, the other going straight to the gurney, the atmosphere thickening with dread.

Marco, hanging in his cell, stared defiantly at his torturers. "Ah. I wondered when we'd get down to things," he said in a voice laced with defiance.

One of the torturers, without a word, swung a bat, striking him on the ribcage with a slap of flesh. The randomness of the act, devoid of any interrogation or demand, was disorienting, breaking down any semblance of predictability.

In another cell, Jenny's eyes darted between her two captors. "You won't get anything from me," she spat.

The torturers ignored her words. "Your name is Jenny Blessing, is it not?" the one in front asked as the other casually played with a pair of pliers by the gurney.

In her cell, Renée tried to maintain composure as her torturers approached. She steeled herself. "How did you find out about Siberia?" one asked in a monotone voice.

In his cell, Marco gasped in pain from the unexpected blow, his body swinging slightly from the impact. He glared at his torturers, his spirit unbroken. "Is that your best?" he taunted, trying to turn his fear into defiance. "Won't get you a trial with the Dodgers."

The torturers, unmoved by his bravado, simply hit him, again and again, each strike a message of their absolute control.

In Jenny's cell, the psychological torment intensified. One of the torturers leaned in close, his breath foul, and whispered, "You do understand that no matter what, you will die here. But only when we let you." The other, in a cruel display of power, snapped the pliers close to her ear, the sharp sound bouncing off the walls.

Jenny clenched her teeth. "Good luck in trying to break me," she hissed.

Meanwhile, Renée's torturers pressed on. "Tell us how you found Morozov."

Renée replied with forced calm, "He matched me in Tinder."

Back in Noah's cell, the leader of Team Camelot was the only one not joined by a pair of sadists. He was all alone, hanging in stoic silence, conserving his strength and willpower.

That was when the door creaked open, and the ominous

entrance of Gruber immediately shifted the atmosphere. His towering presence and raw physicality seemed to dominate the confined space.

Standing before the suspended Noah, Gruber's demeanor conveyed a complex blend of esteem and regret. "Noah Wolf," he began, his voice a deep rumble, "in another life, I would have released you and challenged you to a fight of honor. Man to man. To the death." His eyes held a glint of what might have been respect. "But here, under the Council's orders, my hands are tied."

"As are mine," Noah retorted, glancing up the length of his arms to the chains that held him.

Gruber rolled his eyes. "You really don't know how lucky you are, Noah Wolf," he stated, his voice filling the cell.

"I'm not being smart here," Noah retorted, "but from where I'm hanging, I don't feel so lucky."

"But you are," Gruber replied, undeterred. "Because of all the murderous, soulless bastards in the world, the Council has picked you to be one of our flaming swords."

Noah's eyes narrowed. "You mean be another one of their henchmen, like you?"

Gruber's expression hardened. "Or exactly the same function you perform for E & E, and by extension the American government. Aren't you no more than a henchman serving their purposes?"

Noah remained silent, the gravity of Gruber's words settling in. He knew there was truth in them, a truth he had long avoided confronting.

"Well, that's what's on the table," Gruber continued, his tone more insistent. "And while you consider the offer, I'll leave you with this to remind you that time is of the essence."

With that, Gruber flicked a switch, and the large telescreen on the wall opposite came to life with the images of suffering. The screen was split into three—one section filled with Marco, another with Jenny, the third with Renee, each being beaten mercilessly as they swung about on their chains. Their cries, raw and filled with anguish, reverberated off the cold, hard walls of the cell. Noah could not tear his eyes away from the horrific display, the sounds of the torture enveloping him in a cocoon of agony.

Gruber left, his departure punctuated by the slamming of the door, leaving Noah engulfed in the images and sounds of the telescreen. In that moment, the cramped cell felt like a tomb, sealing him with the cries of his comrades and the harrowing reality of the Council's offer.

TWENTY-EIGHT

SARAH, ALLISON, AND LITTLE NORAH ARRIVED AT the bustling R&D department of E & E. As they entered the War Room, Neil Blessing and Wally Lawson were deeply engrossed in their work. Neil was intently focused on a complex array of monitors, while Wally was tinkering with a device that looked like nothing either of the women had ever seen before.

"Guys, we really need to talk about Noah and the others," Sarah said.

Both men looked over.

"What have they told you?" Allison put to Neil.

Neil sighed. "I've been kept out of the loop," he confessed, his frustration obvious. "Even though it's my own wife who's missing, Parker isn't telling me anything. Doesn't want me involved because of my emotional involvement."

Wally chimed in. "The same goes for me. I'm as completely in the dark as you are."

In the midst of the discussion, Norah, curious and wide-eyed, wandered toward a gadget on a nearby table. It emitted a soft hum, its lights blinking in a rhythmic pattern. Noticing, Wally rushed over, gently pulling the five-year-old back from the device.

"Don't touch that, sweetie," he said softly, "otherwise we'll all go boom."

The adults shared a nervous chuckle, then refocused on the task at hand.

"We may have a plan," Allison said, her tone deadly serious. "But we need your help. In fact, your skills and equipment are vital."

Wally and Neil exchanged a look, nodding. "Count us in," Neil declared, turning back to Allison. "We're not just going to sit here while the people we love are in danger."

"Good," Allison said with an assured nod. "Then let's get started."

TWENTY-NINE

NOAH DIDN'T KNOW HOW LONG IT WAS BEFORE Gruber returned to his cell with two guards. While the big man stayed by the door, the two men who'd accompanied him approached Noah and lowered him to the ground. The relief of touching the cold, solid floor of his cell was immediate, yet it did little to alleviate the sense of foreboding that hung over him.

"Comfortable?" Gruber asked sardonically as one of the guards released his hands from the chains.

Noah, flexing his wrists to restore circulation, replied dryly, "I've had better accommodations."

Gruber ignored the comment, signaling the guards to bind the prisoner's hands behind his back with a pair of solid steel electronic shackles. "Let's take a walk," he said once they were securely fitted.

As the foursome stepped out of the cell, Gruber began leading Noah through the labyrinthine corridors of the base.

"Welcome to the heart of the Council's operations," he announced.

Noah remained silent but observant. The base was a sprawling complex. His senses were immediately assaulted by the sheer scale of it. The air was alive with the hum of machinery and the faint buzz of high-tech equipment. Screens displaying global surveillance feeds lined the walls, glowing with a cold, artificial light.

"This"—Gruber gestured with a sweep of his huge hand —"is where we monitor global events. Every conflict, every shift in power—we see it all here."

They had just stepped into a massive operations room, a nerve center of activity where countless men and women were stationed at sleek, high-tech workstations. It made the War Room look like a broom closet.

Each operator was intently focused on their individual monitors, their fingers dancing across keyboards and touchpads in a rhythm of efficiency. The room hummed with the low murmur of voices and the soft clicking of keyboards. Dominating the front of this bustling hub was an imposing bank of screens, each one streaming real-time data and surveillance feeds from around the globe.

Noah's gaze lingered on the screens, each one a window into different parts of the world. "Impressive," he conceded, though his tone was noncommittal.

Gruber next led him into a vast room filled with military technology, the air buzzing with the energy of concentrated activity. "This is our military tech division. The might of the Council isn't just in information, Herr Wolf."

Noah observed the engineers and technicians at work,

their focus absolute. "Might is one thing," he replied coolly. "Control is another."

Gruber looked at him, a flicker of respect in his eyes. "You understand the stakes, then."

Noah, despite the handcuffs binding his wrists and the guards flanking him, stood tall. "I understand more than you think, Gruber."

They passed an observation window that looked down on a production line where machines made what looked like futuristic tanks. As Gruber led Noah up to the glass, his voice took on a tone of unmistakable pride. "This, Noah, is where we forge the future of warfare," he announced.

Noah's eyes scanned the room beyond the window, taking in the advanced robotics arms assembling intricate machinery and the 3D printers creating components with absolute perfection. "Impressive tech," he commented, his voice betraying no emotion but his mind racing at the implications.

Gruber chuckled. "More than just impressive, Herr Wolf. It's revolutionary. Human expertise combined with machine efficiency—a powerful blend, wouldn't you agree?"

The sight of the Council's military prowess was indeed chilling. Noah took a mental note of the seamless blend of human intelligence and machine precision. It was another reminder of the Council's formidable capabilities. Nevertheless, despite the unease settling in his stomach, he maintained a composed exterior, his discipline keeping his physical reactions in check.

He wasn't about to let these bastards think they'd unnerved him.

The tour continued, Gruber's voice a constant backdrop

as he detailed the capabilities and resources of the Council. Noah absorbed every detail, his mind working tirelessly behind his stoic façade.

"This," Gruber said, gesturing toward a large open area bustling with activity, "is our surveillance department. Each of these analysts is monitoring different parts of the world. You see, we don't just watch; we predict and influence."

Noah's gaze swept across the rows of analysts, each absorbed in their screens, the soft glow of intelligence data illuminating their faces. The scale of the operation was immense, each screen a portal to a different corner of the globe.

"Every conflict, every political or economic shift, every little ripple in the world's fabric—we see it, we analyze it," Gruber continued. "The Council's reach is deep and far-reaching, Herr Wolf. Far more than you can imagine."

Noah's eyes narrowed as he took in the expanse of their surveillance operations. The depth of the Council's reach was indeed far greater than he had anticipated, and the realization added a new weight to his understanding of the situation. The implications of such power and control sent a cold chill running down his spine.

Gruber, observing Noah's reaction, smiled thinly. "Impressive, isn't it? We hold the world in our gaze, Herr Wolf. Nothing escapes our notice."

Gruber's tour was not just informative; it was a psychological ploy. It was obvious that he intended to impress upon Noah the futility of resistance, showcasing the vast resources and influence at the Council's disposal.

They left the analysts and delved farther into the bowels of the base, Gruber leading him into a massive underground warehouse. The sight that greeted Noah was both impressive and unnerving. The warehouse was a cavernous space, stretching seemingly endless in all directions and filled with crates stacked as high as buildings. A stack of crates close to where they walked brimmed with large drones.

Noah's eyes widened as he observed operatives meticulously preparing one of them. This particular drone wasn't armed with conventional weapons. Instead, its payload compartment was being loaded with paper flyers.

As they passed, Noah observed the flyers being loaded into the drone with a critical eye. Each one bore headlines and images meticulously designed to mislead and incite. There were falsified messages claiming to be from China, Iran, North Korea, each alleging responsibility for various global disasters. Other leaflets were adorned with fabricated statements from Islamic Jihadi groups, boasting of orchestrated attacks that had never occurred. These were not mere leaflets; they were potent tools of disinformation, each one carefully crafted to sow chaos and confusion on a global scale.

"The true art of war has evolved, Herr Wolf," Gruber said, watching his reaction closely. "It's not just about bombs and bullets anymore. It's about controlling the narrative, shaping perceptions."

As Noah observed the rows of drones and the operatives meticulously preparing them, a question formed in his mind. "Why use drones for leaflets?" he asked. "We're in the digital age; wouldn't online disinformation be more efficient?"

Gruber remained silent, a knowing look on his face, prompting Noah to think deeper. Then it hit him—a realization that sent another chill down his spine. What if there was no Internet? In order to spread their misinformation, they'd need to do it physically.

They plan to knock out the Internet, he thought. *Cut all communication*. The idea was audacious, almost unthinkable, yet it made a terrifying amount of sense, especially knowing that the Council had at least one powerful EMP at their disposal. In a world suddenly plunged into digital darkness, these drones dropping flyers would be the only source of information for the panicked masses—true or not.

Leaving the warehouse, the enormity of this revelation weighed heavily on Noah. The Council's strategy was clear and chilling in its ambition. This wasn't just about controlling the narrative; it was about completely dominating it in a world stripped of its primary means of communication.

Noah confronted Gruber as they continued their tour through the vast complex of the Council's base. "So you're going to knock out the Internet and the vehicles, then set everyone against each other?" he asked, piecing together the fragments of the Council's plan he had gleaned so far.

Gruber, with a hint of admiration in his tone, responded, "Well spotted. But there's more to it than you think."

"All so you can take over?" Noah pressed, trying to grasp the full extent of their scheme.

Gruber snuffed a laugh, a sound devoid of humor. "You think this is about taking over?" He shook his head, almost pitying Noah's naïve assumption. "If you hadn't been paying attention, Herr Wolf, we've already taken over. We are already in charge. No, this is much more than some petty coup d'état. This is about the new world. The old is in ruins. It must be allowed to burn."

As they moved on, Gruber led Noah into an immense underground chamber even bigger than the one in Siberia that had stored the EMP cannon. They emerged at a balcony overlooking the construction of some giant machine, one that dwarfed the EMP in size and scale.

Noah was lost for words, merely walking up to the railing and staring at it. The immense, cavernous space was bathed in a harsh, artificial light that cascaded from above, casting long shadows that danced across the workers who were meticulously assembling the machine.

The chamber itself, with its towering ceilings, felt almost endless, a testament to the ambitious scale of the project. Scaffolding and various pieces of construction equipment dotted the landscape, surrounding the emerging structure of the machine. This technological marvel, in the heart of its construction phase, boasted large satellite dish-like components and a tangle of wiring and control panels. Each piece was being carefully installed, indicating the machine's advanced capabilities and the precision required in its assembly. Robots, their movements both precise and purposeful, worked alongside human engineers and technicians, each playing a pivotal role in bringing this formidable device to life. The atmosphere was charged with a sense of urgency and focus, as every individual appeared acutely aware of the significance of their work.

"What is that?" Noah asked, his gaze fixed on the imposing structure.

"Perhaps you'll live long enough to find out," Gruber replied cryptically.

The enormity of the Council's plans and the scale of their ambition was becoming clearer with each step Noah took through the base. It was a vision that went far beyond mere political power or control; it was a complete reshaping of the world as it was known. Noah realized he was not just witnessing the inner workings of a powerful organization; he was glimpsing a future that the Council was determined to forge.

Gruber's tour reached its climax back in the vast Operations Room. In the midst of this high-tech nerve center stood an elderly man, his demeanor as they walked up to meet him off-puttingly calm. He had silver hair and wise, knowing eyes that seemed to see much more than they let on. He was almost the complete opposite to Gruber's more overtly menacing presence.

"Sir," Gruber announced as they joined him.

The man smiled, his gaze settling on Noah. "Mr. Wolf," he said, his voice soft yet carrying an undercurrent of undeniable authority. "I've been looking forward to meeting the man who's caused us so much... interest." He held out a wrinkled hand.

Noah looked down at it, then back up, meeting the old man's cold blue eyes. "And who are you?" he asked.

"I am the chief commander of this base. Number Four."

"Number Four?" Noah put to him. "I'm not worthy of one, two, or three?"

Number Four grinned. "Not yet," he said, retracting the hand. "But perhaps in time, you will be."

THIRTY

THE ATMOSPHERE IN THE WAR ROOM WAS ONE OF intense concentration as Allison, Sarah, Wally, and Neil pored over data and cross-referenced intelligence. Their faces, lit by the soft glow of computer screens, were filled with determination, driven by a relentless mission to locate Noah and the others.

For hours, they sifted through mountains of information, piecing together bits of intercepted communications, scrutinizing satellite imagery, and evaluating every piece of intel they could get their hands on using the equipment available to them at R&D. The atmosphere trembled with concentration, broken only by the occasional murmur of discussion or the soft clacking of keyboards.

Suddenly, Wally, who had been analyzing communication patterns, let out a low whistle. "Guys, come check this out," he said.

The others gathered around his station, where he pointed to a series of intercepted messages on his screen.

"I've been tracking these unusual communication spikes going through the router inside the Council's platform. They're heavily encrypted, but Esmeralda has managed to decode part of the communications. It's all pointing to one place—Cuba."

Everyone looked at each other. The tension in the War Room escalated as Wally called out, "Esmeralda, tell them what it says."

The AI's voice, clear and resonant, filled the room. "It appears to be a communication between a concealed facility located on the southern coast of Cuba, in the proximity of the Rio Cauto delta, and an unidentified marine vessel, likely a submarine. The data suggests that this facility has recently received a critical shipment, transferred from the submarine. The coordinates of the location the package was found at is in the Atlantic Ocean, approximately fifty nautical miles from the reported crash site of the plane."

Neil quickly turned to the satellite imagery on his screen. As he zoomed in on the area of Cuba Esmeralda had mentioned, the images revealed not much more than cliffs, sandy coves, and jungle. At first glance, it didn't look like much, but soon they saw signs of it: structures camouflaged within the dense vegetation and rocky coastline. About a mile inland, a large entrance had been dug into the hilly terrain, covered by thick foliage. While they watched the live satellite feed, a huge metal door, barely distinguishable from the surrounding greenery, opened automatically on runners, revealing armed men that began stepping out.

"Must be a service entrance," Neil noted, observing the scene closely. "They have a security checkpoint."

A truck pulled to a stop on the road leading to the wide

shutter door. The armed men approached, checking the driver's papers and ID with thorough scrutiny. They took pictures of him with their phones and lingered for a moment, likely waiting for confirmation from someone inside. Once they received it, they waved the truck in, the metal shutter soon closing after them.

"It's like a fortress," Sarah murmured.

Allison nodded. "They're taking security seriously. Whatever they brought in from the Atlantic, it's important to them."

Wally interjected, "If it's connected to the crash site, it could mean Noah and the others are there."

Allison's eyes narrowed. "This is it. I'm sure of it. This is where they're holding them."

The room suddenly felt charged with a new energy, a mix of hope and apprehension. "We found them. We actually found them," Sarah whispered.

Neil zoomed out slightly, assessing the surrounding area. "Getting in won't be easy. This place is designed to be invisible and impenetrable. We'll need a solid plan."

"We also need to move fast," Allison said decisively. "They won't stay in one place for long. If the Council think they've been compromised, they'll move them somewhere else."

With this hanging over them, Neil, utilizing his technical expertise, delved into the depths of the data they had collected from their recent tap into the Council's communications. He specifically searched for anything pertaining to Cuba: large deliveries, construction equipment, personnel movement. Eventually, he found it, plus the codename for the Cuban facility. They were calling it the Citadel.

Searching more data, he found what they were looking for. The screen in front of him displayed intricate maps and blueprints of the base, the details of which they absorbed with intense focus.

"Look at this," Neil said, pointing to a section of the blueprint on his screen. "I think I found a potential weak point in their perimeter security here."

Sarah leaned in closer, her eyes tracing the layout. "That could be our way in. But what about surveillance in that area?"

Neil zoomed in on the area in question. "There are cameras," he replied, turning to Wally. "Wally, how many quantum cloaks have we got?"

"Camelot and Cinderella took all the cloaked body armor, but I do have three normal cloaks. Should be enough for an infiltration team."

"The armor can go underneath, then," Neil interjected.

"We can do this," Allison said, a firmness to her voice. "We have to."

The team nodded in agreement. They were ready to take on whatever challenges lay ahead to bring their friends and loved ones home. There was a blaze of activity as the foursome, driven by this singular goal, dove headfirst into the logistics of planning their covert rescue operation. The War Room became a hive of strategic planning, the next steps in their mission to rescue Noah and the others from the Citadel beginning to take shape.

THIRTY-ONE

NUMBER FOUR LED THE WAY FROM THE Operations Room, his gait composed and regal. Noah trailed behind him, hands still bound by the electronic shackles. Gruber followed, his presence like that of a well-trained attack dog, close and menacing. They approached a set of grand double doors that swung open silently to reveal vast and luxurious quarters.

As Noah stepped over the threshold, he was immediately enveloped in a world that seemed centuries removed from the high-tech nerve center they had just left. The quarters were a cavernous expanse, bathed in the warm glow of lamplight that shone against the polished mahogany bookshelves lining the walls. The shelves soared toward the high, frescoed ceiling, laden with ancient volumes.

At the center of the room stood a large antique desk, its surface an ocean of dark wood inlaid with intricate golden motifs. Neat stacks of paper and an array of pens lay on top, as if someone sat down there to draft decrees that could change the course of history. Above, a grand tapestry depicting mythological scenes hung, its threads glinting with gold and silver filament, casting golden shadows across the Persian rugs that adorned the parquet floor.

Statues of marble and bronze stood like silent guardians in alcoves, their expressions stoic and eyes empty yet seeming to watch over the room with an air of timeless wisdom. Plush armchairs and chaises were arranged in a semi-circle facing an imposing fireplace, where the crackle of the fire added a comforting yet haunting soundtrack to the majestic silence of the space.

Noah, despite the gravity of his situation, couldn't help but be awestruck by the grandeur of the room. It was a sanctuary that exuded power and intellect, very different from the sterile efficiency of the base outside. It was a room that didn't just display luxury but had its own commanding presence, a space where decisions that affected the globe were made in the comfort of opulence and the quiet company of history's greatest minds.

Gruber's footsteps made a resonating thump as the three of them moved through the quarters, a sound that seemed almost sacrilegious in such a scholarly sanctuary.

Number Four began giving him a guided tour. "This," he said, gesturing to a glass-encased broken cup on a pedestal, "is more than a mere artifact. It is believed to date back to 33 AD. Consider the hands that might have held it... the purpose it may have served."

Noah's eyes were drawn to the relic. "33 AD," he repeated softly. "You mean...?"

Number Four's eyes met his. "Indeed I do. This cup oversaw a period marked by a pivotal moment in history," he continued. "Some say it was the vessel that caught the blood of the man they called a savior."

"The Holy Grail?" Noah asked, a sudden understanding dawning upon him, his previous awe deepening into reverence.

Number Four merely smiled, the gesture rich with unspoken confirmation. "Legends often have roots in reality, Noah. And sometimes, those legends rest in the hands of those who shape the world." His demeanor was friendly, his voice composed, especially when compared to Gruber's silent, brooding form behind them.

They moved to a tapestry that dominated one wall, its threads depicting the glory of Roman emperors. "And this," Number Four continued, "was woven for Emperor Trajan. It's survived centuries, much like the influence of the men it portrays."

Noah studied the intricate weave, the lifelike expressions of the figures immortalized in thread. "You have a piece of history for every era," he noted, his respect for the items battling with his concern for the present.

"History is where the Council has always thrived, Noah. Shaping it, guiding it," Number Four explained.

He led Noah to a glass display where an ancient manuscript lay open, its language indecipherable to Noah but clearly of significant age. "This manuscript predates many civilizations, holding knowledge that shaped the very foundations of modern thought."

Noah leaned in, examining the delicate script. "Who wrote it?"

"Plato. The letters written on it come from his own

hand. It is a dialogue he wrote between himself and his master, Socrates."

Noah looked up at him. "You're saying the Council had a hand in... what? The flow of knowledge? The direction of history?"

Number Four smiled, a cryptic curvature of the lips. "Let's just say, we've always been around, ensuring that history moves in... favorable directions."

As the giant Gruber looked on, Noah took in the magnitude of the Council's reach—not just in distance, but in time. Every artifact in the room was a piece of proof of their longstanding influence, a tale told in hushed tones of power and legacy from beyond the shadows.

"Are you trying to impress me?" Noah asked, his voice edged with a dry skepticism.

Number Four chuckled, the sound warm and unpretentious. "No, my dear boy. I am merely illustrating a point. Wherever there has been civilization, wherever there has been a need for guidance, the Council has existed. In one form or another, the greater minds of man have come together to steer the course of history."

Noah studied him for a moment, a smirk playing on his lips. "Megalomania," he remarked, "pure and simple."

Number Four merely smiled, the way you would at a smart-assed grandson. "Megalomania? A strong word for what is simply the truth. Consider the Illuminati, the Masons, the Knights Templar... all precursors or facets of the Council's influence through the ages. After all, someone must wield power. Why not let it be mankind's golden children?"

They moved into an adjacent sitting room, where the ambiance shifted from academic to one of a more relaxed, yet equally grand, setting. The walls of this comfortable enclave were adorned with oil paintings, their frames as magnificent as the masterpieces they held. Noah's gaze swept across several paintings, and his breath hitched as he recognized the distinct lines and colors of works long thought lost to the world.

"Is that a Caravaggio?" he asked as he gestured to a painting depicting Christ's arrest.

"Indeed," Number Four replied with a nod. "*The Taking of Christ*. Believed lost, but we've kept it safe for posterity."

"And that one?" Noah pointed to another. "It looks like Vermeer's *The Concert*. It was stolen back in 1990."

"Very astute, Mr. Wolf. It's quite the story, how it came into our possession," Number Four said with a hint of pride.

In the background, Gruber remained an ever-watchful, silent presence, his eyes sharp and assessing. Noah, still hand-cuffed, took a seat as Number Four began to weave a narrative that spanned centuries.

"Throughout history, whenever and wherever mankind has thrived, the Council has been there," Number Four began, his voice smooth and measured. "Our role has not been one of domination, but of stewardship—guiding humanity through its tumultuous journey. Consider the discovery of the Americas, European colonialism. We were there, charting the course, aiding in the spread of civilization."

Noah listened intently as Number Four paced the room in front of him, his hands clasped behind his back.

"The American Revolution, the French Revolution,

even the rise and fall of Napoleon. The British Empire, the American Civil War... We've had a hand in shaping the outcomes, aligning them with the greater good as we saw it."

Number Four paused beside a painting that depicted a historical battle, his gaze reflective. "The First World War, the Second World War, the downfall of Hitler, events that changed the world. We were the unseen hand, guiding, correcting."

Noah interjected, "And I suppose you had something to do with Kennedy's assassination and Nixon's exposure during Watergate?"

Number Four turned, his bright eyes locking with Noah's. "Oh, yes, Mr. Wolf. We certainly did. The world is a chessboard, see. Every move requires precision, foresight. Those events... let's just say there are no accidents in the flow of history."

He moved on, his voice growing softer, almost contemplative. "Even the tragedy of 9/11, a day that changed the course of the 21st century, was not beyond our gaze."

Noah felt a chill as he considered the implications. "You're saying the Council has been pulling the strings all along?"

Number Four resumed his seat, his expression serene. "We prefer to think of it as... guiding the human race. It's a heavy responsibility, one we've borne silently, for the betterment of mankind."

Clearly relaxed, Number Four settled into his armchair, his eyes reflecting the light of the lamps. "Mr. Wolf," he began, with the hint of a challenge, "where do you think I come from?"

Noah, leaning back, gave a wry smile. "I'd peg you as

some narcissistic billionaire trying to play God with real people's lives," he quipped, the sarcasm in his voice not quite masking a genuine curiosity about the man before him. "I'd say that your entire Council is made up of similar types. Old men keen to keep their old money and destroying the world to do so."

Number Four chuckled, a sound that echoed softly in the high-ceilinged room. "On the contrary, Mr. Wolf, I come from very humble beginnings. When the Council found me, I was a child, no more than a boy really, in a Nepalese village. They had been led to me after tales had reached their ears of a boy genius who could devour books in hours and recite them by heart."

He paused, his gaze distant as if he could see the mountainous landscape of his youth. "By the age of seven, I was taken in and trained to lead alongside many other children who had been handpicked from around the world. It's a rigorous path, and only a few of us ever make it to the upper echelons of the organization. That is the top fifty."

Noah raised an eyebrow. "A survival of the fittest kind of deal?"

"You could say that," Number Four conceded. "But it is merit that propels us forward, not nepotism. Though there has been many versions throughout history, the Council in its current form was created during the Renaissance, a time of enlightenment, by men who believed in guiding civilization through its most turbulent times. They envisioned an organization that would make the crucial decisions that warring nations were too blinded by their own nationalism to see."

He leaned forward, his eyes capturing Noah's. "They

understood that progress is not a product of chaos but of calculated decisions—decisions that carry the weight of the world on their shoulders."

Noah shifted in his seat, the leather of the armchair creaking beneath him. "So you're the chosen ones, then? The shepherds guiding the sheep?"

"In a manner of speaking," Number Four replied, undisturbed by the sarcasm in Noah's tone. "The Council operates on the belief that the right guidance can prevent catastrophe, can steer humanity toward a brighter future."

"And all the while, you sit in the shadows, pulling strings. Sounds lonely at the top," Noah countered.

Number Four's smile was tinged with a touch of sadness. "Leadership often is, Mr. Wolf. But one does not embark on this path seeking companionship." Number Four shifted subtly in his seat, the flicker of the firelight casting shadows across his face. "Our current strength," he began, "is something you've already had a taste of."

Noah's posture remained relaxed, but his mind was alert, piecing together the implications. "The EMP in Siberia," he stated flatly, not a question but a recognition.

"Exactly," Number Four replied. "That was merely one of many. We have capabilities that span the globe. Technologies in place that ensure our... stewardship remains unchallenged."

Noah raised his eyebrows. "So you're the bullies in the playground with the biggest sticks, then."

Number Four gave a mild, dismissive wave of his hand. "A crude analogy, but if it serves to illustrate the point. Consider the EMP devices not as sticks, but as reset buttons, strategically placed to neutralize any... escalation that may arise."

"Reset buttons for civilization, you mean," Noah interjected, his voice carrying a hard edge.

"Precisely," Number Four acknowledged with a nod. "It's about maintaining balance, ensuring that no single entity can rise to threaten the order we've so meticulously cultivated. If necessary, we can send humanity back to the dark ages to rebuild it correctly if we have to."

Noah's expression tightened. "That's quite the insurance policy."

"It's the assurance of our continued guidance," Number Four corrected. "We're the keepers of the status quo, the defenders of the world's equilibrium. It would be unwise to underestimate the lengths we're willing to go to preserve that. I bet when you left Siberia," he added, a hint of pride seeping into his tone for the first time, "you thought you'd just destroyed the prototype."

Noah remained silent, the truth of the statement hanging heavy in the air.

"Little did you know," Number Four continued, "we already had several up and running, located all over the world. One of which was able to knock your aircraft out of the sky."

It was beginning to dawn on Noah that his and E & E's efforts against a behemoth like the Council were akin to stones thrown against a fortress—a fortress armed with the power to rewrite history itself.

"All of this," he said, "is nothing more than you threatening me. Isn't it?"

"No, no, of course not," Number Four replied, his voice

returning to its earlier congeniality. "I would never make idle threats. Especially not to you, Mr. Wolf. I am simply showing you how futile it is to go against us. For both E & E and for yourself. Please, join us. Be a part of a better future —for you, for your wife, and for your little girl."

Noah had heard enough. He stood up to face the old man squarely. "I'm not about to join a band of schoolyard bullies," he told him.

Annoyed, Number Four also got up out of his chair. "Very well, then. Consider this your new permanent station," he declared, his tone laced with an unspoken threat.

Signaling Gruber to follow suit, he made his way to the exit.

"What about the others?" Noah called out.

The question, loaded with concern and desperation, hung momentarily unanswered.

Number Four paused, his silhouette framed by the doorway as the automatic door slid open. "And what of them?" he retorted, his voice carrying a chilling indifference.

"Are you going to release them?" Noah pressed.

"No," came Number Four's curt reply. "They stay where they are."

And with that, the door sealed shut, leaving Noah enveloped in a silence that was almost suffocating.

THIRTY-TWO

In the shadowy confines of an R&D workshop, Wally, with an air of excitement, was ready to showcase the latest in espionage gadgetry to his eager audience. He stood behind a long table that was covered in high-tech innovation. Allison, Sarah, and Neil gathered around, their faces reflecting a mix of curiosity and anticipation.

"All right, team," Wally began, rubbing his hands together, "let me introduce you to our little helpers for when we reach Cuba." He reached for a case about the size of a ring box and flipped it open to reveal a micro drone that mimicked a honey bee. "You'll remember, Neil, that this little beauty saved our skins against Schultz last year."

Neil raised an eyebrow, a smirk playing on his lips. "If I remember rightly, Wally, your 'bee' got squashed before it could do anything substantial."

A shade of red crept up Wally's neck, but he quickly recovered. "Well, that was a minor setback. This upgraded version is faster, stealthier, and much harder to catch." He quickly moved on, eager to leave the memory of the squashed drone behind.

Next, he picked up a metallic device the size and shape of a fountain pen. "Behold the Sonic Disruptor," he announced. "Non-lethal, but it'll incapacitate anyone within its range."

Wally glanced around, his eyes landing on the tall form of Neil. "Mr. Blessing, care to volunteer for a demonstration?"

Neil furrowed his brow. "Eh, didn't you just say it incapacitates?"

"Yes, but I've got it on a low setting. It will merely disorientate you for a short amount of time at this frequency, while still giving everyone an idea of its capabilities. So what do you say?"

"Eh, okay," Neil said in a dubious tone, bracing himself.

Before proceeding, Wally turned to Sarah and Allison with two pairs of earplugs in his hand. "Before we go any further, you'll need to use these," he said, handing them each a set. "These earplugs are equipped with frequency emitters designed to filter out the disruptor's effects. This way, you won't be affected by what's about to happen."

Sarah and Allison exchanged a quick glance before accepting the earplugs, inserting them as instructed. Wally did the same, ensuring all three were protected from the effects of the Sonic Disruptor.

"Ready?" Wally asked, receiving a nod from both women. "Now," the scientist went on, "you have to be no more than four feet from the target." Wally stepped closer to Neil. "Like so," he added before activating the device.

A low hum, inaudible to those wearing the earplugs,

filled the air. Neil's reaction was immediate; his eyes widened as he swayed on his feet.

"Whoa, that's... whoa!" Neil stammered, his words slurring as he tried to find his balance, much to the concealed amusement of Sarah and Allison.

Wally quickly turned off the Disruptor, and Neil steadied himself, shaking his head. "That was... weirdly enjoyable," he admitted, chuckling.

"Not too shabby, right?" Wally beamed, pleased with the successful demonstration. "Nevertheless, that was it on one. Put it on three or higher and it really packs a punch. On ten, the target might not wake up."

Wally placed the Disruptor down.

His enthusiasm was obvious as he picked up the next gadget, a small, sophisticated device about the size of a smartphone but with various intricate touch dials and a small antenna on the top. It was sleek, with a metallic finish that reflected the dim light of the room.

"This," he announced, holding it up for the others to see, "is my favorite. The Cognitive Harmonizer. It's designed to extract information from a subject without any of the... messiness."

The device hummed softly as he activated it, the lights on its surface blinking in a steady rhythm. As they gathered around the prototype, Wally took a moment to explain its intricacies. "The Cognitive Harmonizer," he began, holding the gadget for them to see, "is designed to temporarily alter brain function in a very targeted way. Let me show you."

He picked up a tablet from the table and pointed to a diagram on it, one highlighting the brain's key areas. "First, it affects the prefrontal cortex, reducing the subject's decision-making capabilities and making them more amenable to suggestion. It's like gently nudging the brain's command center into a more... cooperative state."

Moving his finger to another part of the brain displayed on the screen, he continued, "The amygdala is also targeted, which helps in managing the subject's emotional responses. By doing so, we can reduce panic or aggression, making the interrogation process smoother."

Wally then tapped on the hippocampus on the diagram. "Here's where it gets interesting. The disruption to the hippocampus can cause temporary disorientation, similar to being in a dreamlike state. This makes it difficult for the person to grasp what's happening around them, let alone fabricate lies."

Lastly, he highlighted the thalamus. "And by affecting the thalamus, we're essentially tweaking the brain's sensory relay center, amplifying the overall disorientation effect. It's sophisticated and non-lethal, focusing on making the subject passive and open to suggestion. They'll essentially do whatever you tell them to."

"Like a Jedi mind trick," Neil suggested.

"Yes," Wally agreed. "Or akin to the effects of scopolamine, but without the physical messiness of drug use." He turned once again to Neil. "Round two, Mr. Blessing?"

Neil, a hint of wariness in his eyes, gave a cautious nod. Wally placed the device to the back of Neil's head and activated it. This time, Neil's expression went blank, his eyes glazing over as if he were in a trance.

"What is your guiltiest secret?" Wally asked.

Neil stared blankly for a moment before his lips moved silently. Then, in a voice not his own, he said, "Last month I was doing the laundry when I put Jenny's Dior ballgown on hot by accident. It ruined the dress, shriveled it up. I then drove out to the city dump to get rid of it. Threw it in the landfill. I was too scared to throw it in the garbage at home in case she found it."

"Does Jenny know?" Sarah asked.

"No," Neil replied in a monotone. "I just zipped the garment bag back up and hung it in the wardrobe like it's still there."

Allison, with eyes wide, said, "You might want to reconsider getting Jenny back from Cuba, Neil. I wouldn't want to be you when she finds out."

The room erupted in laughter. Then Wally placed the device back on Neil's head and deactivated the effects. Neil blinked, coming back to his senses with a shake of the head.

"I have this strange feeling that I might be in terrible danger," he said, making everyone grin even more.

Wally looked pleased with the demonstration. "As you can see," he said, "it temporarily disrupts neural pathways, making the subject highly suggestible for up to an hour, and you can reverse the effects by placing it back to the skull and pressing the button twice. It's perfect for quick intel extraction, as well as making potential prisoners more cooperative."

The team nodded, impressed by the device's potential.

His eyes gleaming with excitement, Wally moved on to the next gadget. He reached into his pocket and pulled out a pair of sleek, stylish cufflinks, their polished surface giving no hint of their hidden power. "And now for one of my personal favorites," he announced with a flourish.

"These," he said, holding them up for all to see, "are EMP cufflinks. Don't let their size fool you; these babies pack a serious punch."

Sarah leaned in, intrigued. "EMP? As in electromagnetic pulse?"

"Exactly," Wally replied, his enthusiasm growing. He pointed to a laptop on a nearby table. "Watch this." He slipped the cufflinks onto his wrists and subtly twisted the decorative part of one.

Instantly, the laptop flickered and died, its screen going black.

Allison whistled softly. "That's impressive. It can knock out electronics?"

"Yep," Wally confirmed. "It emits a short-range electromagnetic pulse, strong enough to disable any electronic device within a few feet. Perfect for getting past security systems or causing a little chaos if needed. However, they're a one-shot deal, so you need to use them at just the right moment."

Wally's next revelation was met with eager anticipation as he moved to the end of the table, where a white sheet covered several items. "And now, the pièce de résistance," he declared, whipping back the sheet and unveiling three unique quantum cloaks. "I had my people take the quantum cloaks we were in possession of and tailor each one to reflect the wearer's unique personality."

For Sarah, Wally had crafted a cloak that was a tribute to her rebellious and wild spirit. It was styled like a sleek, black leather jacket with subtle, high-tech enhancements. The fabric gave off an aura of edgy charisma, reminiscent of a rock star's rebellious flair. "It's like wearing a shadow," Sarah remarked, running her fingers over the material as she put it on.

Allison's cloak was distinctly different, designed with a nod to her nickname, the Dragon Lady. It was an elegant single-breasted blazer with a scale-like pattern that shimmered in a gradient from deep crimson to gold. When activated, it flickered with an intensity that matched her fiery reputation. "Fierce and formidable, just like you," Wally said with a respectful nod.

Finally, Neil's cloak was the epitome of hipster chic, blending cutting-edge technology with a trendy, urban aesthetic. The fabric of the sports blazer had a subtle, plaid pattern that shifted colors gently, and when cloaked, it gave off a vibe of cool nonchalance. "It's like stealth mode for the Instagram generation," Neil quipped, clearly impressed.

With the demonstrations complete, the atmosphere in the room softened, a sense of camaraderie settling over the group. Neil and Wally turned to Allison with an air of sincerity that hadn't been there before.

"You know, Allison," Neil began, "it's really cool to be going out on a mission with you again. We really missed having you around."

Wally nodded in agreement, his usual playful demeanor giving way to something more heartfelt. "Yes, it wasn't the same without you. And, uh, about that nickname, Dragon Lady... we're sorry. It was just a bit of fun, you know?"

Allison looked at them, a small smile playing on her lips. There was a softness in her eyes that hadn't been there before. "I always knew about the nickname," she admitted.

"But I took it as a term of endearment. Dragons are strong, fierce protectors. I never saw it as a bad thing."

Sarah, who had been quietly observing the exchange, chimed in. "Dragon Lady suits you, Allison. You've always been our guardian, in a way. And you're definitely fierce."

The group shared a light laugh, the apprehensive respect that had once defined their interactions with Allison now replaced by a deeper understanding and appreciation for her. It was clear that the trials they had faced individually had brought them closer together as a team.

The heartfelt moment, however, was abruptly interrupted by a soft cough. Startled, the team turned sideways to find Molly Hanson standing at the doorway with an amused expression.

"I thought you guys were up to something," she said, her eyes scanning the array of high-tech gadgets spread out before them.

Wally, caught off guard, turned to the room's AI system. "Esmeralda, you should have warned us Molly was here!" he scolded.

The AI's calm voice filled the room. "Molly Hanson possesses a higher security clearance than even yourself, Wally. E & E protocol dictates that she has the right to access..."

Wally, flustered, quickly cut her off with a hushed "Okay, okay, Esmeralda."

Sarah stepped forward. "You're not going back to Doc Parker with this, are you?" she asked.

Molly crossed the room, her steps confident as she surveyed the team. "I should. But I'm not," she replied.

Her declaration brought a collective sigh of relief from the group.

"All right, then," Allison said, a small smile on her lips. "Welcome, Molly, to our motley crew."

Molly nodded, her gaze lingering on each member of the team. "I take it this is all for Noah and the others," she said.

"It is," Allison replied.

"Then count me in."

THIRTY-THREE

In the bleak cells of the Council's base, Marco, Jenny, and Renée each found themselves in the throes of an unending nightmare. Separated and isolated, they continued to face the grueling circumstances of their captivity.

Marco strained against the chains that held him aloft. His interrogator, a man with a bug-like face and hollowed-out eyes, stood before him. His voice was monotonous, devoid of any emotion, as he asked yet again, "How did you and your people find out about Siberia?" Marco's silence brought another attack from the man's partner, a jolt of pain rushing through him as he was struck with the baseball bat.

In the adjacent cell, Jenny gritted her teeth, enduring her own ordeal. Her interrogator, similar in appearance to Marco's, with a face that seemed almost inhuman, murmured his question. "Who told E & E about the hacking factory in the Atlantic?" When Jenny remained silent, the interrogator's partner delivered a sharp, painful jab with a cattle prod, the routine nature of his actions chillingly methodical as she writhed under the electrocution.

Renée, too, faced the same relentless torment. Her cell resonated with the hollow voice of her interrogator. "How many of our bases does E & E know about?" The question hung in the air. Her non-response was met with a calculated infliction of pain.

These cruel men were like the minions of hell, working the late shift down in the Ninth Circle. They were men who had seen so much torture that it had become mundane, a mere task to be performed. Their empty eyes looked out of emotionless faces. Each question, each act of violence, was delivered with the detachment of a person for whom such horrors have become commonplace.

In their separate cells, and in their separate ways, Marco, Jenny, and Renée each battled a growing sense of despair. The barrage of questions, the relentless pain, and the isolation from one another compounded into an overwhelming hopelessness. But beneath the surface, a spark of defiance still flickered. They clung to it, a faint beacon in the darkness of their situation, a silent vow to endure, to survive, no matter the odds.

THIRTY-FOUR

As the evening sun began its descent, casting a soft light through the kitchen window, the moment Sarah had been dreading had finally arrived. Norah sat at the kitchen table, her legs swinging back and forth, blissfully unaware of the gravity of their goodbyes.

Sarah knelt down to her daughter's level. "Sweetheart," she began, "Mommy has to go on a very important trip to help Daddy come back home. And while I'm away, I need you to be very brave for me. Can you do that?"

Norah's innocent blue eyes met her mother's, a sense of understanding flickering in them. "Will you bring Daddy back?" she asked, her voice hopeful.

"Yes, my love. That's exactly what we're going to do," Sarah promised, enveloping Norah in a tight embrace, her heart aching at the thought of leaving her daughter behind.

Allison watched the exchange with a heavy heart. She stepped forward, giving Sarah a moment to compose herself before turning her attention to Norah. "Hey, champ," she said, opening her arms wide. Norah jumped down from the table and ran into them. Allison lifted her up and spun her around, eliciting a giggle from the child. Setting Norah back down, she looked into her eyes. "Mommy and Auntie Allison will be back before you know it, okay?"

"I'll be good," Norah replied, hugging Allison tightly.

Allison then turned to the man and woman who had been quietly observing from the doorway. Both stood with an air of professionalism, yet their eyes held a warmth that was comforting.

"Mark, Linda," Allison addressed them, her tone shifting to one of seriousness, "I'm entrusting you with the most precious thing in my life. You know the stakes. She needs to be protected at all costs, but also, please... let her have as normal a time as possible under the circumstances."

Mark, a sturdy man with a gentle demeanor, nodded solemnly. "We understand, ma'am. Norah will be as safe with us as she would be with you. That's a promise."

Linda, equally as formidable in stature as she was kind in expression, added, "We're trained for this, ma'am. But beyond that, we'll care for her like she's our own. You have our word."

Allison studied them for a moment longer, searching their faces for any hint of doubt and finding none. Satisfied, she gave them a curt nod, her expression softening. "Thank you," she said before turning to Sarah. "It's time."

With one last look at Norah, Sarah whispered a silent prayer for her daughter's safety. Then, together, Sarah and Allison stepped out of the house, leaving Norah in the capable hands of Mark and Linda, their hearts heavy with the weight of goodbye but buoyed by the hope of what they were fighting for.

THIRTY-FIVE

NOAH SAT ALL ALONE INSIDE NUMBER FOUR'S quarters, his eyes scanning the opulent space, each artifact and painting acting as proof of the Council's extensive reach.

The sound of the door opening caused him to turn toward it. Standing there was Number Four, his expression unreadable.

"You must be hungry," he said. "I'd like you to join me for dinner."

At that moment, a procession of staff, all carrying crockery, cutlery, and various steaming pots and containers, entered the room from behind him. They moved with practiced precision, setting a long, ornate table with a luscious feast. The air filled with the aroma of rich, succulent dishes, the clink of fine china, and the shimmer of polished silverware. Gruber was there too, standing in the background, his presence a silent, brooding shadow against all the opulence.

The table groaned under the weight of a veritable feast of

American cuisine. Barbecued ribs, glazed in a smoky, sweet sauce, glistened under the light of chandeliers, while T-bone steaks, seared to perfection, awaited the diners with juicy promise. Beside them, a golden-hued macaroni and cheese casserole bubbled with creamy, rich goodness, its cheesy aroma mingling with the smoky barbecue. Freshly grilled corn on the cob, slathered in butter and sprinkled with a touch of salt and pepper, added a pop of bright yellow to the assortment.

Number Four took his seat at one end, a picture of refined composure as he placed a napkin on his lap. One of the serving staff pulled a chair out from the other end for Noah.

While he observed, the electronic shackles emitted a beep, unlocking and releasing his wrists. Gruber advanced, extending a massive hand, to which Noah relinquished the shackles.

"Take a seat, Mr. Wolf," Number Four gently urged him.

Noah took it, then sat motionless, his hands resting on his lap, his mind a tumult of anger and strategic calculation as the smell of the delicious food hit him.

"Eat," Number Four urged as he began to partake in the feast.

Noah's voice was tight with barely contained rage. "Where are my friends?"

"Eat," Number Four repeated, a note of impatience creeping into his otherwise calm demeanor.

"Are *they* eating?" Noah pressed.

Number Four set down his cutlery and dabbed his mouth with a napkin. "So long as you and I are having this discussion," he said icily, "your friends remain alive. Does that suffice?"

Noah's response was a deafening silence.

A staff member, possibly a waiter, approached Noah with a bottle of exceptionally fine pinot noir. "Would sir like to try some before I pour his glass?" he asked in a polite tone.

His offer was met with stony silence.

"Pour him the wine," Number Four instructed.

As the waiter bent forward, the corkscrew hanging from his belt caught Noah's eye. In a split-second decision, fueled by desperation and rage, Noah sprang into action. He seized the corkscrew, and before anyone could make a move, he had the guy held in front of him, pressing the corkscrew to the waiter's throat while using him as a human shield. In the commotion, the wine bottle had tipped over, its crimson contents spilling across the table and onto the floor like blood.

Guns were instantly drawn, trained on Noah from every corner of the room, including from Gruber's steady hand.

Number Four remained unfazed, almost bored by the display. "Kill him if you must," he said nonchalantly. "He's a committed man and fully aware of the risks involved in being a part of our organization. I'm sure he'd even be thankful to die in our service. His family certainly won't go without."

Noah's eyes met those of the man he held captive. The waiter's eyes were closed, his breathing controlled, his face a mask of serene acceptance.

Disgusted by the resignation and the futility of his own action, Noah let him go, and the waiter stepped back calmly into his role, bending down immediately to pick up the fallen bottle. Noah, feeling the weight of his powerlessness, slumped back into his chair.

"And the corkscrew, Herr Wolf." Gruber's deep voice cut through the air.

With a flick of his wrist, Noah sent the corkscrew spiraling toward Gruber, who, with nonchalant ease, snatched it from the air inches from his face. "Thank you, Herr Wolf," Gruber said as he pocketed the weapon.

"Now will you eat, Noah?" Number Four asked, his tone returning to its friendly cadence.

Realizing the futility of fighting in this moment and understanding that he needed his strength for whatever lay ahead, Noah picked up a fork, allowing the waiter to serve him a T-bone. He began to eat, each bite a bitter reminder of the situation he was in, a game played at the pleasure of an organization that held the world in its grip. The heavy atmosphere in the room remained, a silent witness to Noah's internal struggle and the colossal power of the Council.

THIRTY-SIX

UNDER THE COVER OF THE CARIBBEAN NIGHT, THE rescue party touched down in Havana, Cuba. The plan had been meticulously orchestrated: three separate commercial flights, false identities, and a rendezvous set for a discreet location in the city.

The oppressive heat and humidity of the Cuban night enveloped each of them as they separately navigated the bustling airport, the air thick with the mingled scents of coffee and tropical plants.

Neil, dressed casually in tourist attire, disembarked first, his eyes scanning the crowds with a practiced nonchalance. Merging seamlessly with the throng of travelers, his senses were alert for any signs of surveillance.

Wally and Molly came next. They moved through the terminal, their interactions natural but their eyes sharp. Molly's schooling in espionage had prepared her well for such operations, and Wally, despite having spent his entire career in espionage inside a lab, was every bit the skilled field agent.

Sarah and Allison, the last to arrive, moved with the confidence of seasoned travelers. Allison, in particular, was like a shadow, her eyes missing nothing. Inside the terminal, she noticed a few covert watchers, Council agents blending into the crowds but their purpose betrayed by the intensity of their gazes. Her instincts, honed by years in the field, alerted her to their presence, a silent alarm that set her on edge.

At immigration, the biometric spoof kit Wally had provided them each with came into play. It was obvious the Council would be drag-netting for their fingerprints and retinas. Each member, heavily disguised, stepped up to the booth. One by one, they placed their fingers on the scanner, the kit providing them with false fingerprints that matched the biometric data of normal American citizens. The immigration officers, none the wiser, processed them through.

Once they'd picked up their limited baggage, they each slipped into the humid night of Havana, their faces just another blur in the crowd. The city was alive with the sounds of late-night revelry and the distant rhythm of salsa music. Blending in with locals and tourists alike, they made their way to the local taxi points. The mission to rescue Noah and his team from the clutches of the Council had begun, and every second counted.

The team arrived separately at their designated hotels in different parts of the city, prepared for the next phase. The hotels, each a blend of Cuban architecture and modern comfort, offered brief respite and a moment to blend into the flow of tourists and locals alike.

Neil, staying in a modest hotel near the impressive edifice of El Capitolio, absorbed the vibrant street life from his balcony. He watched as classic American cars from the 1950s cruised past, their colors as vivid as the city itself. Below, vendors sold aromatic street food, the scents of frying plantains and spiced meats wafting up to him.

Wally and Molly, in a more upscale hotel by the Malecón, marveled at the ocean view, the moon casting a silver sheen over the water. They shared a quick, inconspicuous toast with tiny cups of strong Cuban coffee before heading out into the night.

Sarah and Allison, opting for a boutique hotel nestled in the heart of Old Havana, soaked in the historic charm of their surroundings. The cobbled streets and colonial buildings whispered stories of the past as they moved through them, the air rich with the sound of distant music.

Leaving the hotels a few hours after arriving, their paths converged at a lively jazz club. The exterior, awash in the warm glow of neon, promised a night of rhythmic escapism. But that wasn't why they were there.

As each member of the team entered the club at different times, their arrivals staggered so as to put off potential surveillance teams, they were greeted by a whirlwind of sensory experiences. The air was thick with the scent of white rum and cigar smoke, an intoxicating blend that set the scene. The sultry sound of a trumpet player filled the air, the notes rising and falling with an effortless grace that only a true master could achieve.

Dancers moved across the floor with a fluidity that was mesmerizing. Their bodies swayed to the beat of Latin soul, the rhythm seeming to flow through them like a current.

Women in flowing dresses spun and twirled, their laughter mingling with the music, while sweat-heavy men guided them with a confident, gentle hand. The club was a kaleidoscope of life and color, each patron a character in the ever-unfolding story of Havana's nightlife.

Sarah was the last to arrive. She made her way through the crowd to the bar, her presence drawing a mix of curious and snide looks from some of the men in the club. Undeterred, she leaned against the bar and ordered confidently, "A Cobra's sting."

The bartender, a woman with a knowing look in her eye, paused for a moment, her demeanor turning serious. She reached for an old, dusty bottle behind the counter. The bottle was intriguing, with a scorpion and a cobra preserved inside, floating in whatever booze filled it. The bartender poured a shot of the thick, red liquid, which resembled blood more than a drink.

As Sarah reached for the glass, the bartender's hand shot out, stopping her. "Don't drink it," she warned in a low, urgent tone. "Take it to the bathroom and give it to the blind man."

Puzzled but trusting her instincts, Sarah nodded and took the glass. She turned and began to navigate through the thick crowd, the club's atmosphere electric with the rising crescendo of the music, the air thick with the heat of dancing bodies, the scent of sweat mingling with the fragrances of rum and perfume.

The bathroom door eventually came into view, a beacon in the dimly lit club. Sarah pushed through, the noise of the crowd fading behind her as she entered the quieter space.

Her mission was clear: find the blind man and deliver the mysterious drink.

Upon entering the restroom, Sarah spotted him immediately. Her curiosity piqued, she made her way to the corner of the room, past the cubicles to the sinks and mirrors, where a middle-aged man sat, his eyes hidden behind a pair of blacked-out glasses. His presence seemed out of place in the lively club—he was some type of attendant, surrounded by bottles of perfumes and colognes, a purveyor of scents in a place of sound and rhythm.

She approached him cautiously and handed over the shot glass. "I was told to give you this."

The man, alerted by her voice, took the glass with practiced ease, bringing it to his nose for a brief sniff. Then, with a knowing smile, he tossed the contents down his throat, savoring the taste. "Mmm," he murmured contentedly, wiping away a stray drip with the back of a finger.

Standing up, he offered his elbow to Sarah. "You able to follow instructions?"

"Yes," she replied.

"Then I want you to take us left when we leave this bathroom," he instructed.

Guided by the blind man, Sarah navigated them back through the club, his confident strides belying his supposed lack of sight. They moved behind the bar to a backroom, a storage area cluttered with various items. Once inside, the blind man locked the door behind them, securing their privacy.

"You see that chest freezer?" he asked, his tone businesslike.

"Yes," Sarah responded, moving toward it and opening

the lid. Inside, it was filled with bags of ice and slabs of frozen meat, ordinary items for the club's kitchen.

"Did I tell you to open it?" the blind man scolded her.

Sarah closed it, stepping back and mumbling, "Sorry."

The man, muttering under his breath, shuffled over to the freezer. "Thirty years working this gig," he grumbled, "first for CIA, now for E & E, and you agents always thinking you know best."

Arriving at the chest freezer, he slid a panel on the top to one side, revealing a hidden keypad. His first attempt at entering a code was incorrect, prompting him to lift his glasses to get a better look at the keys, revealing that he was not completely blind.

With the correct code entered, the freezer opened again, but this time, there was no meat or ice. This time there was a set of stairs leading downward, a faint light glowing from below.

"Voilá!" the man declared, a hint of triumph in his voice.

He gestured toward the stairs. "Go on, your friends are waiting for you."

With his assistance, Sarah climbed into the freezer, cautiously making her way down the steps.

At the bottom, the sound of the hatch closing up above her, she found herself in a secret passage hidden beneath the lively façade of the Cuban jazz club. Walking toward the dull light a little farther on, Sarah emerged into a surprisingly well-equipped underground operations room, complete with living facilities. It couldn't be any more different from the vibrant club above. The space was efficiently organized with screens lining the walls and equipment neatly arranged.

Neil was the first to spot her. His face broke into a wide

grin as he stood up from a console. "Sarah!" he exclaimed, his voice filling the enclosed space. He crossed the room with a few quick strides and enveloped her in a hearty hug.

"All in one piece, I see," he joked, pulling back to look at her.

Sarah returned the smile. "Wouldn't miss this for the world," she replied.

Wally, who had been rummaging through a crate of gadgets, looked up and beamed. "Hey, Sarah! The gang's all here now!"

Molly, standing a little off to the side, offered Sarah a warm, if somewhat reserved, smile. "Good to see you, Sarah," she said.

Allison, who had been overseeing the setup, walked over with a smile. "Sarah, glad you made it safely," she said. "We've got a lot to get done."

"Feels like old times, doesn't it?" Sarah remarked, looking around at the group.

"It does," Neil agreed. "Except this time, the stakes are even higher."

THIRTY-SEVEN

THE DINNER, AN EXTRAVAGANT YET TENSE AFFAIR, concluded with Number Four leading Noah, followed by Gruber and their entourage, to a secluded room within his quarters. The center of the room was dominated by a large, intricate hologram of the Earth.

As they approached, the hologram sprang to life, displaying vivid, swirling colors that represented the various conflicts and environmental crises plaguing the planet. Number Four began to speak, his voice carrying a somber weight. "Look at our world, Noah. See the oil fields burning, the ozone layer thinning, the ice caps melting. Witness the rapid industrialization of developing nations, the Amazon shrinking, deserts spreading."

The hologram zoomed in on different parts of the world, each image more distressing than the last. "The grim calculation is clear," Number Four continued. "Our planet has a limited time left at this rate. The world is choking, suffocating under the weight of its own progress."

Noah watched, the scale of the problems laid bare before him in harsh, unyielding detail. He could see the entire globe suffering, its beauty marred by human activity.

Number Four's voice grew more intense as he spoke of the world's governments. "Their reactions are futile, chaotic, and contradictory. They can't even find common ground within their own cabinets, let alone with leaders of other nations. They all think they're right, yet none are willing to listen to the other."

Noah, his gaze still fixed on the hologram, reminded him, "You forget. I've spent the last six months watching you people. Much of this conflict is fueled by the Council's misinformation campaigns."

"We merely aim to speed up the process," Number Four retorted sharply. "They're the ones who refuse to listen, who refuse to see beyond their own narrow sets of interests."

The hologram shifted, showing a rapid timeline of human population growth. "Two hundred years ago, there were a billion people on this planet. Eighty thousand years of homo sapiens had accumulated no more than a single billion. But then came the Enlightenment and the Industrial Revolution. In the two centuries of rapid advancement in medicine, science and technology, we've multiplied to over eight billion. Our planet was never meant to hold so many. It is why we are being driven to madness and extinction."

Noah's eyes narrowed as he absorbed Number Four's words. "And what's your solution?" he asked.

Number Four paused, a small smile playing on his lips. "I'm glad you asked. I'll show you."

He gestured to the hologram, and the image shifted again, this time to a series of locations across the globe, each marked with a distinct symbol. "Our solution is radical, yes, but necessary. The Council has a plan to restore balance, to reduce the strain on our planet, and to place mankind back on course. It's a plan that requires sacrifice but one that will ensure the survival of our species into the next millennium."

Number Four, with a sense of gravity, began to outline the Council's master plan. As he spoke, the hologram morphed, illustrating each phase with chilling clarity.

"Phase One: Disseminating False Information," he began. The hologram displayed a network of digital connections, symbolizing the media and social networks. "Over the years, we've manipulated these platforms, sowing discord on sensitive topics. Creating division, distrust. Essentially what you and your team have been trying to stop these past months."

Noah's jaw tightened as he watched the network pulse and spread across the hologram, a visual representation of the Council's insidious influence.

"Phase Two: Destruction of Internet and Satellites." The image shifted to a global scale, showing satellites orbiting the Earth before being engulfed by a wave of electromagnetic energy. "We will use the EMP cannons to create a global communication blackout. Imagine the hysteria, the confusion when the world suddenly goes silent."

He moved on. "Phase Three: Dissemination of Post-Blackout False Information." The hologram now showed images of drones dropping flyers, pirate radio transmissions crackling into life. "With no Internet, no satellites, we resort to more traditional means of misinformation. The drones and flyers you saw are part of this strategy.

"Phase Four: EMP Weapon Against Transportation."

The hologram depicted various modes of transportation—planes, ships, cars, trains—all coming to a catastrophic halt. "It's not just about planes falling from the sky or the disruption of global communications," Number Four explained, his tone almost casual. "Cargo ships, ferries, autonomous vehicles, trains—all of them are vulnerable to our EMP weapons."

Noah could almost hear the screams, the sounds of destruction, as the hologram illustrated the devastation such an attack would cause.

Then came the worst. Horror, pure and simple.

"Phase Five: Microwave Weapon in Urban Areas." The image changed to show several cities, each marked with a target. The machine Gruber had shown Noah before was now visible, its ominous form rising up inside a huge underground chamber. "This will allow us to clear the cities," Number Four said with chilling certainty. "Imagine, Mr. Wolf, a weapon that could end all life within a city without damaging any of the infrastructure or the plant life. Nuclear weapons, while powerful, are blunt instruments—destroying everything and leaving an area uninhabitable for centuries." Number Four's voice was even, almost clinical. "But the weapon you see here can clear an area the size of Manhattan in mere minutes. Then people can come in, bag up the bodies, and you've got yourself an empty city."

The room went silent. Noah, standing before the image of a planet in turmoil, felt a cold sense of dread. The Council's plan was not just an attack or a coup; it was a complete restructuring of the world order, a plan executed with surgical precision and utter disregard for human life. Noah now realized the true scale of the battle he was facing—it was not just a fight against an organization, but a fight for the very future of humanity.

Number Four's presentation continued to take a darker turn as he detailed the aftermath. "Clearing out the bodies," he began, the hologram shifting to show teams systematically removing human remains from the cities. "It's a grim task but necessary for what comes next."

He gestured, and the hologram changed again, displaying the methodical dismantling of the world's infrastructure. "Revitalizing the planet," he proclaimed. "Ending the reliance on oil fields, breaking down the now superfluous buildings and infrastructure and disposing of them safely while turning those spaces back over to nature. That will be our next goal. Watch," Number Four urged as the hologram showed the Sahara and other deserts transforming into lush oases, water redirected from the Red Sea through repurposed oil pipelines. "Without mankind's constant emissions, weather patterns will normalize, and the oceans will replenish."

The hologram then accelerated into a timelapse, showing the Earth over the next five, ten, twenty, thirty, fifty years. Each stage was a drastic transformation—industrial areas reclaimed by nature, the holes in the ozone layer healing, and a world where the scars of human civilization were slowly erased.

Fifty years into the future, the planet was unrecognizable. Vast estates dominated the landscape, each controlled by a single family, the remnants of humanity living in a state of eco-conscious luxury. The hologram depicted a world where commerce and need were no longer the driving forces.

Machines did the heavy lifting, and humanity focused on intellectual and cultural pursuits.

As Noah absorbed this radical vision, Number Four placed an arm around his shoulders. "They won't have died for nothing," he said softly. "They will have given their lives so that their species can live on. A necessary sacrifice for a sustainable future."

Noah stared at the utopia, feeling a mix of horror and allure at the vision. It was a future built on the ashes of billions, a paradise with an unimaginable cost.

"Now, tell me, Mr. Wolf; where would you like your family's estate to be?" Number Four asked, his voice gentle yet laden with the gravity of the question. "Colorado, perhaps?"

Noah's mind reeled at the proposition, the weight of the decision, and the brutal reality of what this 'new world' entailed. It was a choice between joining a vision he found morally repugnant and resisting an almost omnipotent force. In that moment, standing before the hologram of a future Earth, Noah realized the true depth of the Council's ambition and the monumental scale of the battle he faced.

THIRTY-EIGHT

Beneath the Havana jazz club, Allison, Sarah, Wally, Neil, and Molly were in the final stages of their preparation. The room was a hive of focused activity, each member meticulously packing their backpacks and making last-minute adjustments to their disguises.

As they finished gearing up, the man who had guided them there descended the stairs, moving with a confidence that belied his supposed blindness.

"Everything is ready in Santa Clara," he informed Allison, his voice low and steady. "Your things have already reached their destination and are waiting for you."

"Good. Then if all goes to plan, we should reach the base by nightfall," Allison responded.

"Good luck, mi amiga," he said, tapping her gently on the arm.

As he turned to leave, Allison reached out, touching his elbow. "Thank you, Manuel," she said, her smile genuine.

Manuel lifted his glasses, revealing damaged eyes that saw

more than most. "You know, you're still as beautiful as you were the first day you came strolling into this bar back in '83." Lowering the glasses, he added in an undertone, "I should've known you were trouble the second I laid these old eyes on you. Especially that night, in bed, when you recruited me." A flicker of emotion filled his gravelly voice as he told her, "I almost felt better thinking you were dead. At least that way I had closure."

With those words, he turned and left.

Allison watched him go, a pang of cold sadness momentarily crossing her features. Then with a deep breath, she pushed the emotion aside. After all, she was the Dragon Lady, and there was no room for sentimentality in the field.

She turned to her team, who quickly averted their eyes, pretending not to have witnessed the exchange. "Come on," she barked, glancing at her wristwatch, "it's only three minutes until we leave. Make sure everything is right. We won't get another chance at this."

The team sprang into action, each member checking their gear with renewed focus. The air was thick with anticipation, the weight of the mission pressing upon them. They were ready to embark on a journey that would test their skills, their resolve, and their dedication to the cause.

One by one, the members of the rogue rescue team emerged from the basement of the jazz club, each taking a separate exit and blending into the early morning streets of Havana. The city was just beginning to stir, the first rays of sunlight casting long shadows on the old, colorful buildings.

Allison was the first to leave, her steps purposeful yet casual as she navigated the quiet streets. She kept her head down, a large sun hat shielding her face, aware of the ever-present threat of the Council's agents.

Sarah followed a few minutes later, taking a different route. She moved with the ease of a seasoned traveler, a back-pack slung over one shoulder. Yet despite her relaxed demeanor, her eyes darted around, scanning her surroundings for any sign of surveillance.

Neil was next, his Che Guevara T-shirt blending in with the tourist crowd as the streets began to fill. He kept his hands in his pockets, his posture relaxed but alert. The early morning light cast a golden hue over the city, but Neil's attention remained fixed on the potential dangers hidden in plain sight.

Molly and Wally departed last, each in a different direction, their paths converging toward the Viazul bus station.

The depot was a hub of activity with buses coming and going and tourists milling around. The team members arrived from different directions, their timing staggered to avoid drawing attention.

As they boarded the tourist bus, Allison and Sarah found seats together, pretending not to know each other. "Is this seat taken?" Sarah asked casually. "No, of course not," Allison replied, offering a polite smile.

Molly and Neil also sat together, engaging in light conversation to maintain their cover. Wally, meanwhile, found himself seated next to an elderly Canadian woman who immediately engaged him in chit-chat.

"You're American, right?" she put to him after they'd exchanged names.

"Well spotted," he put back.

The bus quickly filled with noisy tourists, a cacophony

of different languages filling the air. Camera phones clicked, and excited chatter mixed with the hum of the engine as the bus set off across the island in the direction of Santa Clara.

The plan was simple. Until they got close to the city, they couldn't drop their cover as ordinary tourists. Manuel's sources claimed that Council agents were out on the highways stopping all rented vehicles, or just those carrying foreigners. They were also staking out the towns and villages, setting up checkpoints outside some. The only way to get close enough to the Citadel without alerting the Council was to do it as tourists, mingling and unseen within the faceless swell of the thousands of tourists that flood the island.

As the bus rolled toward Santa Clara, the team edged closer to their destiny, ready to face whatever challenges awaited them.

THIRTY-NINE

The stale air of Jenny's cell was thick with the acrid smell of burnt flesh. Her interrogator continued his relentless barrage of questions. "How did you know about Siberia?" he droned on, his voice grating on her nerves like a piece of wire being dragged across her bones.

Beside him, the other man wielded the cattle prod, its use leaving angry, red burn marks on Jenny's skin.

"How?!" the interrogator shouted so hard he covered her face in spittle.

Jenny enjoyed that she had him rattled. She just smiled, showing off her bloodstained teeth.

The angry-faced interrogator nodded at the other man, and she was hit with the prod. The jolt of electricity sent waves of excruciating pain through her body, but all it did was harden Jenny's resolve. She drew upon her extensive knowledge of meditation, focusing through the pain—preparing for her escape.

Because everything was part of her plan.

For the past hour, she had been using the cover of her spasms to dislocate her wrists from the shackles that held them. As the electricity coursed through her again, the pain was immense, a searing fire that raced up and down her arms, but she gritted her teeth and pushed through it. With a grimace of agony and determination, she finally slipped her hands out of the cuffs.

The prod suddenly sputtered and died, its charge spent. The torturers, taken aback, began discussing among themselves which tool to use next, their backs turned on the captive. This was Jenny's opportunity.

With the grace and silence of a panther, she lowered herself to the ground. Inside the cell with them was a third man, an armed guard by the door. Unfortunately for him, his attention was on the other two men rather than his duty. He didn't notice her move.

In a flash, Jenny was upon the two torturers, her movements precise. Taking the backs of both men's heads, she savagely smashed them together, face first, once, twice, until they collapsed onto their knees.

Jenny grabbed ahold of the heavy cattle prod. The guard by the door was just unshouldering his bullpup when she reached him with it. In one fluid motion, she brought the substantial weight of the device down on his head. A loud crack signaled his skull fracturing as he fell backward into the wall, the assault rifle dangling from his shoulder, his empty hands raised for protection.

Jenny's eyes were blank as she brought the cattle prod crashing down on him again and again until he crumpled to the floor in a heap.

Adrenaline coursing through her veins, Jenny quickly

gathered the IWI Tavor bullpup, her hands moving with practiced ease as she checked it over, ensuring it was in perfect working order. She then chambered a round, the soft click sounding loud in the quiet cell.

Her mind was already racing ahead to her next obstacle —the retina scan required to exit the cell.

She glanced at the gurney with all the torture implements on it, specifically the set of scalpels. Then she turned to the lifeless eyes of the guard on the floor. A grim realization set in; she would have to take a gruesome next step to secure her escape.

FORTY

THE TOUR BUS EASED TO A STOP AT THE EDGE OF Santa Clara, pulling into a picturesque rest stop that overlooked a sprawling valley. The stop itself was a beautiful example of Spanish colonial architecture, with its ivory white structures and red terracotta tiled roofs. The area buzzed with activity as tourists from several buses milled around, taking photos with selfie sticks, all vying for the perfect shot. Others headed for the restaurant or to the restrooms.

Amidst this bustle, Allison, Sarah, Wally, Neil, and Molly began the next phase of their plan. They casually made their way to the restrooms.

In the men's, Neil and Wally scanned the line of cubicles. Wally's attention was drawn to one particular cubicle where a pair of loafers, identical to his own, were visible through the gap beneath the door.

He exchanged a knowing nod with Neil, who had just spotted another cubicle with a pair of checkerboard patterned Vans visible beneath its door—shoes identical to his own. Each man approached their respective cubicle, giving a discreet, coded knock.

The doors opened, and in stepped Neil and Wally, coming face to face with their absolute doppelgängers.

Inside Neil's cubicle, he couldn't help but comment, "Impressive. You look just like me." The doppelgänger responded with a silent gesture, placing a finger to his lips.

Wordlessly, they exchanged rucksacks that were identical in looks but not in weight. The doppelgängers then left the cubicles and the bathroom and seamlessly blended into the crowd of tourists outside.

In the women's restroom, a similar scene unfolded. Allison, Sarah, and Molly each encountered their own lookalikes. There was no conversation, just an efficient exchange of gear.

Once alone, each member of the team quickly changed out of their tourist attire. Inside the rucksacks was black, nondescript clothing, as well as Neil, Sarah, and Allison's personalized quantum cloaks. The transformation was swift and methodical, each member keenly aware of the time ticking by.

The five doubles, having seamlessly assumed their identities, emerged from the restrooms with a casual ease that belied the meticulous planning behind their actions.

The first to step out was Wally's double. He adjusted his Hawaiian shirt and ambled into the crowd with a practiced nonchalance. His demeanor was a mirror image of Wally's relaxed tourist guise, right down to the way he paused to admire the view of the valley.

Moments later, Neil's doppelgänger emerged, the Che Guevara T-shirt worn with the same casualness as Neil's. He also blended into the crowd, his posture and mannerisms indistinguishable from the man he was impersonating.

Allison's double stepped out of the restroom, pausing to adjust her sun hat and scanning the area with a carefully measured gaze before moving toward the main tourist throng.

Sarah's and Molly's doubles followed suit, and together, the doppelgängers mingled with the tourists. To any onlooker, they were just another group of foreigners enjoying the sights of Santa Clara, their presence unremarkable amidst the diverse tapestry of people at the rest stop. They moved with a purpose that was hidden in plain sight, their role crucial to maintaining the illusion that Allison, Sarah, Wally, Neil, and Molly were still part of the tour group.

Nevertheless, dark clouds loomed. The arrival of two Council agents in a Jeep marked a sudden shift in the atmosphere. Dressed in clothing that screamed official business—radios and pistols clipped to their belts, earpieces snugly in place, and mirrored sunglasses masking their eyes —their movements, purposeful and distinct, sliced through the tourist revelry.

They began their inquiries immediately, approaching each tour guide with an air of authority. Pictures of Sarah and Neil were shown. The first tour guides they showed them to responded with shakes of their heads and shrugs of confusion.

But the agents' search soon led them to the tour guide responsible for the group Allison and her team were supposed to be with. The guide studied the pictures carefully. Sarah's disguise drew no recognition. However, Neil's image made the guide pause. "Maybe," he muttered, squinting at Neil's photo. "It looks a little like one of the gringos."

"Where is he?" one of the agents demanded, his tone sharp.

The tour guide scanned the crowd, his gaze landing on Neil's doppelgänger, who was lounging on an upstairs terrace. He pointed, and the agents wasted no time. They marched up to the terrace, their rapid approach drawing curious glances from the tourists.

Upon reaching Neil's double, they demanded to see his passport. The doppelgänger, maintaining his role, produced the fake passport with a hint of indignation. Unsatisfied, the agents then produced a retina scanner, insisting on a scan.

The doppelgänger's protests grew louder, a perfect act of the aggrieved tourist. "Don't you know I'm an American?" he exclaimed, his voice tinged with anger and disbelief. "This is outrageous!"

"You are in Cuba, and it is the law," the agent retorted.

Reluctantly, the doppelgänger complied, allowing his eyes to be scanned. Across the terrace, one of the other doppelgängers, observing the scene, made a discreet phone call.

Inside Allison's cubicle, as she was finishing her transformation, her phone rang. The warning was clear and urgent. "You better watch it," the doppelgänger informed her. "Two men have just arrived. They're hassling Christophe."

Allison's response was calm but firm. "We'll stay tight, then," she said.

"You better," came the reply, laced with concern.

Back on the terrace, the agents, having completed the

retina scan, found that the man was not Neil. With a mix of frustration and reluctance, they left the scene. The doppelgänger watched them go, a sense of relief washing over him, before he quickly sent a text to Allison: "You're all clear, but be careful. Very careful."

The message underscored the gravity of their situation. They were deep in enemy territory, and the margin for error was nonexistent. Allison pocketed her phone, understanding the weight of the mission more than ever. It was time to move. The next phase of their plan awaited, and they needed to be extremely cautious.

The rest stop, a hubbub of activity and chatter, suddenly shifted gears as the tour guides began herding everyone back to the buses. In the seclusion of the cubicles, the team readied themselves as the sounds of bus engines rumbling to life filtered into the bathroom.

With the tourists all leaving, each member emerged transformed, their nondescript clothing and quantum cloaks replacing the tourist disguises. They were also packing M17 sidearms.

Fully equipped and dressed for the operation ahead, they were now the complete opposite of the casual tourists they had been moments ago. Moving with precision, they regrouped at the back of the property. Without a word, they scaled a low wall, landing softly in the alleyway on the other side. The mid-morning light cast long shadows in the narrow passage, providing cover as they moved stealthily toward their next destination.

The dirt road at the end of the alley was typical of Cuba's rural landscape, especially in the southeastern part of the island. Lined with lush vegetation, it offered the perfect route for a covert approach. As they navigated their way, the surroundings transitioned to a more rural setting, the sounds of nature replacing the bustle of the tourist stop.

It wasn't long before they came across their ride out of here, hidden under tarps and loose vegetation, carefully concealed from prying eyes. Without hesitation, they uncovered two vehicles, revealing rugged, all-terrain Jeeps that looked ready for the rough journey ahead.

Sarah confidently took the wheel of one, with Allison settling in beside her. In the other vehicle, Neil assumed the driver's seat, Wally taking the passenger side, and Molly climbing into the back.

With a nod to each other, they started the engines and set off, the Jeeps kicking up dust as they began navigating the dirt road. The route they were taking would be a network of back roads and rural tracks, a path carefully chosen to avoid detection and to make the most of Cuba's less-traveled routes.

As they drove, the team remained vigilant, their eyes scanning the horizon for any signs of pursuit or danger. They were a unit in motion, each member focused on their role, their minds set on the task at hand. The journey to the Citadel had begun, and with each mile, they drew closer to confronting the formidable enemy that awaited them.

FORTY-ONE

Noah awoke in the solitude of Number Four's quarters, the silence enveloping him like a thick blanket. The faint hum of the station's life support systems was the only sound disturbing the quiet. Feeling an inexplicable pull, he found himself drawn to the operations room, coming to a stop before the hologram of the world.

It cast an otherworldly glow that illuminated Noah's contemplative figure as he used the control panel to move the holographic globe, watching the projected future of humanity unfold before him.

He scrolled forward through the six phases the Council planned to unleash. He saw cities darken, societies crumble, and the population dramatically decrease. Within twenty-five years, the world transformed into something unrecognizable. The relentless tread of mankind, which had for so long trampled over the earth, seemed to lift, giving way to a world where nature thrived in the absence of human overcrowding and exploitation.

Where there was human infrastructure, it was bold and beautiful in its imagination. Civic squares entwined with nature to form architecturally phenomenal spaces. In these cities of tomorrow, buildings curved and rose like the trunks of mighty trees, their surfaces a mosaic of living green walls and solar panels, shimmering with a self-sustaining glow. Rooftops were transformed into gardens, buzzing with insects and dotted with the bright colors of wildflowers, contributing to the biodiversity that thrived in the heart of these urban forests.

Transportation was a seamless blend of efficiency and environmental consciousness. Networks of underground and overground trains moved silently on magnetic tracks, their energy sourced from renewable power. Personal vehicles, now redundant, were replaced by shared, autonomous pods that glided along designated lanes, their paths intertwined with green corridors to allow wildlife to cross safely.

Noah's heart ached at the vision of a planet unburdened from human excess. Outside of these cities, he saw forests regrowing in areas that were once concrete jungles, the air becoming cleaner and wildlife flourishing in a way it hadn't for centuries. The Earth in this future breathed freely, healing from centuries of scars.

But this idyllic vision was shattered by the next sequence of images that Noah brought up. The toll of human lives lost in achieving this utopia was staggering. The hologram displayed chilling statistics and images of chaos and suffering that would follow the Council's plan. Millions of children and adults alike would perish in the collapse of society, like patients suddenly deprived of life support. Whoever survived the initial catastrophes would be forced to wander the planet, cut off, completely open to relentless suffering.

Noah's hand hovered over the control, his mind racing. The microwave weapons—the final phase—were particularly haunting. Entire cities wiped clean of life, leaving behind eerie, uninhabited shells. The scale of the genocide was unimaginable, a cold and calculated culling of the human race.

He was torn between the vision of a healed planet and the unspeakable cost it entailed. The dilemma weighed heavily on him, each option a labyrinth of moral and ethical implications. On one hand, the lifting of humanity's footprint from the natural world was a chance for the earth to recover. On the other, the method to achieve it was nothing short of catastrophic, a nightmare of suffering and death.

Noah longed for Sarah's presence, aching for her counsel, her voice of reason. He needed someone to talk to, to help him navigate the storm of thoughts raging in his mind. The loneliness of the room amplified the ferment in his head, each thought bouncing off the walls, unanswered and hollow.

However, the stillness outside of Noah was suddenly shattered by the blaring of a security alarm. The sound jolted him from his reverie as a voice boomed over the tannoy system. "Attention, all personnel! We have a prisoner escape. Repeat, a prisoner escape. All staff, be on high alert and report any suspicious activity immediately."

Noah's heart raced as the announcement reverberated through the quarters. The possibility that one of his team members had broken free sparked a glimmer of hope amidst his turmoil.

JENNY WAS A SHADOW AMONG SHADOWS, moving with a predator's grace through the Council's sprawling Citadel. Her many years as an assassin were evident in every silent step she took, every calculated breath she made. She navigated the gloomy corridors with an ease born of years in the field, her movements blending seamlessly with the environment.

Jenny's path soon led her to the ventilation shafts, a network of hidden routes within the base. Using the flat edge of the scalpel, she removed several screws belonging to a grill, then slipped inside. The narrow, metallic tunnels became her silent highway, guiding her unseen above the heads of her enemies.

As she crawled through the shafts, Jenny's keen eyes scanned the rooms below through the grills, her mind attuned to the task at hand. She found what appeared to be a busy walkway, people moving back and forth, and waited over the grill like a bat preparing to swoop down on its prey. Then she saw him—a lone guard with a comms unit in his ear, momentarily isolated from his comrades. Just what she was waiting for.

Having already removed the screws from the grill, she positioned herself above him, her body coiled and ready. Through the grating, her eyes locked on to her target, waiting for the perfect moment. Then, with the swiftness of a striking viper, she dropped down behind him. Before he could react, she had snapped his neck with a prompt, clinical movement, the guard slumping to the ground, lifeless.

Without hesitation, Jenny bent down and retrieved the

fallen man's sidearm: a Beretta M9, adding it to the Tavor assault rifle she already had.

She then retrieved the comms unit from the guard's ear and placed it in her own. Pausing, she listened intently to the chatter that filled the airwaves, and it wasn't long before she heard what she needed—a mention of tightening security around the cellblock they were keeping Marco and Renée in, as well as what floor it was on. A cold smile touched her lips. She now knew where to find her team.

FORTY-TWO

As dusk began to settle over the Cuban landscape, the rescue team was driving through rural landscape toward the banks of the Rio Cauto river. The journey had been arduous, their Jeeps maneuvering through dense jungle over rough terrain. The craggy paths had tested the vehicles' limits, but they had persevered, bringing the team this far—to the last phase of their journey.

Neil maneuvered the rear Jeep with a practiced hand, but his usual focus was tinged with a sense of introspection. His eyes, usually sharp and alert, held a forlorn expression as he navigated the rugged path leading toward the river.

In the back seat, Molly observed Neil's demeanor in the rearview mirror. She reached forward, placing a comforting hand on his shoulder. "You okay, Neil?" she asked.

Neil's gaze flickered to the mirror, meeting Molly's eyes briefly before returning to the road ahead. "Just thinking about Jenny was all," he admitted.

"You're worried about her?" Molly prodded gently, her hand still resting on his shoulder.

A small smile curved Neil's lips. "That's the thing," he said, his voice tinged with a sense of pride. "I miss my wife terribly. But am I worrying about her safety? I'm not so sure." He paused, the smile growing. "If I was being honest, I worry more for the fools who have her."

Wally nodded in agreement. "They have no idea what they've gotten themselves into," he chuckled.

The two Jeeps reached the outskirts of a small riverside settlement. The village itself seemed to be in a tranquil embrace with the river, the modest one- and two-story buildings hugging the shoreline. It was a picturesque scene of rustic simplicity and natural beauty. The Rio Cauto, wide and meandering, flowed gently by, its waters reflecting the deepening hues of the twilight sky, a series of wooden fishermen's shacks on stilts lining the water's edge.

As they drove through the village, the shadows of the trees and buildings stretched longer and longer, like dark fingers reaching across the ground. The air was filled with the sounds of the evening: the gentle lapping of the river against the shore, the distant calls of birds settling down for the night, and the sound of voices mingling in the bars that were just opening.

In the lead Jeep, Allison's eyes were fixed on a tablet's screen, analyzing the map displayed on it with keen attention. "This should be it," she murmured to Sarah, who was focused on navigating the lead Jeep. "The third hut on the right."

Sarah steered the vehicle toward their destination, pulling up outside a long shack that bore the sign *San Carlo*

Excursións. Neil, following closely, brought the second Jeep to a stop just behind them.

Just inside the hut, a middle-aged man dozed in a ratty old leather armchair, the wear and tear of the chair evident in the stuffing peeking out at various spots. A straw hat was perched over his face, moving slightly with each snore that escaped from beneath it, and his feet were propped up on a cabinet that also supported an old TV, the flickering images of a Cuban soap opera playing across the screen.

As Allison stepped out of the Jeep and approached, her shadow fell across the sleeping man. The snoring ceased abruptly as he sensed her presence looming over him. Without a word from Allison, he lifted the hat off his face, his initially sleepy eyes widening in recognition and snapping to full alertness.

"Señora Dragón," he greeted, a tone of respect coloring his voice as he stood up rapidly, almost toppling the TV in his haste. He straightened to attention, his posture transforming from relaxed to rigid in an instant.

"Good to see you, Santiago," Allison responded. "It's been a long time."

"It has," the Cuban replied, the two of them continuing to look at each other for a few anxious seconds.

Allison eventually shrugged it off, getting down to the business at hand. The evening air was thick with the scents of the river and the jungle as she quickly got to the point with Santiago, the urgency in her voice clear. "Manuel has told you everything?" she asked.

"Of course. It is all ready," Santiago replied. His gaze shifted past Allison, landing on the two Jeeps they had arrived in. "Quickly," he urged, pointing across the dirt street to a shuttered garage. "You need to hide the vehicles in there."

The team sprang into action, following Santiago's lead. Neil assisted him in sliding open the heavy shutter door, revealing a spacious, dimly lit garage. Santiago's eyes darted around cautiously as he instructed them. "Hurry," he said with a low intensity. "Even though this is my village, I still can't tell you who to trust and who not to. Money has a way of quickly making allies."

They maneuvered the Jeeps inside, their movements swift and efficient. Once parked, Santiago quickly closed the shutter, the sound of the metal door echoing briefly in the quiet street.

Without wasting a moment, the Cuban then led them through the modest interior of his shack. Like the fishermen's huts, it opened directly onto the river. They emerged onto a wooden veranda, where tied to the railing was a small boat that bobbed gently on the water.

"Your base of operations is seven miles down the river," Santiago informed Allison, assisting them aboard the boat with practiced ease. "I will take you to it. Then you are on your own."

"And all our equipment?" Allison inquired.

"It arrived six hours ago. It is all there waiting for you," Santiago confirmed.

"Thank you, Santiago," Allison said, her gratitude genuine.

"Anything for Señora Dragón," he replied, a twinkle in his eye. "Especially now that she has risen like Lazarus. Even if the man from Bethany could only manage four days compared to the six months we all believed you dead."

"Well, Lazarus only had Jesus. I've got Noah Wolf," Allison quipped, a rare smile flickering across her face.

With the team settled in the boat, Santiago started the outboard motor. They began to glide away from the shore, the sound of the engine softly breaking the evening stillness. The sun was dipping below the tree line, casting the river in shades of orange and purple, a serene backdrop to the covert urgency of their departure. As night fell, they moved silently down the river, the next phase of their mission lying ahead in the darkness.

FORTY-THREE

Time was of the essence. With one or more of his team on the loose, Noah needed to find some way of joining them. In the opulent confines of Number Four's quarters, he methodically searched for any means of escape. His hands glided over polished surfaces, feeling for hidden panels or seams. Every inch of the lavish space was scrutinized, from the ornate furniture to the exquisite art that adorned the walls. But every screw head was covered, every gap sealed, leaving no hint of a secret passage or hidden doorway.

The omnipresent cameras in each room tracked his every move, their unblinking electronic eyes following him relentlessly. In times like this, he really wished he was wearing a quantum cloak. The feeling of being constantly watched was adding to the oppressive atmosphere, a reminder that he was under the Council's control.

Frustrated by his fruitless search, Noah found himself in the study at a drinks cabinet. He poured himself some expensive cognac from a fancy crystal decanter, the rich aroma of the liquor momentarily distracting him from his predicament. Taking the decanter with him, he settled into an armchair, swirling the amber liquid in his glass.

That was when the door opened and the giant Gruber entered, observing Noah with a combination of curiosity and disdain. "I see you've given up on searching for a way out," he commented dryly.

"Care to join me?" Noah offered, raising his glass in a half-hearted toast.

"Why not," Gruber replied. "A drink before death, Herr Wolf."

"Whose? Mine or yours?" Noah challenged, their eyes locking in a silent battle of wills.

Gruber took a glass from the cabinet, then a seat opposite Noah, his movements cautious, like he was sitting across from a wild animal. He leaned forward with the glass, Noah meeting him halfway as he poured Gruber his drink, their gazes never breaking.

Relaxing back in his chair, Gruber took a sip and then broke the silence. "You know," he mused, "I fail to understand what they see in you, Herr Wolf. Back in Siberia, you were mine. If it hadn't been for your friends, you wouldn't be here."

"Maybe that's what makes me stronger, Herr Gruber," Noah retorted. "My friends." He took another sip of his cognac, and then added, "As well as your lack of them, of course."

Gruber's response was a gulp of cognac, downing the glass in one go. He held it out for a refill, his huge hand almost swallowing the tumbler whole.

Noah leaned forward with the decanter, meeting the glass and pouring the giant another drink.

———

THE LEVEL five cell block of the Citadel was a place of despair. In separate cells, Marco and Renée hung from their restraints, their bodies wracked with the fatigue of their prolonged ordeal. The block was on lockdown, an oppressive silence reigning over the area, broken only by the occasional footsteps of the guard patrolling the corridor.

In her cell, Renée tried to shift her position slightly, seeking a moment's respite from the relentless pain as she hung there by her arms. Her spirit, though worn, remained unbroken.

In the cell adjacent, Marco's spirit, though battered, hadn't dimmed. His jaw was set in a defiant line, a silent rebellion against their captors.

It was then, as they hung there shivering, that the quiet was pierced by a soft, almost imperceptible sound from above. A faint rustling, like a whisper. Both of them lifted their gazes toward the ceiling, bodies tensing in anticipation.

In the labyrinth of ventilation shafts, Jenny moved with calculated purpose. She had navigated the maze of ducts with the precision of a predator stalking its prey. Her movements silent but swift, she was driven by the urgent need to locate and rescue her team.

She quickly located them, her heart tightening at the sight of her comrades through the bars of the grills overlooking their cells. With a silent vow, she began working on the vent cover above the corridor that ran through the cell block, her fingers deft and sure. Below was a single guard, stationed between their cells.

The vent cover fell with a muted thud, Jenny calculating her drop from the shaft with absolute exactitude, her body cutting through the stale air. She landed silently, her posture poised and ready.

The guard, alerted by the sound of the vent cover, turned toward the noise. His eyes widened at the sight of Jenny, right there, a figure emerging out of nowhere like a ghost. His hand moved instinctively toward his Tavor, but Jenny was already in motion. In a swift, decisive movement, she closed the distance between them. Her left hand shot out, striking the guard's wrist, knocking the bullpup aside. Simultaneously, her right hand delivered a sharp upward strike to his throat, a targeted blow designed to incapacitate without lethal force. The guard's eyes bulged, his breath catching in his throat as he struggled for air.

With the guard momentarily stunned, Jenny executed a precise judo throw, using the guard's own momentum to bring him crashing headfirst into the wall. The impact was solid, the guard's body bouncing back and hitting the floor with a thud that resonated through the cell block.

In an instant, he lay motionless on the ground. Jenny didn't waste a second. Her eyes darted to the security cameras monitoring the cell block. She raised the Tavor bullpup rifle in her hands, her aim steady despite the adrenaline coursing through her veins. In quick succession, she fired at each camera, the sharp reports of the gunshots bouncing off the walls. One by one, the cameras exploded in showers of sparks.

Turning her attention to releasing her friends, she

rushed to Marco's cell. "Hang in there, Marco," she said, digging a hand in a pocket of her fatigues and pulling out the two eyeballs she'd removed from the guard earlier. She held them to the retina scanner, a light going green above the door as it slid open, then placed the eyeballs back in the pocket, running inside the cell.

She immediately helped Marco down from the chains, his legs unsteady from the prolonged suspension as he leaned on her for a moment.

"You are a sight for sore eyes," Marco managed to say, a weak smile on his face despite the pain.

While Marco leaned against the wall taking a breather, Jenny moved across the cellblock to Renée, pulling the eyes back out and holding them to the scanner.

When Jenny got her down, Renée's relief was beyond doubt as she flexed her wrists to restore circulation.

Reconvening in the corridor, Marco instantly took his wife in his arms. Then, after he and Renée were done embracing, Jenny handed Marco one of the Tavors. "You think you can still handle one of these?" she asked.

"Always," Marco replied, gripping the weapon with a newfound resolve.

Next, she handed Renée the M9—just as the sound of marching feet approached the door to the cell block. The three of them took cover as it began to open, their backs touching the cold metal walls.

Over the tannoy, a stern voice commanded, "Surrender immediately or face lethal consequences. This is your only warning."

Jenny exchanged a glance with Marco and Renée. "Not a chance," she whispered. "We fight our way out."

"It's not just your physical feebleness," Gruber continued in a voice filled with contempt. "It's your mental feebleness, too. Look where you are. Right where we want you. At our mercy. At our..."

Just as Gruber was about to continue his verbal assault, a sharp crackle from the tannoy system cut through the study, interrupting him mid-sentence. The voice that boomed over the speaker was urgent. "Attention all personnel, attention. This is a Code Red situation. We are initiating a full lockdown. All security doors are to be closed immediately. I repeat, initiate full lockdown. All available security personnel, report to level five cell block on the double. This is not a drill."

Gruber's eyes narrowed as he processed the announcement. Noah's expression, however, shifted subtly, a flicker of satisfaction crossing his features. He took a slow sip of his cognac, savoring the moment.

"Looks like you might be right where my team wants *you*," he remarked with a wry smirk.

Gruber's reaction was a mixture of irritation and begrudging respect. "Your friends... they're more resourceful than we gave them credit for," he admitted. "But you are all mere fleas running up the back of a tiger. Our organization predates Christ himself. We are the masters of the world. We would never allow ourselves to be captured as carelessly as you. To be tricked as easily. Look at how easy it was for us to hide the Dragon from you. How easily Henrik Schultz took her from you. Do you know that it was I who personally oversaw her interrogation?"

Images of Allison's body after they'd gotten her back filled Noah's mind. The bruises, burn marks, the chemicals they found swimming around in her blood, the hollow look in her eyes when she woke up.

Noah's own eyes clouded over. His grip on his glass tightened as he placed it to his lips. He said nothing.

"You are not worthy of joining us," Gruber went on. "And yet he treats you like a prince. Why?"

Noah narrowed his eyes. "Who's he?"

"Number Four."

Noah frowned. "I'm sensing some daddy issues here," he taunted. "If you're jealous of how your master is treating me, you need to take that up with him later on when he's tucking you into bed."

Gruber's tone darkened. "You will not join us. You lack the foresight. You are only interested in yourself, your wife, your child."

At the mention of his family, Noah's expression hardened. "Easy, big man," he growled. "You leave Sarah and Norah out of this."

"On the other hand," Gruber countered, "maybe you will join us. If only to protect them."

"I'll protect them by destroying you and your masters," Noah shot back.

"You'll try. But in the end, when the inevitable is happening, you will beg for our mercy for the sake of your wife and child."

The temperature in the room turned up a notch as Noah slowly rose from his chair, Gruber rising to match him. They stood feet apart, their bodies rigid, scowling at each other. Each man was coiled like a spring, ready to unleash violence at the slightest provocation. Their eyes locked in a fierce glare, muscles tensed and jaws clenched, an unspoken challenge hung in the air between them.

But just as the atmosphere was reaching boiling point, the door opened, and Number Four stormed in, his presence immediately commanding the space. His usual composed demeanor was replaced by visible frustration, a rare crack in his otherwise controlled exterior.

"Your friends are trying my patience," he snapped. "I may have to kill them whether you join us or not," he grumbled, casting a dark look at Noah.

Gruber, sensing the shift in dynamics, took a step back, allowing Number Four to take the lead.

At the mention of his team, Noah's expression had hardened, his gaze never leaving Number Four. "I didn't think you were the type to make idle threats," he retorted, his voice steady but edged with a cold anger. "Or are you losing control of your own game?"

Number Four's eyes narrowed. "This is no game, Mr. Wolf. The stakes are real, and your friends are becoming a liability. Make no mistake: If they interfere further, they will be dealt with... permanently."

A moment of tense silence followed, one that was abruptly disturbed when two armed men entered the study, their presence adding a new, ominous layer to the already charged atmosphere. Both were clad in tactical gear and wore gas masks that obscured their faces.

Without a word, they walked straight over to Number Four and Gruber, holding out gas masks. The two Council men accepted the masks without hesitation, fitting them over their heads with practiced ease, the dark lenses and filtered respirators adding a sinister aspect to their already formidable appearances.

Noah watched this development, his expression unreadable but his mind racing to assess this new threat.

Number Four then took another mask from one of the armed men. He tossed it casually toward Noah, where it landed with a soft thud by his feet. The action was nonchalant, but the underlying message was clear and menacing.

"I suggest you put it on," Number Four said, his voice muffled behind his mask. "Unless, that is, you want to join your friends in unconsciousness."

Noah's eyes narrowed as he picked up the mask, weighing it in his hands. The threat was unmistakable—a gas attack. His mind raced with possibilities and contingencies, but the immediate choice was starkly clear.

With a resigned yet defiant motion, Noah fitted the mask over his head, a terrible foreboding gnawing at his stomach.

———

JENNY, Renée, and Marco moved cautiously through the deserted corridors of the Citadel, their senses on high alert. The gunfire and bedlam that had filled the air moments ago had abruptly ceased, replaced by an eerie silence that seemed to press in on them from all sides. The guards they'd fought at the cell block had suddenly retreated, leaving the corridors deserted.

As they wandered the facility, Marco spotted a group of guards up ahead, moving quickly out of there before heavy security doors slammed shut behind them, sealing off the passage. The sudden evacuation of the guards was alarming —it was too easy, too convenient. Something must be happening. But what?

"I don't like this," Marco muttered.

"Me neither, baby," Renée agreed, her eyes scanning their surroundings for any sign of what might be coming next.

Jenny's instincts told her that they needed to change their approach. "I think it's time we hit the ventilation," she suggested, pointing to a grate above their heads.

Without hesitation, the trio sprang into action. They climbed the wall with practiced agility, reaching the grate in mere moments. Jenny pushed it open and was the first to haul herself into the narrow space of the ventilation shaft.

But as she pulled her legs up, a sudden rush of gas billowed from the shaft, hitting her full in the face. She choked, eyes stinging, lungs burning. The gas was disorienting, its effects immediate and overwhelming. With a groan, she collapsed back into Marco's waiting arms, dropping from the shaft.

Marco threw her over his shoulder. Weak from the beating, he struggled, but through grit and stubborn willpower, he managed to move with her as gas flooded the corridor.

"It's everywhere," Renée said.

A suffocating wall closed in on them from all directions. Cut off, they gave up trying to escape. Marco gently placed Jenny down, taking Renée's hand firmly in his. They stood together, united even in the face of the encroaching gas. "Well, here we go," Marco groaned with resignation as it hit them, gripping Renée's fingers tightly until they both lost consciousness.

FORTY-FOUR

THE NIGHT ENVELOPED THE RIO CAUTO LIKE A shroud, the only light coming from the faint glow of the moon and the stars scattered across the sky. The boat, equipped with an electric motor, moved silently through the water, its hum barely audible over the chorus of cicadas and nocturnal insects that filled the air.

The overgrown vegetation along the riverbanks was a shadowy mass, occasionally illuminated by the moonlight. Tall trees loomed overhead, their branches swaying gently in the night breeze, creating dancing patterns of light and shadow.

Santiago navigated the boat with a practiced hand, sitting at the back, his eyes fixed on the dark waters ahead. Allison, Sarah, Wally, Neil, and Molly sat quietly, each lost in their own thoughts. The rising angst of the mission slowly wound each up tighter as they got closer to their final destination, but there was also a sense of unity among them, a shared purpose that bound them together.

As they glided along, they occasionally passed fishermen heading in the opposite direction. Santiago exchanged nods with them, a silent acknowledgment between locals. To the fishermen, it was just another tour guide taking foreigners for a nighttime excursion.

Rounding a bend in the river, Santiago reached forward, touching Allison on the back of the shoulder. She turned to him, and he whispered, "We'll be there soon. Just on the other side of this bend."

Allison smiled as Santiago returned his eyes to the river and resumed steering the boat, a thoughtful expression on her face. "You want to ask something?" Santiago said without turning, sensing her gaze.

"Yes," Allison replied softly.

"About Manuel," Santiago guessed, his voice low.

"Yes," she confirmed.

"You want to ask if he is okay," he continued.

"And if you are."

"And me?"

Allison nodded silently.

Santiago sighed. "First I will answer for my brother," he began. "He is as good as he can be after he got caught spying for you. The state eventually let him out of prison and gave him his club back. They can't give him the rest of his sight back—not after they poured bleach in his eyes for being a traitor—but they did return him the club our grandfather left him. So he didn't lose everything."

The bitterness in Santiago's voice was clear, a reminder of the harsh realities faced by agents like himself in foreign lands. Working undercover, often in hostile environments, the price of betrayal or discovery was steep. The dangers were real, the sacrifices immense. Being a US agent in a foreign country, particularly one with strained relations, was a constant balancing act of risk, trust, and survival.

"And you?" Allison asked next.

"Me?" the Cuban said, his gaze never leaving the bending river. "I will be happy so long as this time your stay in Cuba doesn't end with my brother not speaking to me for the next ten years."

After that, Allison said nothing, letting him be.

They eventually reached their destination: a secluded shack that sat over the water like most of the fishing shacks lining the Rio Cauto. The structure was half-perched on the riverbank and half-supported by stilts. Its weathered wooden exterior gave it a camouflaged appearance against the backdrop of the jungle foliage.

"This is your base of operations," Santiago announced as he expertly maneuvered the boat toward a small jetty that jutted out from the structure. The jetty, made of the same weathered wood as the shack, creaked gently under their weight as they disembarked.

This humble wooden building, however, for all its outward simplicity, concealed state-of-the-art security features. Santiago approached a seemingly innocuous wood panel near the door and struck it with the edge of his hand. The panel fell in, revealing a hidden keypad. He swiftly entered a code, and a series of beeps followed, accompanied by the sound of mechanical bolts retracting in the doors and shutters, which were only covered in weathered wood, but steel underneath.

The door swung open, and they all filed into the 'shack.' The inside was spacious, akin to a hunting lodge, with a clean but basic interior. Wooden beams supported the roof, and the simple furnishings gave it a utilitarian feel.

"All your things are in the bedroom," Santiago informed Allison, nodding toward a door at the far end of the main room.

Inside the bedroom, two large aluminum cases lay on the bed. "Help me get these into the other room," Allison said to Neil. Together, they hefted the heavy cases and carried them into the adjacent room, setting them on tables before flipping the latches open.

The first case revealed an arsenal of weaponry. Inside were several M4A1 carbines and SIG Sauer M17 pistols, their matte black finishes gleaming under the room's lights. Hunting knives were neatly lined up next to compact gas masks. Body armor vests, sleek and lightweight, were stacked alongside night vision goggles, their green lenses staring up at them. Added to this were Wally's gadgets: the bee drones, the Sonic Disruptors, the Cognitive Harmonizer, and the EMP cufflinks.

Wally meticulously reviewed the array of gadgets laid out before the team, his attention to detail evident in his thorough examination. Satisfied that everything was in order, his gaze settled on a glossy, rectangular container that seemed unassuming at first glance. With a flick of his wrist, he opened it, revealing its contents: three bee drones.

"I've updated these drones," Wally announced, elevating the case to eye level, allowing the team to get a closer look. "They're now equipped to assist with specific elements of our mission." His eyes sparkled with a blend of pride and excitement as he regarded the tiny machines. "They are now capable of interfacing with and infiltrating computer systems. And not just that," he added with a sinister smirk. "These bad boys now pack a serious punch. Each one is fitted with a Cognitive Harmonizer. Meaning it can attach itself to someone's head and mess with their brain functions." And with that, Wally snapped the container shut.

The second aluminum case was a hub of communications and computer equipment. It contained high-powered laptops, their screens and keyboards ready for operation. A satellite phone lay next to a set of encrypted comms, essential for secure field communication. There were also several hard drives and USB sticks, containing valuable data and software for hacking or intelligence analysis, as well as a high-powered dongle for communicating with Esmeralda.

Molly inspected the contents of the second case, her eyes assessing each item. "We'll set up a comms station here," she decided, pointing to a corner of the main room where a small desk and chair sat. "This equipment will give us eyes and ears outside and keep us a step ahead."

The interior of the shack buzzed with a focused energy as everyone got to work. Allison, taking charge, turned to Wally. "Wally," she said, her tone firm, "is it all here?"

"It looks like it," he confirmed, scanning the equipment laid out before them.

"Good. Then we need to get set up. I want us out on foot in less than an hour."

Allison's command set them all in motion. The team worked rapidly, unloading the cases and assembling the gear. Molly set up the communications station, her fingers flying over keyboards as she brought screens to life. Neil and Sarah checked the weapons, ensuring each was ready for use, while Wally checked over the gadgets.

As they prepared, Santiago pulled Allison aside, holding a small tablet. The screen displayed a map of the area around the Citadel, a red dot prominently marked. "A pathway leads from the back of the Council's place to these caves," he explained, pointing to the map. "They are less than a mile from where the Council is keeping your friends. The dot is your transport out of here. It is in one of the caves."

"Is it what I asked for?" Allison asked.

"Yes. It is," Santiago replied, handing her the tablet. "Each of your fingerprints has been uploaded to its security system. So only you and your team will have access to it."

Allison took the tablet, her eyes studying the map closely. "Thank you, Santiago. This will be invaluable."

Santiago nodded. "Now I must leave," he said, turning to exit the shack.

Allison reached out, stopping him for a moment. "Santiago, I am thankful for the help of you and your brother. Truly."

Santiago paused, his expression softening slightly. "Then help rid this place of these *bastardos*," he said with a quiet intensity.

With those parting words, Santiago left, disappearing into the night. The second the door closed on him, Allison turned back to her team. This humble little shack, once a mere speck in the vastness of the Cuban jungle, now throbbed with the life and energy of their mission. The cases of weapons and gear stood as silent reminders of the battle to come, the team poised on the brink of a confrontation that would test their limits and define their destiny.

FORTY-FIVE

THE WORLD SLOWLY SWAM BACK INTO FOCUS FOR Marco, Jenny, and Renée, each emerging from the depths of unconsciousness like divers surfacing from the deep. Their heads throbbed with a dull, persistent ache, a testament to the potency of the knockout gas they had inhaled. Blurred images gradually sharpened, the gray walls of their cell solidifying into grim reality.

As their vision cleared, they saw a guard standing about three meters in front of them. Initially, he appeared as three overlapping figures but soon merged into one. His hand was resting on the pistol holstered at his hip, and he was also wearing a gas mask, the eyes behind its screen cold and resolute as they fixed on the prisoners before him.

The mask was a menacing sign that any escape would be met with an immediate gas attack.

This time, they were being held together in the same room, fixed to chairs by mechanical clasps. For Jenny, the restraints were exceptionally thorough. A restraint mask covered most of her face, inhibiting her ability to bite anyone, and they'd even gone so far as to fit her in a straight-jacket beneath the clasps. They were taking no chances with her this time. Not with two men already dead and another three in the infirmary.

The air in the cell was heavy with a sense of finality. The realization that escape was no longer an option hung over them like a shroud. Each of them struggled against their bonds, but the restraints held fast.

As they sat facing each other, Marco's eyes met Jenny's and then Renée's, a silent communication passing between them. The message was clear: they were in deep, and getting out would not be easy.

———

IN NUMBER FOUR'S STUDY, the air was thick with uncertainty and the lingering traces of the knockout gas. Number Four, Gruber, and Noah sat in an uneasy triangle, each wearing a gas mask, their gazes locked in a silent stand-off. The room's ventilation system hummed in the background, methodically purging the air of the last remnants of gas.

As the system completed its cycle, a voice suddenly crackled over the tannoy: "Attention all personnel. The air has been successfully purified, and it is now safe to remove your masks. The security breach has been contained. Resume normal operations."

At the signal, the men slowly removed their masks, revealing expressions that ranged from annoyance to steely determination. Number Four's eyes were cold as he regarded

Noah. "Looks like your friends are back in their cages," he remarked. "Now," he added in a darker tone, "patience, Mr. Wolf, is a virtue. One which I'm afraid is running out on my part."

Before Noah could respond, the door opened, and two guards entered, one of them holding a pair of electronic cuffs. Gruber stood up, his towering presence more threatening than ever, his eyes fixed on Noah. The guards moved toward Noah to cuff him, but Gruber intervened with an outstretched arm, stopping them in their tracks.

The big man then took the cuffs from them and tossed them at Noah, who caught them effortlessly. "Let him put his own cuffs on," Gruber commanded in a voice filled with disdain.

Noah, maintaining eye contact with Gruber, slid his hands through the electronic handcuffs, which automatically tightened around his wrists. The gesture was one of resignation but also of unspoken challenge.

"Take him to his cell," Number Four ordered.

The guards each took ahold of Noah's shoulders, guiding him to the exit. As they reached the door, Number Four called out, "And Mr. Wolf?"

Noah turned.

"Just to let you know. You have an hour to decide. Join us or die. That goes for your team, too."

With that ultimatum hanging in the air, the guards escorted Noah out of the room, his future—and that of his team—hanging in the balance.

FORTY-SIX

IN THE DEEP HEART OF THE CUBAN NIGHT, THE jungle was a noisy symphony of nocturnal life. The incessant chirping of insects, the distant calls of night animals, and the rustle of leaves created a continuous backdrop that enveloped Allison, Neil, and Sarah as they moved stealthily through the undergrowth. The ghostly green glow of their night vision goggles (NVGs) pierced the darkness around them, transforming the world into a monochromatic landscape of shadows and light.

Each of them was clad in state-of-the-art tactical gear, essential for the mission at hand. In their hands, they carried M4A1 carbines equipped with suppressors, ensuring that any shots fired would be as silent as possible. Their helmets were of the special forces variety, equipped with mounted NVGs, the ocular lenses pulled down over their eyes. Over their mouths and noses, they wore compact gas masks, and beneath their quantum cloaks, they had on Level IV-rated body armor, low-profile plate carriers, lightweight yet with enough stopping power to protect against rounds from a .30 caliber rifle.

Allison led the way. Neil followed next, his eyes scanning the terrain, alert for any signs of danger, while Sarah brought up the rear. As they drew closer to their target, the thermal settings on their NVGs began to reveal hidden cameras, cleverly concealed among the foliage. These electronic eyes, invisible to the naked eye, glowed with telltale heat signatures, betraying their locations to the well-equipped trio.

Back at the shack in the makeshift operations base, Molly Hanson and Wally Lawson were immersed in a world of screens and communications equipment. The wooden structure, perched on the edge of the Rio Cauto, was alive with the sounds of the surrounding jungle. Inside, the creaking ceiling fans labored tirelessly, doing little more than circulating the hot, humid air that pervaded the sweltering space.

Molly, with her eyes fixed on the satellite imagery displayed on her screen, whispered into her comms, "You're getting close."

Wally, examining a different monitor, suddenly tensed. "Wait, I'm getting something on the thermal," he announced. On his screen, a significant heat signature emerged—a large vehicle moving toward the trio in the jungle.

In the undergrowth, Allison instinctively raised a hand, signaling the team to halt. All three froze in place.

On Wally's thermal screen, the vehicle appeared as a bright blob of orange and red, stark against the cooler greens and blues of the surrounding environment. "Looks like a Jeep," he observed.

Hidden among the trees, Allison, Neil, and Sarah began to hear the low growl of its engine. They watched as the headlights cut through the night, casting elongated shadows along the narrow dirt road that ran a few meters from where they stood.

"Eyes on it," Allison whispered into her comms, her gaze locked on the approaching vehicle.

The Jeep came to an abrupt stop on the track, mere feet from their concealed positions. All three of them crept farther back into the thick vegetation, pushing themselves even deeper into the brush. They then watched through the green tint of the NVGs as the men sat there for a few seconds.

In an instant, the area was bathed in harsh light as floodlights along the track snapped into life, illuminating the jungle in harsh, unforgiving brightness. Each of them was forced to flip the ocular lenses of their NVGs up, their eyes throbbing from the sudden burst of light.

With the team caught in the sudden glare, their cover was compromised. The sound of the Jeep's engine idling became a menacing presence. In the operations base, Molly and Wally watched the scene unfold on their screens, powerless to intervene.

In the illuminated jungle, Allison, Neil, and Sarah remained motionless. Their next move was critical in the face of this unexpected development. Hidden amidst the undergrowth, they watched three guards emerge from the Jeep, dressed in body armor and green jungle camouflage.

The trio crawled deeper into the swampy brush, each finding a suitable spot to conceal themselves, the air thick with the smell of damp earth and vegetation.

The guards, however, appeared lax, their movements lacking urgency, suggesting a routine patrol rather than an active search. Each was armed with an IWI Tavor bullpup, but they carried their weapons with a casualness that spoke of routine rather than expectation.

"So tell me," one of the guards joked to another, a grin spreading across his face as he turned to a third, more sheepish-looking guard. "Where is it you saw the"—he paused, exchanging a snigger with his companion—"the ghost?"

"It wasn't a ghost," the sheepish guard defended himself. "It was a distortion. And I saw it on multiple cameras."

"You said ghost," the other guard said.

"No. I said it looked like one. It's like the memo we got said," the sheepish guard continued, his voice growing more confident. "Be on the lookout for any distortion in CCTV footage. If it is some type of cloaking, then it might be what I was seeing on the feeds."

Allison, Neil, and Sarah exchanged worried glances from their hiding places. The mention of a distortion in the CCTV footage and the reference to a memo about being on the lookout for such anomalies indicated that their quantum cloaks might have been detected.

"So that's why we've gotta come all the way out here to check things," another guard grumbled.

"Whatever it is should be here, in this area," the sheepish guard affirmed.

The two other guards rolled their eyes but complied as one of them, probably the leader, commanded, "Fan out." They unslung their Tavor bullpups, their demeanor shifting from casual to alert as they prepared to enter the jungle at the side of the track.

From their camouflaged positions, Allison, Neil, and Sarah watched them disperse into the jungle, their hearts pounding. The situation had escalated rapidly, and they knew they needed to remain undetected. Each of them stayed perfectly still. They were digitally invisible under the cover of their quantum cloaks, but to the naked eye, the threat of discovery was real and immediate.

Through their earpieces, Molly's voice whispered a quiet but urgent reminder of the stakes. "Remember, you need to get to the perimeter without raising any alarms. Security officers are required to check in every ten minutes. If they don't, it triggers an immediate search team response and a Code Red situation at the base. As well as that, their vitals are monitored remotely. Any flatlining, and we'll have the same scenario. Code Red. So you can't kill them. Not until you're inside the base."

As Molly spoke, one of the patrolling guards received a radio call. "Check in, Ten-Five," a voice crackled.

"Checking in," Ten-Five responded, his voice calm. "Just searching those spots Eight-Sixteen was talking about. Over."

"Copy that. Over," the voice responded.

The trio dug themselves farther into the mud, trying to become one with the earth as the guards drew nearer. The swampy ground was cold and wet against their skin, but they remained motionless, knowing that any movement could betray their presence.

Neil felt something slither across his body, and when he looked, he saw the snake, its patterned scales sliding over his camouflaged gear. He remained still, controlling his breathing, a model of self-discipline and focus, taking it to tantric levels as the snake went on its way.

The guards continued their methodical search, their bullpups at the ready, their eyes scanning the floodlit jungle, searching the shadows.

One of the guards got dangerously close to Sarah's position. His eyes narrowed, staring right at her, sensing something amiss. As he raised his radio to call the others, Allison acted.

With a sudden, silent movement, she burst from her hiding spot behind him. In her hand was a Sonic Disruptor. She set it to seven, pointed it at the guard, and activated it.

He barely made a sound, instantly crumpling to the ground, rendered unconscious by the Disruptor's powerful sonic waves.

With the first guard silently downed, the urgency of the situation spiked. Allison gave a quick, sharp signal to Neil and Sarah, who were still partially submerged in the swampy underbrush.

Neil targeted the guard closest to him, leaving his hiding place. The guard, however, was not as oblivious as he had hoped. Just as Neil got close enough to engage his Disruptor, the man turned sharply, catching a glimpse of movement in the corner of his eye.

In an instant, the situation escalated. The guard lunged at Neil, a struggle ensuing as the two men began grappling in the darkness.

The sounds of their scuffle alerted the third guard. He turned around, only to find Sarah right there, her Sonic Disruptor pointed at him. She pressed the button just in time, sending the guard into unconsciousness.

The man struggling with Neil was strong and had managed to wrestle the Disruptor away, throwing it into the darkness. They fell to the ground, locked in a desperate fight.

Allison acted quickly. She rushed toward Neil and the guard, her own Disruptor in hand. The guard, focused on Neil, didn't see her coming. Allison pointed the Disruptor at him and activated it.

The effect was immediate. The guard went limp, the fight draining out of him as he fell unconscious. Neil, panting heavily, pushed him off and sat up.

The trio regrouped. The unexpected scuffle had been intense, but they had managed to avoid raising an alarm. They had to move fast now, knowing that time was against them.

———

THE GRAY WALLS of the cell closed in on Noah as he sat alone. Mechanical clasps, identical to those restraining the rest of his team at that moment, clamped him to a chair bolted to the floor.

Suddenly, the door swung open, and Gruber's massive frame filled the cell. In his hands, he carried a chair, which he placed directly in front of Noah, his eyes never leaving the captive's face. The giant of a man then sat down, crossing his arms over his grotesquely wide chest, his posture exuding a menacing calm.

"He's promised me that I will get to be the one to do it," Gruber began.

The 'he' he was referring to was clearly Number Four, and the 'it' was unmistakably a reference to some form of personal execution. Gruber leaned forward slightly, his eyes gleaming with a dark anticipation.

"So let me tell you just how I'm going to do it, Herr Wolf," he continued, his tone almost conversational but laced with a chilling promise of pain. "How I'm going to break you apart, one bone at a time."

Gruber began unfolding his plan with cold precision, numbering each step as if reciting a well-thought-out recipe for destruction.

"One," he began, raising a finger for emphasis, "I'm gonna start with your fingers. I'll snap each one, slowly, savoring the sound of the bones cracking.

"Two," he continued, his voice steady, "I'll move to your toes. I'll crush them, one by one, until you can't even stand the thought of walking again.

"Three, your arms and legs. I'll break them in multiple places. You won't be able to move without feeling excruciating pain.

"Four," Gruber went on, his face a mask of brutality, "your ribs. I'll break them so every breath you take feels like a knife twisting in your lungs.

"Five, I'll shatter your kneecaps. You'll beg for mercy, but by then, it'll be far too late.

"Six, your spine. I'll leave that for last, so you can feel every other pain in your broken body before I finally paralyze you.

"Seven..."

———

WITHIN THE COVER of the Cuban jungle, Allison, Neil, and Sarah had restrained the three guards. The leader of the men, still unconscious, lay bound on the ground. Time was of the essence. They needed him awake and coherent for his mandatory check-in with the Citadel, which was due in less than a minute. And it was no good responding to it themselves. The base employed voice recognition technology, making it crucial that the leader himself make the call.

Allison quickly administered smelling salts under the guard leader's nose. His eyes fluttered open, confusion and panic evident as he found himself bound and surrounded by his captors. As he opened his mouth to shout, Allison was ready with the Cognitive Harmonizer. She pressed it against his temple and activated it.

The effect was immediate and dramatic. The guard's eyes glazed over, his body slackening as the device emitted a low hum. It was as if his conscious mind had been momentarily switched off, leaving him in a dazed, highly suggestible state.

"Now," Allison said calmly, addressing the disoriented guard. "You're going to answer a few questions."

Under the influence of the Harmonizer, the guard's usual resistance melted away. His responses were slow but cooperative, his voice distant as if he were speaking from a dream. When Allison inquired about the presence of more patrols in the area, he replied, "No... no more patrols for a while... At least an hour."

Satisfied with his answers, Allison directed him to make his check-in call. She guided him through the process, instructing him precisely on what to say. The guard complied without question, his voice monotone as he reported to the base that he had found nothing of interest in the area—just as Allison had instructed him to.

With the immediate threat of discovery averted, Allison made her next move. "Now," she said firmly, "you can drive us all a little closer to your base."

The trio quickly loaded the two still incapacitated guards into the back of the Jeep. The leader, under the effects of the Cognitive Harmonizer, was exceptionally malleable. He climbed into the driver's seat without resistance, his movements automatic and uncoordinated.

Allison, Neil, and Sarah followed him into the vehicle, keeping a close watch on their coerced driver. The engine rumbled to life, and they set off, the night enveloping the Jeep as it wound its way through the Cuban jungle, drawing ever closer to the heart of the Council's operations.

It was less than five minutes later when Allison, Neil, and Sarah caught their first glimpse of the Citadel. Hidden within the natural landscape, the base revealed itself not through overt structures but through subtle signs detectable only through their NVGs' thermal settings, signs that hinted at the scale of operations hidden within the foliage.

As they approached, air vents camouflaged among the trees expelled gas into the night, their presence betrayed only by the gentle disturbance of the surrounding vegetation. The integration of the base within the jungle was seamless, unsettling evidence of the Council's ingenuity and endless resources.

Under the influence of the Cognitive Harmonizer, the leader drove mechanically, his voice a continuous, unfiltered stream of information. He began to divulge details about the base, painting a picture of its immense size and sophistication.

"It has multiple levels," he mumbled, eyes fixed on the road ahead. "There's a staff of over a thousand... it even has its own school, hospital, and living quarters for families. After all, they don't like us leaving the base."

"I bet they don't," Allison quipped in an undertone.

The guard continued, "There are tennis courts, swimming pools, gyms... It's like a small town buried underground. I've worked at four of them," he revealed. "There's even one underneath London... massive, sprawling beneath the city."

The two guards in the back, now awake but gagged and bound, could only listen in helpless silence as their leader unwittingly betrayed their secrets.

The Jeep came to a gradual halt at a safe distance from the Citadel's southern entrance. Tucked away in foliage that concealed them, Allison, Neil, and Sarah quickly disembarked.

Allison turned to the guard. "Now you remember what you've got to do, right?" she asked, ensuring that their plan was clearly understood.

The guard nodded slowly. "Yeah. Drive around, checking in every ten minutes."

Just then, a call came through on the Jeep's radio, another routine check-in request. The guard reached for the radio with a sluggish motion.

"Everything's okay with me and the others," he reported in a steady voice, maintaining the ruse. "We're now heading out to San Bernardo Cove to check out the coastline. Over."

His response was met with a curt acknowledgment from

the base, and he placed the radio back. The trio watched him, each aware of the delicate balance they were maintaining. By having the guard continue his patrol with regular check-ins, they were buying themselves precious time to infiltrate the base unnoticed.

Allison gave the guard a final nod, a silent signal of approval. He nodded back, starting the engine again and driving off.

As the sound of the Jeep faded into the distance, the team took a moment to assess their next move. The Citadel lay ahead, its true extent hidden beneath the jungle. The night was still young, and the mission was reaching a critical phase.

Allison, Neil, and Sarah disappeared into the underbrush, seamlessly blending into the shadows. As they moved, Wally's voice crackled through their comms. "You better be quick," he cautioned. "The Harmonizer will wear off in an hour, and all he'll be left with is a big headache."

After a rapid trek, they found a concealed vantage point that offered a clear view of one of the base's ventilation shafts. It was an unassuming feature in the vast complex, but for them, it was a potential entry point, a silent gateway into the heart of the enemy's lair.

Settling into their positions, Allison reached into her kit and pulled out a small, nondescript box. She opened it to reveal the three bee drones.

Neil and Sarah watched in silent anticipation as she carefully activated them. With a gentle hum, the tiny machines came to life, their wings fluttering with an almost natural rhythm. The drones buzzed around for a moment, getting their bearings before Allison directed them toward the ventilation shaft.

Using a small tablet, she guided the bee drones through the grate and into the shaft, their tiny cameras transmitting live footage back to her tablet. The screen showed a dark, narrow passage, the drones' minute size allowing them to navigate it with ease.

As they ventured deeper into the ventilation system, the trio watched the screen intently. The feed provided them with valuable reconnaissance, allowing them to map out the internal layout of the base and identify potential obstacles.

With the bee drones disappearing into the darkness of the ducting, Allison, Neil, and Sarah remained in their hidden spot, eyes fixed on the screen, ready to make their next move based on the intelligence gathered by their tiny allies. The night was deepening, and so was their infiltration of the Citadel.

FORTY-SEVEN

The heavy door to Noah's cell swung open, and Number Four entered. Gruber, who had been busy going over his intricate plans for Noah's death, snapped to attention, standing up sharply from the chair.

Number Four approached Noah. "This is your last chance, Mr. Wolf," he began, his gaze fixed intently on the captive. "Join us or be wiped out with everyone else."

"I've heard your spiel," Noah replied, his voice steady. "A world under your control. A new order."

"It's more than control," Number Four countered. "It's about creating a world where chaos is replaced by order, where the senseless squabbles of nations are replaced by unified direction."

"And at what cost?" Noah challenged. "Freedom? Individuality? The lives of billions of innocent people?"

"Consider the bigger picture, Noah," Number Four urged. "Imagine a world without hunger, without war, where resources are managed wisely and everyone has their place."

"A place handed to them by you," Noah retorted.

"It is a better world," Number Four repeated.

"A world where you play God?"

"Not God, Mr. Wolf," Number Four corrected. "Stewards. Caretakers of a world teetering on the brink of its own destruction."

"You're talking about a dictatorship," Noah countered, his voice laced with skepticism.

"A benevolent one," Number Four insisted. "Under our guidance, humanity will reach its full potential."

"And those who disagree?"

"They'll come to see the wisdom of our ways, in time."

Noah shook his head. "You're asking me to turn my back on everything I believe in."

"We're offering you a chance to be part of something greater. To save humanity from itself."

Noah's gaze never wavered. "And if I refuse?"

Number Four's expression hardened. "Then you leave me no choice but to consider you an enemy of our cause."

———

In their secluded vantage point, the trio of Allison, Neil, and Sarah watched the tablet intently as their bee drones buzzed through the Council's base, weaving a digital map of its complex interiors. Each drone, a marvel of micro-engineering, flitted silently through the corridors and ventilation shafts, their tiny cameras capturing every detail.

On the screen of Allison's tablet, the layout of the base

began to take shape in the form of a three-dimensional map. The drones' feeds revealed the positions of guards, the layout of key facilities, and the intricate network of passages that made up the Citadel.

One of the drones, navigating through the maze of vents, came upon the installation's security server room. Wally's voice, clear and focused, crackled through their comms. "That's it. I need you to get one of them inside," he instructed.

Skillfully, Allison guided the drone into the server room, slipping through the ventilation grate with ease, its small size allowing it to enter undetected. Inside the room, the drone hovered for a moment, analyzing its surroundings before making its way to the main router.

With precise movements, it 'attached' itself to the router, creating a crucial connection that would bridge Esmeralda to the base's internal systems.

"Okay." Wally's voice broke the silence. "We're in. Now go find Noah and the others."

The drone, firmly attached to the router, was now granting Esmeralda access to the Citadel's internal security systems. Meanwhile, Allison masterfully maneuvered the other two drones through the intricate rabbit warren of the underground base. With each passing second, the map on her tablet grew more detailed, painting a clearer picture of the complex terrain they would soon be navigating.

Everything appeared to be going to plan. So far.

———

Number Four stood in front of Noah, his piercing blue eyes attempting to penetrate the resoluteness of the man before him.

"You continue to resist the inevitable, Mr. Wolf," Number Four began, his voice calm yet edged with a hint of impatience. "But you must see the futility of your stance. Our vision is the only path to a sustainable future."

Noah, fastened to the chair, met Number Four's gaze with unyielding defiance. "Your vision is nothing but a dictatorship disguised as salvation," he retorted. "You talk of sustainability, but at what cost? Freedom? Humanity?"

Number Four sighed, a gesture of exasperation. "Freedom is an illusion, Noah. A naïve concept that has led humanity to the brink of its own destruction. We offer guidance, a chance to correct the course before it's too late."

"And who decides what's right? You? Your Council?" Noah challenged. "You speak of guidance, but I see control. I see a world where choice is stripped away, where people are nothing but pawns in your grand design."

The old man leaned closer, his tone becoming more insistent. "You underestimate the gravity of the situation, Mr. Wolf. Our planet is dying, societies are crumbling. We offer a solution, a way to restore balance."

Noah's response was firm. "Balance through fear, through manipulation? That's not a solution; it's subjugation. I won't be a part of it."

Number Four straightened. "Your idealism is commendable but misguided. You cling to a notion of a world that no longer exists."

"No," Noah countered. "I cling to the belief that people

should have the right to choose their own destiny, not have it dictated by a self-appointed elite."

Number Four's eyes narrowed, a flash of anger momentarily crossing his features. "Your refusal puts everything at risk, not just for you, but for your loved ones. Consider the consequences of your defiance."

But Noah's will remained steadfast. "I've made my choice," he said. "I stand against tyranny, against your vision of a controlled world. I'll fight it with everything I have."

A heavy air of defeat hung in the room, a finality in his tone that made the declaration final.

Number Four turned to face Gruber. His voice was low, tinged with resignation. "Okay," he said. "He's all yours. Do what you must."

The words were barely more than a whisper. Yet in the silence of the cell, they rang loud like a siren.

Gruber's response was a slow, menacing smile. He stood up, his massive frame casting a shadow over Noah. As Number Four made his way out of the cell, the mechanical clasps began releasing Noah from the chair, signaling the beginning of a deadly confrontation.

Number Four paused at the door. His back to the two men, he said, "Make it quick." And with that, he left, the door closing behind him with a definitive click.

Gruber turned his attention to Noah, an unmistakable glint of excitement in his eyes. "It seems we are finally here, Herr Wolf," he said, his voice a low rumble of thunder.

Noah stood up, his body tense and ready. "I guess talking was never your style, Gruber," he replied.

Gruber's smile widened. "Why talk when action speaks louder?" he taunted, slowly circling Noah like a predator.

Noah kept his focus, watching Gruber's every move. He took a fighter's stance and began moving around the room, using the chair bolted into the center of the floor as a shield, keeping it between them.

Gruber's voice was a growl. "Breaking you will be a pleasure."

Noah's gaze never wavered. "You'll find I'm not so easily broken."

Some primal urge was calling them to battle, the air charged with the anticipation of the impending clash. Then it happened. Gruber made the first move, lunging at Noah with a speed that belied his massive size.

FORTY-EIGHT

As Marco, Jenny, and Renée sat bound to their chairs, something strange happened. The stale air of the cell began to reverberate with the distinct, low buzz of a bee. While they searched for the source of the sound, it deftly maneuvered through the ventilation grill above them, hovering down into the room.

Their heads turning to it in unison, they tracked the drone's flight with a mix of curiosity and cautious hope.

The lone guard in the cell, already on edge, adjusted his gas mask, his eyes narrowing at this buzzing intruder as he, too, saw it. With clumsy swipes, he began attempting to capture the bee, each attempt more frantic than the last. With the drone's advanced agility allowing it to easily evade his grasp, the guard's efforts seemed futile.

As the man's frustration reached its zenith, his actions grew increasingly erratic. In a particularly desperate swipe, he lost sight of the drone entirely. Frantically, he spun around, his gaze darting in all directions in a fruitless search for the elusive intruder. His eyes swept over the room in a panic, momentarily fixing on his three captives, as if hoping that one of them might point it out to him.

It was at that moment the bee quietly crawled across the screen of his gas mask. Panic set in as he spotted it—inches from his face.

He whipped off the mask in a frenzy, but it was too late. The drone was now crawling across his face. His fingers were right on the point of seizing it as it reached his temple, but the bee beat him to it when it activated its built-in Cognitive Harmonizer. The device emitted a pulse that instantly put the guard into a stupefied state, his hand freezing mid-air as his eyes glazed over, completely immobilized by the sudden and severe cognitive dissonance. The room fell into an eerie silence, the guard now rendered harmless, a victim of the drone's most unexpected weapon.

In the chairs, Marco, Jenny, and Renée watched with a mixture of astonishment and relief as the drone left the guard's head and made its way to Marco, hovering close to his ear. A familiar voice emanated from the drone's tiny speaker. "Good to see you, Marco," Allison's voice said, crisp and clear.

"Dragon Lady," Marco replied with a knowing grin.

Jenny and Renée shared his grin, understanding dawning on their faces.

Allison's voice continued through the drone. "You need to be quick," she instructed. "That guard has just been hit with a Cognitive Harmonizer. It should keep him malleable and open to suggestion for the foreseeable future. Use him wisely."

"What about these clasps?" Marco asked, looking down his body at the mechanical straps holding him to the chair.

"Easy," Allison replied. "Ta-da!"

At her command, the clasps clicked open, freeing their limbs. The three operatives sprang into action, their movements filled with purpose.

As the door to the cell unbolted as automatically as the clasps, Allison warned them, "I'm not sure how long Esmeralda can stay in their system before they notice her. So you need to move fast."

———

THE AIR in the cell was charged, the fight immense, a struggle for survival. In the tight space, Noah moved smoothly and accurately, occasionally using the chair bolted to the room's center as a barrier against his much larger opponent.

Gruber, embodying raw power, launched a series of ferocious Muay Thai elbow strikes. Each one was a thunderous blow that aimed to crush his opponent's skull.

Noah countered with sidesteps and low sweeps. He spun away from each attack, his movements a blur, creating just enough space to avoid the pulverizing impact.

Gruber adjusted his strategy, adopting the stance of a seasoned Pencak Silat fighter. He unleashed a rapid succession of palm strikes and knee thrusts, turning his entire body into a weapon—a huge, thunderous weapon.

Drawing on Aikido, Noah redirected his momentum, using Gruber's force against him. He executed swift, circular movements, attempting to unbalance the giant as he pushed his huge fists away. But it was like Gruber's feet were rooted to the concrete. He didn't even sway.

As they fought, their breaths ragged, their bodies slick with sweat, the cell reverberated with the sounds of their battle. It was a clash of wills and skills, a fight where every move carried the weight of survival. Gruber, towering and immense, was a formidable adversary. His fists, like sledge-hammers, swung in powerful arcs, aiming to connect with crushing force. His legs, like tree trunks, launched devas-tating kicks, their impact capable of snapping bones.

The stale air shook with a symphony of grunts, thuds, and the sharp exhalation of breath. It was a fight where only the strongest, the most adaptable, would emerge victorious.

———

MARCO, Renée, and Jenny edged their way through the cellblock, their progress marked by the uneven footsteps of the 'cognitively harmonized' guard leading them. His grip on his Tavor bullpup was lax, his movements sluggish and erratic, nothing like the rigid alertness of the trio following him.

Their hands dangled in front of them, each adorned with a pair of electronic handcuffs that had been rendered ineffective, the three of them feigning captivity. As they neared the end of the block, the guard's confusion became more evident. Abruptly, he halted, turning to face them with a dazed expression. "Sorry, what am I supposed to be doing?" he slurred, his words barely coherent.

Marco, his eyes darting to the two armed guards stationed at the door ahead, leaned in and whispered urgently, "You're moving us to another cell block. Gruber's orders."

The guard nodded slowly, a flicker of understanding crossing his clouded eyes. "Oh yeah. Right," he mumbled. With a labored effort, he resumed leading them forward.

Upon reaching the guards at the door, they came to a stop. "Need to move these prisoners to another block," the man leading them mumbled. "Gruber's orders."

The two guards exchanged skeptical looks. "We haven't heard anything about this," one of them said, his tone laced with suspicion. "You sure about that?"

"Gruber's orders," the incapacitated guard repeated, his voice trailing off as he swayed on his feet. "Said it's urgent..."

"Are you drunk?" the second guard interjected, eyeing him critically.

The guard, his coordination faltering, began to sink slowly to the floor. "No, no, just... really tired," he mumbled, his words barely coherent. "Maybe if I sit down for a bit."

The two guards at the door glanced at each other, their concern shifting from suspicion to the welfare of their colleague. "What's wrong with him?" one guard whispered to the other, all his attention on the unusual scene unfolding before them.

"To hell with this," Jenny muttered. Using the distraction, she made her move. With speed and precision, she flicked off the useless cuffs, reached behind her, and drew the guard's pistol she was keeping tucked in her waistband, firing twice. The two guards fell to the ground, bullet holes running through their foreheads, silenced before they could react.

As the sound of the shots echoed through the cellblock,

Marco and Renée exchanged a brief, grim look, acknowledging the necessary brutality of their situation. Without a word, they stepped over the fallen guards, stripped the men of their weapons, and followed Jenny as she led the way through the now unguarded door. The incapacitated guard, oblivious to what he had unwittingly helped create, slumped against the wall, his consciousness fading into an induced haze as the effects of the Cognitive Harmonizer overwhelmed him.

————

UNDER THE CLOAK OF DARKNESS, Allison, Neil, and Sarah crouched at their concealed vantage point just outside the Citadel. The jungle around them buzzed angrily with life, completely at odds with the silent, looming structure of the base.

Wally's voice crackled through their earpieces, breaking the nervous silence. "Esmeralda's gotten control of the base's functions. She's opening the outer blast doors now."

As they watched, the massive doors of the base began to slide open, the unseen hand of Esmeralda manipulating the security protocols.

"Okay, good," Allison whispered into her comms. "Now, Esmeralda, initiate the next phase."

As they waited to enter, the AI's synthesized voice emerged through the base's communication system, imitating the head of security with perfect accuracy.

"All security personnel, report to your nearest cell block immediately for an urgent briefing," Esmeralda commanded through the speakers.

The trio waited, observing as figures hurriedly moved inside the base, following the false orders.

"This is our window," Allison whispered. "Let's move."

The three of them moved rapidly through the now unguarded perimeter, their quantum cloaks rendering them mere shadows in the night to the watching cameras. As they entered a deserted corridor, Allison relayed her plan in a hushed tone.

"Right, we know what to do. Neil, head for Jenny and the others. Sarah, find Noah."

Neil glanced at her. "And where are you going?"

"To find the scumbag in charge of this place," Allison replied, her eyes steely.

Without another word, they split up, each disappearing into different parts of the sprawling complex. Their steps were silent, their presence unnoticed as they delved deeper into the heart of the enemy's lair, each on their own critical mission.

———

THE CELL CONTINUED to shudder with the grunts of the fighters. Noah's strategy of evasion and targeted attacks had kept him alive so far, but it wasn't really hurting his opponent.

Gruber was a force of unstoppable strength, coming at Noah like a wrecking ball, each of his strikes offering death. But help was on its way.

Amidst the flurry of strikes and dodges, Noah's sharp eyes caught a flicker of movement from the ventilation shaft above. A bee drone, no larger than a thumb, emerged stealthily, its wings a soft hum in the charged atmosphere. For a fleeting moment, Noah's heart surged with a glimmer of hope, recognizing it as one of Wally's.

But Gruber, ever the vigilant predator, detected the drone's presence almost instantly. His reaction was yet more evidence of his battle-honed instincts. In a sudden, fluid motion that belied his size, Gruber's hand shot out like a striking cobra. His fingers closed around the tiny drone with lethal precision.

There was a brief, almost imperceptible crunch as the drone was crushed within the vise-like grip of Gruber's hand. Its potential assistance, the hope it represented, was extinguished as quickly as it had appeared.

Nevertheless, it wasn't the only attempt at help coming Noah's way. As the metallic fragments of the drone fell to the floor, a second interruption came via the cell door. With a hiss and a mechanical whir, it slid open unexpectedly. Both men froze, their fists raised, eyes darting to the doorway.

They then exchanged a quick, calculating look, each man gauging the other's intent, before, in that split second of mutual assessment, Noah saw his chance. Without hesitation, he bolted toward the open door, his muscles aching but driven by a surge of adrenaline.

Gruber roared in frustration and charged after him.

Noah's mind raced as he ran, his path lit only by the sparse, flickering lights of the base's narrow hallways. He needed to find a way out, to regroup, to plan his next move. His heart pounded in his chest, a drumbeat of survival urging him on.

The bee drone. The bee meant something; it meant he had friends here.

But Gruber was a relentless force, closing the distance behind Noah, his breaths heavy, his determination verging on the manic. He was not just chasing Noah; he was hunting him, fueled by a relentless desire to complete his mission: to break Noah Wolf into little pieces.

The corridors of the base turned into a high-stakes maze, a deadly game of cat and mouse. Noah's agility was his only advantage in this race against time and brute force. His mind worked overtime, calculating turns, looking for obstacles to slow Gruber down.

As they rounded a corner, Noah glimpsed a network of pipes running along the ceiling. Without a second thought, he leapt up, grabbing on to them, swinging his body up to climb on top. He scrambled along, trying to put distance between himself and Gruber.

Gruber, undeterred, followed suit, his massive frame surprisingly agile as he climbed after Noah. The chase was on in earnest, a deadly pursuit in the bowels of the Citadel. Noah's only hope was to outmaneuver Gruber long enough to find a way out—or at least a way to turn the tables on his remorseless pursuer.

FORTY-NINE

NEIL EDGED HIS WAY ALONG THE TANGLED corridors of the Council's base. Clutching his M4A1 carbine tightly, one eye glued to the scope, he scanned the area for any signs of Marco, Renée, or his beloved Jenny. They should be coming right his way.

Esmeralda's tannoy call had cleared the area of guards, but there were still people around that he had to avoid.

"They should be close," Molly whispered through his comms.

And so they were. As he turned a corner, Neil's heart leapt into his throat. There, in front of him, were Marco, Renée, and Jenny. The relief that washed over him was so manifest that a wave of emotion momentarily overtook his usually composed demeanor. His hands let go of the M4A1, the carbine swinging down on its strap and dangling from his neck as he broke into a run. "Baby!" he murmured, rushing toward his wife.

On seeing Neil, Jenny's eyes widened. In an instant, the

hardened façade she usually maintained melted away. She too dropped her weapon, the Tavor falling to the ground with a clatter. The husband and wife embraced tightly, their hands gripping each other in a rare display of raw emotion. Jenny nestled her head into Neil's shoulder, her voice a soft whisper. "I knew you'd come find me."

Neil held her, his eyes closed as he savored the moment, feeling her warmth, her presence. For a rare few seconds, they allowed themselves to acknowledge the depth of their feelings and the very real fear that they might never have seen each other again.

Marco and Renée watched the reunion filled with happiness and relief. It was a brief respite in the midst of the brutal circumstances they'd found themselves in, a reminder of the personal stakes involved in their perilous mission.

After a moment, Jenny and Neil separated slightly, their eyes locking in a silent conversation of understanding and shared resolution.

"Is the cavalry coming?" Marco asked Neil, breaking the brief silence.

Neil turned to him and shook his head, his expression turning serious. "No, it's just us. Me, Sarah, and Allison. Molly and Wally are overseeing things about eight miles away. Apart from that, we're on our own."

A heavy silence fell over the group as the weight of Neil's words sank in. They were deep in enemy territory, vastly outnumbered and outgunned. But in that moment, united in their purpose and their bond, they felt a surge of determination.

"We'll make our own cavalry," Jenny said firmly, her hand squeezing Neil's.

Marco and Renée nodded in agreement, a sense of determination hardening in their eyes. They were a team, and they would face whatever came next together.

———

ALLISON STEALTHILY NAVIGATED the Citadel's web of corridors. Clad in her scaly quantum cloak, she was a crimson and gold ghost in the heart of the enemy's lair. Her every movement was a silent dance in the darkness.

As she moved, security personnel rushed by her, the sound of their rapid footsteps filling the sterile halls. They were responding to the pandemonium elsewhere in the base, unaware of the predator in their midst, and ran straight past.

Finally, she reached her destination: Number Four's quarters. The door was ajar, an invitation she accepted with a silent nod. Inside, the room was opulent, not like the utilitarian design of the rest of the base. At the center stood Number Four, his back to the door and his attention fixed on a large monitor displaying security footage from around the base.

Allison slipped into the room unnoticed, her presence as quiet as a whisper. She positioned herself strategically behind Number Four.

Her voice broke the silence. "You don't have your attack dog, Gruber, anymore," she said.

Number Four spun around sharply. The surprise on his face was fleeting, quickly replaced by a calculated calm. Number Four was a master of composure, but Allison could see the flicker of concern in his eyes.

"Ah, the Dragon Lady," he said. "This is a somewhat unexpected visit."

Allison's stance was relaxed, yet her eyes were sharp, a predator sizing up her prey. "Just thought I'd drop by," she replied coolly. "Seems like your base is having quite a night."

Number Four glanced briefly at the monitor, his expression unreadable. "Indeed," he conceded. "But it's nothing we can't handle. You, on the other hand, are quite the wildcard."

Allison smiled thinly. "I always aim to surprise."

Number Four's gaze returned to Allison, eyes narrowed slightly, analyzing, calculating. "And what is it that you want, Allison? Why come here?"

Allison pierced her own eyes at him. "I'm here to get my agents back."

Number Four chuckled, a sound devoid of humor. "A noble goal, but you must know it's futile."

Allison took a step forward, her expression darkening. "We'll see about that."

Her hand moved slowly, deliberately, as she reached into her pocket and pulled out the Cognitive Harmonizer. The device, compact and menacing in its design, seemed to hum with potential.

Number Four's eyes followed her movements, his usually unflappable demeanor showing the first signs of uncertainty. "What's that?" he asked.

Allison's expression was one of grim determination. "You're about to find out," she said.

The room seemed to grow colder as Allison activated the device. It came to life with a soft, ominous whir, the sound a prelude to the chaos it was designed to unleash.

FIFTY

THE BATTLE BETWEEN NOAH AND GRUBER intensified as they crashed from a ventilation shaft into a corridor, both combatants quickly scrambling to their feet, the momentum of their fight undiminished. Noah engaged Gruber with a series of Taekwondo low, turning kicks aimed at the giant's knees, attempting to destabilize his base.

Gruber countered, launching a powerful elbow strike aimed directly at Noah's head. Ducking under the blow, Noah felt the rush of air, the strike narrowly missing, jumping back to get distance between them as another elbow thrust at him, ready to rip his head off his shoulders.

Getting away, Noah took a second to breathe air into his lungs, leaning against the wall of the corridor and panting. The strain of continuous evasion was wearing on him both mentally and physically. His muscles screamed in protest, his breathing labored. Only the meal he had consumed earlier fueled his resilience, keeping at arm's length the exhaustion that threatened to claim him.

They went again, Noah pushing off the wall as Gruber came at him.

Despite the disparity in their physical attributes, Noah's durability shone through. He executed a series of Pencak Silat sweeping hand strikes, aiming for the eyes in a bid to disrupt Gruber's sight, disorientate him, inflict pain. The precision of Noah's strikes were proof of his time with an Indonesian grand master and his indomitable will. They were perfect. They should have blinded the giant.

Yet they only forced Gruber to momentarily falter, taking a few steps back and blinking his battered eyes, shaking his head, sweat showering off his hair.

Then he corrected his feet and came at Noah again.

For every maneuver Noah executed, Gruber responded in kind, his strikes a deadly ballet of power and accuracy. A particularly vicious capoeira kick from Noah was met with a counter from Gruber, who employed Wing Chun to deflect and deliver a punishing counterattack, a palm strike aimed at Noah's chest that sent him staggering back, winded, struggling to breathe.

As he stood there, leaning against the wall, battered and gasping for air, Noah realized that this monster was just too strong; science had gifted Gruber an insurmountable advantage. He needed a different tactic. Hand-to-hand combat in close quarters wasn't doing it.

Then, in the heat of their duel, Noah's opportunity was gifted to him. A wide, reinforced door suddenly opened several feet away, two technicians walking out into the corridor. Beyond them was the vast room that housed the colossal microwave machine.

Noah seized his opportunity. With Gruber distracted by

the technicians, he burst toward the heavy door as it began closing, Gruber hot on his heels.

On the other side, Noah found himself running along a metal walkway that bisected the chamber. The vastness of the room, with its towering machine, was vastly different than the claustrophobic intensity of the corridor. Here, within the shadows, components, and equipment, Noah hoped to level the playing field, using the jutting machinery as both shield and battleground in the next phase of their confrontation.

Any advantage was welcome. Because Noah was beginning to feel the strain of the fight. His body was covered in the signs of the conflict's ferocity—left eye swollen shut, a deep gash across his cheek, his movements hindered by a pronounced limp. He found himself pushed to the brink against Gruber, whose own visage had been grotesquely altered by the fight, the giant's nose crushed to the point of non-recognition.

Noah's survival instincts guided him to the colossal machinery dominating the room, his boot heels tramping down the metal steps toward it. All the time, Gruber was right there behind him. With agility borne of necessity, Noah maneuvered through a maze of machinery and equipment that littered the main floor of the room.

Placing a little distance between himself and Gruber, he finally reached the tower block-sized machine, propelling himself up a scaffold tower to reach its base, his eyes searching for sanctuary among the machine's innards. Climbing with difficulty, driven by sheer will, Noah found what he was looking for: a gap to hide in. With Gruber beginning his own ascent of the machine, Noah quickly threw himself into the gap and ensconced himself within an alcove of wires and machinery—an uncertain hideout within the mechanical behemoth.

The space, cramped and lined with the innards of technology, offered Noah a momentary shield from Gruber's physical superiority. He used this brief pause to assess his dwindling options, his breathing ragged, each inhale sharp against the backdrop of throbbing wounds. Below him, Gruber's frustration boiled over as he realized he'd lost him, the sound of his fury filling the cavernous room. "Where are you, Wolf?!"

This cat-and-mouse game amidst the machinery not only provided Noah with a tactical advantage but also symbolized the contrasting styles of the combatants—one leveraging the environment and intellect, the other an unnatural force using superior power, relentless and unyielding. As Noah plotted his next move, hidden within the machine, the stage was set for a cunning counterattack, Noah's determination to overcome this monster against all odds hardening by the second.

———

HAVING ESCAPED the clutches of the Citadel, Neil, Marco, Jenny, and Renée made it back to the hidden vantage point in the jungle. Their arrival was marked by a mix of relief and apprehension.

"What now?" Marco asked.

"Now we wait for the others," Neil replied.

"But shouldn't we be helping them?" Jenny interjected.

Neil, however, insisted on pragmatism. "You're not

helping anyone," he told his wife firmly. "That goes for you two, as well," he added, turning to Marco and Renée. "You can hardly hold yourselves up. We're better off waiting for the others out here."

"But they might be in danger," Renée pointed out.

"I'll find out," Neil said. Placing a finger to his ear, he sought an update. "Wally, what's the situation with the others?"

Wally's voice was instant. "Allison is in the quarters of Number Four while Sarah has almost reached Noah. He's currently trying to avoid Gruber."

"You think they need our help?" Neil pressed.

"I'm not... I... he... Neil?..." Wally's voice was swallowed by static and then gone.

"Wally? Wally?" Neil repeated, but no answer came.

That was when things took a sharp turn.

Inside the Citadel server room, members of the Council had just removed Wally's drone from the router, having found it after detecting Esmeralda's presence in their system. The Council once more had full control over the base.

Neil and the others could only watch as the blast door they had just left through slammed shut. The sudden roar of sirens then sent the jungle birds scattering from the trees.

The base had just gone into a Code Red lockdown.

"This isn't good," Neil said, looking at the others. "We need to move. Rendezvous with the getaway vehicle."

"But what about the others?" Renée put to him.

Neil gave her his most solemn look. "Noah, Allison, and Sarah are three of the most gifted agents on this planet," he told her. "If anyone can get out of there, it's them. Now," he added nervously, "we really do need to move."

Stranded, with their communication severed and the enemy on high alert, they braced for the challenges that lay in wait within the unforgiving embrace of the jungle.

———

GRUBER PROWLED AROUND THE MACHINERY, his voice echoing through the vast space of the multi-storied chamber. "You know, I had your Dragon for a whole three months," he began, a sinister pleasure in his tone. Noah, concealed within the alcove, felt a jolt of anger. His eyes pierced, fists clenched tightly as Gruber continued, "It was pretty obvious from the beginning that her body wouldn't survive much physical torture. So we had to turn to pharmacology for our results."

Noah's breath caught in his throat.

"Your Dragon was putty in my hands," Gruber taunted, his words like daggers, trying to poke Noah out of his hiding spot. "You know as well as I do, Herr Wolf," he continued as he walked around the machine in search of his prey, "how people under those types of drugs open right up for you. How they will tell you anything you want to hear. They will even reveal things that they themselves are unaware of. Things they have kept long buried within their psyche."

As Gruber went on, Noah's resolve crystallized. He began to work a length of heavy metal from its fitting, the task demanding all his focus. The metal screeched quietly against the tension, a sound that did not go unnoticed by Gruber, who paused momentarily, trying to discern the sound's origin.

The giant went on, "Over those months, we got to know

one another, I and your Dragon. I learned to mold her subconscious to my will." Gruber's voice grew colder, more menacing. "She told me much about you, Herr Wolf. Told me that you've changed since the birth of your daughter. That it has activated parts of you that had ceased when you were seven years old due to your previous condition of histrionic affect disorder. She told me she genuinely fears that you're not the same man you once were. Having studied you for so long, Herr Wolf, I had always been under the impression that you were as cold as ice. That killing to you was like flipping a switch to others. That you never questioned orders—especially when those orders were to kill. But the Dragon told me that since your daughter, you've become more... emotional. That you care too much." Noah, struggling with the piece of metal, felt a surge of protective rage. The metal finally gave way, a soft groan that felt like relief to Noah as Gruber continued his psychological assault. "That is why," the malevolent creature went on, "I'd like you to know that after this is done, after I have killed you, I am going to find your wife and little girl, and I am going to drown them in that lake you live next to."

This final, sick threat to his family was the last straw. With the metal now free, Noah, fueled by a primal fury, erupted from his hiding place above. He descended on Gruber like a bolt of lightning, wielding the piece of metal with the skill of an expert bōjutsu practitioner. With a series of calculated strikes, Noah drove Gruber backward onto a platform suspended meters above the ground.

Even the big man couldn't block Noah's relentless assault forever. Eventually, the piece of metal found its mark on Gruber's disfigured nose, eliciting a rare display of vulnerability from the giant as he flailed, caught off guard. Seizing the moment, Noah delivered a punishing blow to his torso, the impact audibly fracturing ribs, before targeting Gruber's knee, effectively bringing the colossus down.

He sat there crumpled, legs folded underneath him, his wide back leaning against the railing of the platform, one eye closed over, the other staring up at Noah. He was wheezing, struggling for breath, and for the first time since Noah had lain eyes on him, he looked utterly defeated.

As Noah raised the metal for a final, fatal blow, a voice pierced the air. "Noah!"

It was Sarah. Distracted, Noah hesitated, turning toward her call. This momentary lapse allowed Gruber to seize his chance. Hauling his injured body up, he scrambled through the gap in the platform's railing, dropping down to the floor below and disappearing through a door.

"Noah!" Sarah called out again as she ran toward him.

Noah forgot about Gruber, at least for now. Instead, he turned to his wife. His heart surged, a sense of relief washing over him, momentarily eclipsing the horror and madness of their surroundings. They embraced tightly, and in that embrace, Noah felt the weight of what they had endured apart from one another and what still lay ahead together.

Breaking the moment, Sarah handed Noah her M4A1 carbine, a silent acknowledgment that things were far from over. She then armed herself with her M17 pistol, her movements efficient and familiar.

"I missed you so much, baby," she told Noah as they prepared to face the Council.

"Norah?" Noah asked.

"She's safe."

Their brief respite was shattered as security guards began flooding into the vast room, their presence signaling the onset of a new challenge.

———

UNDER THE RELENTLESS din of sirens that filled the jungle air, Neil, Jenny, Marco, and Renée ran with everything they had, getting the last from their battered and weary bodies. With their communications severed and the compound locked down, their singular hope lay in reaching the rendezvous vehicle concealed deep within the jungle's embrace.

Neil led the way, his tablet illuminating a path. The jungle around them was alive, not just with the natural cacophony of its animal inhabitants but with the ominous rumble of Jeeps patrolling the dirt tracks that criss-crossed the terrain.

Just as they hit a rocky slope, a group of soldiers in the back of a passing truck caught a glimpse of them running through the foliage. Shouts pierced the air as the vehicle ground to a halt, and within moments, the quiet dread of anticipation was shattered by the sound of radios crackling. The situation escalated as more vehicles converged on their location, spilling out men armed and ready to pursue them into the jungle's depths.

As the team quickened their pace down the incline, Neil called out, "It's up ahead," he promised. "Just a little farther."

The pursuit was a desperate bid for survival. With every labored breath and step, the vehicle—their lifeline—loomed ever closer. But as the terrain became more rocky, the caves looming closer, the jungle suddenly lit up with machine gun fire, the bullets cutting through the vegetation after them.

From the perspective of one of the chasing guards, the pursuit intensified. He was closest to them, trailing Neil, Jenny, Marco, and Renée through the jungle from less than twenty meters away. As the terrain shifted beneath his boots, descending into a rocky declivity that led toward an ominous series of caves, the guard spotted his targets. Marco, lagging slightly behind, became the focus of his aim.

Dropping to one knee, the guard steadied his Tavor, then unleashed a volley of shots, the harsh report of gunfire shattering the jungle chorus. Yet as quickly as he had them in his sights, they had vanished, his bullets finding nothing but rock, the group disappearing over a ridge.

Meanwhile, Neil and his team plunged into the darkness of a tall cave, the entrance marked by the steady drip of water. "It's in here somewhere," Neil asserted. As he activated his night vision goggles, the cave's interior revealed itself in shades of green and black. "Wow!" he exclaimed, taken aback by what lay hidden from the naked eye. "Remind me to thank Santiago when I next see him."

Back on the chase, the guard was navigating the treacherous descent, carefully and cautiously. "They went into the cave," he whispered into his radio, the grip on his Tavor tightening with anticipation.

As he approached the cave's mouth, he was met with nothing but darkness, the hissing sound of falling water filling his ears. Step by cautious step, he advanced, the weight of his mission heavy upon him, until, suddenly, the cave burst into life, illuminated by the blinding glare of headlights. But not the headlights of any normal vehicle, oh no. These headlights were innumerable and high voltage, blinding to the man standing in the entrance of the cave.

Because there, in front of him, was an LAV-25—a fast, eight-wheeled amphibious light armored vehicle used by the US Marine Corps for rapid assaults and equipped with an M242 Bushmaster 25mm chain gun. Confronted with the unexpected appearance of this heavy-duty beast, the guard's heart raced, his body trembling.

In a desperate, futile gesture, he raised his Tavor, aiming at the behemoth that towered over him. But before he could act, the chain gun roared to life, a devastating burst of fire silencing him forever.

As the guard's colleagues neared the cave, intent on capturing their prey, they were met not with the expected darkness but with the LAV-25 charging forth from its concealment, its huge tires clawing at the rock for traction. The tables turned, the hunters became the hunted, their fate sealed by the overwhelming firepower and tactical superiority of those they had only moments ago pursued.

FIFTY-ONE

MORE AND MORE MEN FLOODED INTO THE VAST chamber. Surrounded on all sides, Noah and Sarah, acutely aware of the dire straits they found themselves in, made the difficult decision to throw down their weapons, raising their hands high. The odds were just too overwhelming.

With the cold metal of numerous firearms trained on them, they were cornered, their options dwindling rapidly. Recognizing the gravity of their situation, Noah attempted a final, desperate plea for understanding. "Listen, we can work this out," he began, aiming his words at the leader of the armed group, a stern figure who stood with an unwavering gaze at the other end of the platform. "Just take us to cells. Your Number Four wouldn't want either of us dead. Trust me."

"Screw you!" the lead guard cut him off. "You're Noah Wolf. We're taking no chances."

The air thickened as the sound of weapons being cocked

filled the void, the unmistakable click of barrels locking into place.

Noah took hold of Sarah by the arm, bringing her close to him as he edged backward toward the handrail of the platform, ready to jump with her, follow Gruber's escape, before the firing started.

But just as the situation seemed to plummet to an inevitable conclusion, a voice pierced through the edgy atmosphere, resonating with authority from above. "Officer!" the clear voice of Number Four called from an upper platform.

The chief commander of the Citadel was standing in an open doorway. Beside him was an unexpected ally—Allison Peterson, her stance bold against the backdrop of unfolding drama.

Whispering with an urgency that belied her calm demeanor, Allison leaned close to Number Four. "Tell your men to bring them here," she murmured, her words laced with the invisible force of the Cognitive Harmonizer. Without a moment's delay, Number Four, his will ensnared by the device's influence, issued the command with an uncharacteristic edge of compliance. "Bring them to me. Now!"

Noah's eyes locked with Allison's from across the distance, a silent exchange of hope and strategy passing between them. The guards, visibly unsettled by the abrupt change in orders, exchanged wary glances.

"I said bring them to me!" Number Four insisted loudly.

The guards did as they were asked, ushering Noah and Sarah toward the stairs, then following closely behind. As they ascended to the upper platform, there was a pervasive and uneasy mood inside the chamber. Guided past more guards toward the enigmatic Number Four, they moved at a cautious pace, acutely aware of the Tavor rifles at their backs. With their hands raised, they trod the path laid out by Number Four's unforeseen directive, a mix of apprehension and hope marking their journey.

Upon reaching Number Four and Allison, they steeled themselves for what would come next. "Okay. Now hand them over," commanded Number Four as they arrived at the door. The guards exchanged uncertain looks, their eyes darting between their leader and the imposing figure of Allison standing just behind him.

"That's an order," Number Four added sharply. Reluctantly, the guards stepped aside, allowing Noah and Sarah to move past him and join Allison in the corridor beyond.

"May I ask, sir," the lead guard ventured, his curiosity overcoming his discipline, "who is this woman with you?" The question hung in the air, charged with an uneasy undercurrent. Number Four, momentarily caught off guard, turned to Allison, his expression clouding with confusion as the effects of the Cognitive Harmonizer began to wane, his grip on the situation visibly loosening.

Facing his men once more, Number Four managed, "Her name is Allison Peterson."

The guards turned their scrutiny toward Allison, the lead guard's voice carrying a mix of suspicion and intrigue. "And who is that, sir?"

In a quick motion that brooked no hesitation, Allison took charge of the situation. "I'm the Dragon Lady," she said before tugging Number Four back into the safety of the corridor and firing two shots at the guards with her M17, hitting one in the chest, the other in the throat. Then, with a calculated press of the door button, she sealed the entrance, the heavy blast door closing with a definitive thud.

As the final act of her plan, Allison activated her EMP cufflinks, sending a pulse that fried the door's opening mechanism, effectively locking it against the onslaught of guards now desperate to breach it and come after them.

Allison turned to Noah and Sarah, her M17 still smoking. She handed them each their own pistols, ensuring they were armed for what lay ahead, then grabbed ahold of Number Four. Holding on to him, she noticed the questioning looks Sarah and Noah directed at the Citadel's leader, who now seemed out of sorts and under her grip.

"What's wrong with him?" Noah asked.

Allison explained, "A little device of Wally's creation. Cognitive Harmonizer. But it won't last forever. And neither will that door. We need to move."

With the urgency of Allison's words propelling them forward, they quickly set off down the corridor, their steps echoing in the empty hallway.

———

BACK AT THE riverside base of operations, dawn was breaking, the sky transitioning to a deep blue and the birds beginning to stir. Wally Lawson and Molly Hanson faced the unnerving silence of their communications equipment. "Allison, come in. Neil, come in. Sarah, do you copy?" Wally's voice, tinged with desperation, filled the room, only to be swallowed by the static. He turned to Molly. "Nothing. It's like we're being jammed."

Molly's mind raced at the implications. "But if we're being jammed, that would mean..." Her words trailed off as an ominous realization set in. "We need to move!" she snapped.

But before they could, the sudden appearance of men at the windows, guns poised and ready, cut through their nerves like a knife. The uniforms were unmistakable—Council guards.

"Stay where you are and put your hands up," commanded the leader of the five men, his voice cold and authoritative as they fanned into the shack.

Wally and Molly exchanged a look of resigned understanding, their hands raised in surrender.

"Well, this isn't good," Wally muttered under his breath.

———

NOAH, Sarah, Allison, and Number Four advanced rapidly through the corridors, the latter's steps uncertain and sluggish, as if his body was struggling to obey the commands of a distant mind. Allison's grip on his suit jacket was iron-tight, her fingers twisted into the fabric, pulling him along with a force that tolerated no resistance. As they approached a locked door, Allison maneuvered Number Four in front of the retina scanner, a sharp shove against his back ensuring compliance. His head was then forcibly tilted toward the device, his eyes blinking rapidly as the scanner emitted a soft, whirring sound, the green light flashing in acknowledgment.

"What's happening?" Number Four said as the door slid open, revealing an expansive underground garage, its existence hidden beneath the deceptive tranquility of the Cuban jungle. "What has happened to me?" Number Four demanded as Allison pushed him through the door.

"Shut up," she snapped. "We only need you a little longer, then you're dead."

The air was much cooler in the garage, tinged with the metallic scent of machinery and the faint, musty odor of rubber. Armored Humvees lined the space in precise rows, their dark forms looming like silent sentinels ready for battle, machine gun turrets poking out of their roofs. Overhead, fluorescent lights flickered intermittently, casting long shadows across the concrete floor and reflecting off the vehicles' matte surfaces.

A large set of blast doors dominated the far end of the garage, a formidable barrier between the rebels and the lush, untamed wilderness of the jungle outside. They marched past walls lined with racks of equipment and tools. Here and there, cables snaked across the floor, connecting to various charging stations, while digital displays flickered with the base's internal communications and security statuses. Most of them carried the Code Red symbol.

Allison guided the stumbling Number Four toward the retina scanner beside the blast doors. Her hands were firm on his shoulders, jockeying him as if he were nothing more than a puppet. With a forceful push, she held his face up to the scanner, waiting for the brief moment it took to recognize him. The doors began to slide open, revealing the dense, vibrant Cuban jungle that lay beyond, very different from the sterile environment of the Citadel.

Without hesitation, Allison shoved Number Four down onto his knees on the threshold between their man-made confines and the wild freedom outside. Pulling her M4A1 from her shoulder, she readied it, aiming directly at him, her intentions clear, her nerve never in question.

It was at this moment, under the imminent threat of death, that Number Four's senses fully returned to him. "Wait," he pleaded, his voice a mix of confusion and urgency. "I remember now." His eyes darted around, taking in the faces of Noah and Sarah and finally resting on Allison, who stood resolute beyond the barrel of her carbine. A frown creased his brow as he struggled with the reality of his situation. "What are *you* doing here?"

"Shut up!" Allison's response was sharp, a verbal snap that mirrored her willingness to act.

But just as her finger tightened on the trigger, Noah intervened, stepping forward and placing himself between the gun and Number Four. His eyes locked on Allison's, conveying a depth of conviction that challenged her resolve without uttering a single word.

"What are you doing?" Allison asked, her brow furrowing.

"We need him," Noah told her in an even tone.

"You think he's going to tell you anything?" Allison countered.

"He knows more about the Council than anyone we know of," Noah argued. "He could be vital in fighting them."

Allison remained unconvinced. "It doesn't matter," she said. "They won't let him leave this island alive. They'll do everything to stop it. He's just a piece of it, Noah. A small part. He may call himself Number Four, but there is no real leadership in this organization. Just lots and lots of little pieces. He's probably fitted with something that's rigged to explode the second he leaves this place."

Fully recovered by now, Number Four joined the conversation, addressing Noah specifically. "She's wrong about me being fitted with something. There is no bomb. But she is right about them not letting me leave in your company alive. And she's also right when she says I won't tell you anything. I certainly won't. Not anything that you don't already know, at any rate. I have played my cards pretty openly, Mr. Wolf," he declared, acknowledging the stalemate between them.

"You're still coming," Noah said, grabbing him by the arm and lifting him up off the ground.

"Hold it there!" a voice suddenly boomed.

All eyes shifted to the far end of the garage, beyond the row of Humvees. There, in all his brutal glory, stood Gruber. Leaning heavily on one leg and with a face so beaten it was barely recognizable, he was still an imposing figure as he held a Tavor bullpup rifle aimed at the group.

More men, weapons ready, silently filed into the room behind him. "Sir?" Gruber called out to Number Four. "Get away from them and come join us."

Number Four made a move to comply, but Noah's firm grip stopped him in his tracks. "You're staying here with us," Noah growled at him.

"I see you found your dragon again, Herr Wolf," Gruber taunted, a malicious glee in his reptilian eyes as they scanned Noah. "Oh, and look, you have your wife, as well. Isn't that sweet. Now you can all die together."

Noah's response was calm but laced with defiance. "We're not dying today, Gruber. Not today, not here. And not before *you*."

Allison, her eyes darting to the encroaching men gathered behind the behemoth, added, "Your confidence is misplaced, Mr. Gruber. You do understand it's Noah Wolf you're talking to?"

Sarah murmured to them, "Keep moving back slowly. We need to get to the jungle."

As they inched back toward the blast doors, Gruber and his men continued their slow advance across the garage. Finally stepping into the fresh air of the jungle, the three of them felt a momentary sense of relief.

But then things turned from bad to worse.

Amidst the standoff and their careful retreat, the sharp snap of a twig cut through the air. They turned sharply, only to be met with the sight of more Council guards emerging silently from the jungle, effectively encircling them. This sudden appearance instantly heightened the danger. Surrounded with no clear path to escape, the group felt the weight of their predicament settle in, their fleeting hope shattered.

Reluctantly, they lowered their weapons to the ground. The guards stepped forward, tightening the circle around them. Gruber's taunting voice broke in. "Looks like our fight gets to continue, Herr Wolf. But no metal bars this time. Just our fists." He burst into laughter, deep and mocking. It echoed out of the garage and through the jungle, a sound of victory that seemed to seal their fate.

But maybe Gruber was proclaiming victory just a little too soon. Maybe fate wasn't quite so certain. Because his laughter was suddenly challenged by another sound—a distant roar that grew louder and more formidable with each passing second. It was the unmistakable sound of an engine, powerful and relentless, tearing through the silence and the dense foliage. Just as Gruber's laughter reached its peak, it was abruptly cut off by the sight of the LAV-25 exploding out of the jungle, its headlights bursting on, blinding the guards.

It charged into the clearing, its arrival turning the tide in an instant. The front wheels crashed over a ridge of rock, launching the mechanical monster into the air. As it landed, the guards in the jungle were flattened under its heavy frame, ground into the dirt by the eight wheels of the LAV as it came to a sudden, skidding stop.

That was when the 25mm chain gun erupted on top of it, its deafening roar filling the trees, cutting down the exposed men inside the garage with ruthless efficiency. Birds scattered into the air, a flurry of movement against the chaos, while in the garage, those who didn't get to cover in time were turned to pink mist by the mighty chain gun.

Gruber wasn't one of them, however. He and several others had managed to dive for the cover of the armored vehicles. They now watched in dismay as their numerical advantage disintegrated before their eyes.

The chain gun ceased as quickly as it had begun, leaving behind a sudden silence punctuated only by the distant calls of the now distant birds. With the immediate threats neutralized, the side door of the LAV flung open. Jenny leaned out, urgency etched into her features. "Come on!" she shouted at them, her voice a beacon of hope amongst the bedlam.

They sprinted for the LAV, Noah firmly grasping Number Four, ensuring he was part of their desperate escape. The second they all tumbled inside, the door slammed shut, effectively isolating them from the madness outside. In the driver's seat, Marco wasted no time, engaging the vehicle in reverse. As the diesel-powered monster roared to life, it began its retreat, pulling a three-point turn, then heading back the way it came.

With the LAV disappearing into the jungle, Gruber, his determination as unbreakable as ever, barked commands at his men, his furious voice filling the garage. "After them! Don't let them escape!" he roared, clambering into the turret of an armored Humvee. His hands gripped the machine gun. "This isn't over, Wolf!" he shouted into the jungle as the driver brought the vehicle to life.

———

MEANWHILE, Wally and Molly found themselves in their own precarious situation, zip-tied and seated on a small boat navigating the dark, meandering waters of the Rio Cauto. The dawn air had a nervousness about it, the only sounds being the gentle lapping of water against the boat and the distant calls of awakening animals. Armed guards, their faces stern and watchful, sat beside them, ensuring there was no chance of escape.

Wally's curiosity was piqued when he spotted Molly subtly lean down, seemingly to scratch her foot, then slyly fiddling with the sole of her boot.

When she caught him looking, he mouthed, *What are you doing?*

Just wait, she responded silently, the focus of her fingers on a hidden compartment in her heel, despite the clumsiness enforced by her zip-tied wrists.

A guard caught the unusual movement. "Hey!" he barked, eyeing the panel that she had managed to partially slide from the heel. "What's that?" he demanded, stepping closer, reaching out to grab her, to stop her.

In that moment, Wally acted. Bursting up from his seat, he sent the guard tumbling overboard with a sudden charge. Molly seized the opportunity, pulling the panel all the way out and pressing a button on the revealed device.

It emitted a soft beep.

Instantly, the other guards snapped to attention, their eyes fixed on the small gadget now fully exposed. One of them, quicker to react and driven by a surge of panic, shouted, "It's a bomb!" Without a second thought, he snatched the device from Molly's grasp and hurled it into the river. It disappeared with a soft splash, the ripples quickly swallowed by the waters of the Rio Cauto.

The atmosphere aboard the boat shifted dramatically. The guards, now perceiving Wally and Molly not just as captives but as threats, quickly regrouped. They turned their weapons on the pair, their expressions hardening even more.

"Don't move!" one guard commanded.

Both captives froze as a sudden, charged silence fell over them, the only sounds coming from the gentle lapping of water against the boat and the distant splashes of the man overboard swimming back to them.

Simultaneously, a new sound entered the river. The rhythmic sound of an approaching engine melded with the twilight, unnoticed at first by the guards as they converged on Wally and Molly, weapons drawn and demanding answers. With the confrontation escalating, the distant hum of the engine grew steadily closer, until the silhouette of an unassuming fishing skiff was visible cutting through the water, its presence innocuous against the drama unfolding on the boat.

"What did you just pull from your shoe?" one guard demanded, pressing his rifle into Molly's neck. "Tell us! Now!"

The guards, their focus narrowed on Molly and Wally, failed to notice the approaching vessel, the night swallowing the skiff's silent approach, as well as the fisherman onboard, his face hidden beneath a straw hat, his hands hidden beneath a large poncho that covered his body.

Just as the guards prepared to exact their punishment, it drew parallel, its approach masked until the very moment it was poised alongside their boat.

Noticing the fisherman's skiff for the first time, the armed men's suspicion quickly escalated into aggression. "¡Sigue tu camino!" one of them shouted in Spanish, his voice sharp, commanding the fisherman to move on. The fisherman, seemingly unperturbed, turned slowly toward them, his movements deliberate under the guards' watchful eyes.

The moment his eyes met theirs, the guards were unnerved. In the fisherman's gaze, they detected a steely resolve, the unmistakable look of a killer.

In an instant, the tranquil night air was shattered. The fisherman burst up from his seat, throwing back his poncho and revealing an FN Minimi in his hands. With a swift, practiced motion, he unleashed a hail of bullets toward the guards, fanning his fire from one man to the next. The sudden eruption of gunfire caught them off guard, their attempts to retaliate cut short as they scrambled for cover within the limited space of their boat. Wally and Molly threw themselves onto the floor, pressing their bodies against the cold, hard surface. The boat rocked violently with the sudden shift in weight, but they held on as bullets whizzed overhead, splintering the boat's structure and puncturing the night with more chaos.

The deafening gunfire finally ceased, allowing Wally and Molly to cautiously release their ears and blink their eyes open. The anxious silence felt almost as loud as the shots had. Slowly, with the caution of those not yet sure the danger had passed, Molly turned over to survey their surroundings. That's when she saw him—Santiago, standing with a presence that felt both surprising and immensely reassuring. He leaned over the side of the boat, extending a hand to them, a silent promise of safety in his eyes.

"It seems I've found you just in the nick of time," he said.

The Cuban assisted them onto his skiff, his focus first on Molly. "Ladies first," he said as he helped her aboard. The scene around them was grim—motionless guards riddled with bullet holes. Some were strewn about the boat, others floated in the water, the blood flowing out of them like a red mist.

After ensuring Molly was safely on board, Santiago then turned and helped Wally.

With all three aboard the skiff, the Cuban pulled the throttle of the motor back and performed a one-eighty in the river, heading in the direction they had come from.

Once a safe distance away, Santiago began explaining, "I spotted those guys a while back heading your way. You're lucky your old pal Santiago was still looking out for you."

Molly smiled gently at him. "And glad, too," she said. "Really glad."

Wally, still reeling from the events, then turned to Molly. "Ms. Hanson," he began, "are you going to tell me exactly what that was you pulled from your heel? Because I can't recall giving you any such contraption from the offices of R&D."

"It's a beacon," she told him. "That's why it wasn't good that he threw it in the river."

"A beacon?"

She nodded.

"And who does this beacon call?"

Looking him in the eyes, she said, "The cavalry."

———

UNDER THE AZURE expanse of the Caribbean sky, three US submarines emerged silently from the depths, a mile off the southwest coast of Cuba, where the Rio Cauto meets the sea. Onboard the lead vessel, the captain pulled away from his periscope, the seriousness of the mission reflected in his eyes. He turned to face the individual seated behind him, none other than Doc Parker, the acting head of E & E.

"So she's sprung the signal," the captain stated, breaking the charged silence that filled the submarine's control room. "Now what?"

Doc Parker, ever the picture of calm, met the captain's gaze squarely. "Now we get them out of there," he responded without a hint of doubt. "All of them."

FIFTY-TWO

THE ENDLESS VEGETATION OF THE CUBAN JUNGLE blurred past as the LAV-25 barreled through the under-growth. Behind them, the menacing rumble of Humvees, commanded by Gruber, shattered the dawn's tranquility. Machine gun fire rattled the air, a deadly percussion to the high-speed chase.

The LAV's armor plating sang with the impact of bullets, a relentless wave of pings. Inside, the atmosphere was one of focused chaos. "Noah, take the chain gun!" Renée shouted over the cacophony of pinging metal. "Otherwise they're gonna blow us off the road!"

Noah climbed up into the turret, taking his position. The chain gun roared to life under his control, spitting fire into the twilight. His eyes narrowed as he tried to pick off the five Humvees chasing them through the dim light of dawn. The drivers, all seasoned in combat driving, used every trick in their arsenal to avoid his targeting, weaving through the trees and over the rough terrain with practiced ease.

From five different angles, their mounted M2 Browning heavy machine guns fired continuously, sending a hail of bullets toward the LAV.

Visibility was poor in the dim light, the teeming plant life creating shadows that danced and shifted, making it difficult for Noah to land his shots. The eight wheels of the LAV hit rocks and rough patches, jostling him violently as it maneuvered over fallen trees and smashed through thick underbrush.

Gruber, the most elusive of all the chasers, managed to land the most hits on the LAV, his shots ringing out with deadly precision.

Noah changed things up. He attempted to force the Humvees into each other, sweeping the spray of the M242 chain gun across the jungle, the tracer rounds lighting up the foliage, forcing the Humvees to move sideways. This technique quickly brought rewards.

One Humvee, trying to get a clear shot and avoid the spray of machine gun fire, swung recklessly in front of Gruber's vehicle, causing its driver to brake sharply, almost throwing the giant out of the turret as he was left behind.

Seizing the moment, Noah targeted the aggressor, the chain gun tearing through the dawn, a multitude of bullets striking the grille, hitting the engine block, causing the Humvee to swerve uncontrollably. With a tug of the triggers, Noah sent another devastating barrage of bullets into the stricken vehicle's fuel tank, the explosion filling the trees with fire.

The frenzy of crashing metal didn't stop there; two other Humvees, caught in the crossfire and confusion, collided with each other, their destruction lighting up the early morning sky as one exploded in a spectacular fireball, the other careening off the path into a tree.

"Gotcha!" Noah shouted.

But just as the tide seemed to be turning in their favor, the unmistakable whir of helicopter blades sliced through the morning air, adding a fresh layer of dread.

"Helicopter inbound!" Sarah's warning was punctuated by the hiss and whistle of missiles being launched. Just missing their mark by mere feet, their explosions illuminated the dawn and set the dense foliage ablaze.

"We've got to lose it!" Marco barked, swerving the LAV.

More missiles exploded around them, sending out shockwaves and debris. The AH-64 Apache attack helicopter, nimble and elusive, was also an expert in dodging Noah's attempts to target it with the chain gun. Nevertheless, determined and focused, Noah waited for the perfect moment. As the helicopter dipped low, trying to get a clear shot through the canopy, he targeted its tail rotor, the chain gun's rounds shredding the delicate machinery and sending the helicopter spiraling out of control. The pilot, caught off guard, struggled with the stick, but it was too late; the damaged rotor failed, and the helicopter crashed into the jungle with a deafening explosion.

Cheers erupted from the LAV. The remaining two Humvees, including Gruber's, had disappeared from sight, seemingly no longer in pursuit.

As the wreckage of the attack helicopter lay behind them, the team shared a moment of exhausted relief. "Good work, everyone," Noah said, breathing heavily. "Now let's get out of here before they send reinforcements."

The LAV pushed forward, deeper into the jungle's

embrace, their spirits bolstered by the successful escape but aware that the danger was far from over.

Bursting from the thick undergrowth onto a winding road carved through hilly terrain, the LAV's emergence was rapid, its presence on the asphalt out of place among the usual traffic that traversed these hills.

The relative openness of the road did not offer reprieve, however. No; instead it introduced new threats. Gruber, leading a new convoy of Humvees, was right there, his vehicle taking the lead as they pursued Noah and his team with renewed vigor.

A towering figure even from a distance, Gruber manned the machine gun turret of his Humvee with a predatory focus. His first barrage of bullets clanged against the LAV's armor, a metallic hailstorm intent on breach and destruction.

But the Browning wasn't enough; he needed something stronger. That was when, with a calculated calm, one of his men handed him up a box of grenades. Gruber's hand closed around one, pulling the pin with a practiced ease, his eyes never leaving the LAV as it swerved along the serpentine road ahead of them. He counted under his breath, timing his throw with an exactness born from experience.

As Noah swiveled the chain gun toward Gruber, a moment of anticipation hung in the air. Gruber, acting with a calm honed through countless skirmishes, launched the grenade with deadly accuracy.

The world seemed to slow as the projectile neared its mark, detonating in a blinding flash just a fraction before it reached the chain gun. The timing was impeccable; the explosion unleashed a maelstrom of shrapnel. Metal fragments, propelled at lethal speeds, peppered the chain gun's intricate mechanism. The gun's external housing, designed to protect against small arms fire, was punctured and torn open by the onslaught, exposing the vulnerable internal components to the destructive force of the blast. The chain gun's feeding mechanism was shattered, with gears and springs ejected from their positions, rendering the weapon incapable of cycling ammunition.

Within the confines of the LAV, the force of the blast propelled Noah away from the chain gun's controls, sending him tumbling backward into his companions. Regaining his bearings amidst the madness, he managed only a terse "We're in trouble" before another grenade detonated against the vehicle's armored side. The explosion rocked the LAV, jostling its occupants with a ferocity that underscored the gravity of their predicament.

With some way still to go, they were vulnerable, the LAV's primary weapon disabled. The explosion's reverberations marked a pivotal shift in their chase. With Gruber and his men pressing their advantage, the road ahead promised nothing but further peril.

———

As WALLY, Santiago, and Molly navigated the dark river toward a long concrete bridge that dissected it, the distant sound of chaos began to reach their ears—gunfire intertwined with the guttural roar of engines.

The three of them exchanged worried glances.

Peering up the ridge to their left, they saw it: the LAV-25, now a fireball, hurtling down the hill with Gruber's

Humvees in hot pursuit. While they watched, another of Gruber's grenades struck the LAV, intensifying the flames as it neared the bridge.

"Hand me that box," Santiago said, nodding toward a long, narrow crate on the floor of the boat. Molly quickly passed it to him, noting its surprising weight. "Take control of the skiff," the Cuban commanded Wally, who steadied it as Santiago unveiled an RPG launcher from the crate. "Keep her steady," Santiago instructed, loading the RPG with practiced hands. He stood, the launcher resting on his shoulder, his eyes fixed on the bridge.

The LAV blazed across it, the vehicle's reflection a streak of fire on the water. Santiago's focus didn't waver; he waited for Gruber's Humvee to enter the bridge. The structure was old, built during Batista's days before the revolution, a length of road straddling concrete legs.

It wouldn't take much to bring it down.

As the Humvee hit the halfway point of the bridge, Santiago fired. The rocket, a bright streak in the dawn, found its mark. The bridge erupted in a deafening explosion, its structure giving way under the force of the RPG. As the flaming LAV made it to the road on the other side, the bridge's midsection began to collapse, sending chunks of concrete and twisted metal plummeting into the water below.

The chasing Humvees found themselves on a rapidly disintegrating path. Gruber's Humvee, mere seconds behind the LAV, got it worst. The driver slammed on the brakes, but it was too late—the road beneath them crumbled, sending the vehicle crashing into the sudden debris. The impact was catastrophic, the Humvee's forward momentum halted abruptly as it slammed into the fractured, collapsing remnants of the bridge.

Gruber, who had been standing in the turret, was catapulted out by the force of the crash. He landed on the other side of the river, tumbling down the asphalt, a mix of rolling and cartwheeling, smashing into the ground over and over, his limbs going slack as the bones inside them broke apart.

He finally came to a stop and lay there motionless among the debris of the shattered bridge, the smoldering wreck of his vehicle bursting into flames behind him.

———

THE LAV-25 GROUND TO A HALT, its side door flinging open. Everyone except Noah sprang into action with fire extinguishers, battling the flames that threatened to consume the vehicle.

Amidst the frenetic effort to quell the fire, Noah emerged, his demeanor calm yet resolute, a SIG Sauer M17 pistol firm in his grip.

Without a glance at the efforts to douse the flames, he made his cautious approach to the aftermath of the explosion. Gruber lay there, a heap of battered flesh, the brutality of his landing painted in a smear of blood along the road.

Gently, Noah nudged him with his foot. Gruber spluttered back to consciousness, a wheezing, broken figure with injuries that were grotesquely visible. He was horribly misshapen, bones sticking out of him, including his collarbone, which poked out of his shoulder.

"Herr Wolf," Gruber managed to gasp, a twisted grin forming despite the blood oozing out of his mouth. "You know... whatever happens today... you can't escape the Council. They will get you in the end. They are too big and too old to be defeated. You are only postponing... the inevitable." With a last, laborious effort, he puffed out his chest, adding, "Now do what you must."

The air was pierced by a single shot, a grim finality to Gruber's unholy existence. As the others paused their frantic firefighting to look over, Noah was already walking away, the pistol now hanging loosely at his side.

As a silence settled over the group following Noah's action, their focus was abruptly shifted by calls from the river. "Over here!" came Santiago's urgent voice. Wally and Molly, from aboard the skiff, waved frantically to catch their attention.

Quickly, Noah and the others, including their captive, Number Four, made their way down to the riverbank, where Santiago expertly maneuvered the skiff closer. The group then carefully boarded the vessel, Noah shoving Number Four forward, aware of the added danger his presence brought.

"Who's he?" Santiago asked.

"A liability," Allison answered with clear annoyance.

Despite the crowding, the skiff proved capable of carrying them all. Each person found a spot, all eager for a speedy journey to relative safety.

As Santiago steered them away from the smoldering remains of the bridge and the night's turmoil, a sense of relief began washing over everyone.

"We thought we lost you," Molly said.

"We had a bit of trouble," Noah replied, glancing back at the fading fires.

"Yeah, I'll say," Wally added, managing a weary smile.

Allison simply nodded. "We stick together. That's how we get through this."

The skiff cut through the water, leaving behind the darkness for the promise of safety and the next phase of their journey.

———

INSIDE THE CONTROL room of the USS *Chicago*, Doc Parker stood among the crew, his eyes scanning the banks of equipment that lined the walls. The room buzzed with the low hum of machinery and the occasional crackle of radio communications, an encapsulated world of steel beneath the waves.

One of the communications officers, headphones still around his neck, turned to Parker and the captain with a report. "I'm getting a lot of chatter from the base," he began, his gaze fixed on Parker. "Looks like your people got away. It also looks like they took a lot of the Council guys with them."

"Sounds like them," Parker remarked in an undertone.

"There was a chase through the jungle which ended with the destruction of a bridge. Their vehicles couldn't follow. After that, they lost track of them. No idea where they are now."

Before Parker could respond, another officer, headphones pressed to his ears, swiveled in his chair to face the captain and Parker. "Captain, I've got Corporal Davis on the radio. Shall I patch him through?"

"Go ahead," the captain responded, nodding.

The room fell silent as Davis' voice, hushed and urgent, filled the space. "We found the location of the beacon," he whispered, the sound of foliage rustling softly in the background. "It's in the river. However, that's not the most interesting part. The most interesting part is the boat we found drifting near the beacon's location. The one filled with bodies wearing bullet hole polka-dots. Your peeps aren't among them. So I'm thinking it was them who did the shooting. You want us to keep looking?"

The captain, his expression grave, leaned forward slightly. "You better make a sweep of the area, Corporal," he said, his voice steady and commanding. "See if you and your men can't find any more signs of them."

Davis' reply crackled through the speakers. "If they're in trouble, they'll be heading north along the river to avoid the base. It's their best shot at staying... under the... where I'd... radar." As the Marine spoke, the line began to degrade, morphing into static.

The communications officer, now frowning, adjusted dials in an attempt to clear the connection. After a moment, he looked up at the captain, concern written across his features. "Sir, our communications are being blocked. All of them."

A charged silence enveloped the control room, broken only by the persistent hum of machinery. All eyes turned to the captain, seeking his insight into the unfolding mystery. The captain's gaze then met Doc Parker's, a silent question hanging between them.

Parker, his brow furrowed in thought, finally spoke. "There's only one reason why they would be blocking communications."

FIFTY-THREE

With dawn rapidly turning into morning, the jungle river became a corridor of light and shadow, the sun threading through the trees in blades of gold. For almost an hour, the skiff's gently humming engine was the only intrusion into the natural world. But this didn't last.

The relative quiet was pierced by the distant thrum of helicopter blades, a sound growing ominously louder within the midst of this secluded paradise. It reminded them of the danger pursuing them, their unseen hunters drawing ever closer.

With the first light touching the waters of the river, Noah's keen eyes spotted a man waving to them from the bank. He pointed him out to Santiago. Recognizing the signal, Santiago expertly maneuvered the vessel to the river's edge.

"They are searching up ahead," the man warned in rapid Spanish when they were close enough. "Patrol boats scouring the river. Men with guns."

Understanding the gravity of the situation, Santiago addressed his companions, "We'll have to walk from here." With decisive action, they disembarked, and Santiago, ensuring no trace of their passage remained, pushed the empty boat back into the current, letting it drift away.

Leaving the river behind, the group embarked on a challenging trek through the jungle. The thick canopy overhead turned the growing daylight into a dim twilight, intensifying the sense of isolation. Every step was fraught with difficulty; the underbrush clawed at their clothing, and the air hung heavy with humidity, making each breath a laborious effort. The relentless sound of the jungle was a constant reminder of the vibrant life around them.

The trek lasted less than an hour. Emerging from the jungle, the group stumbled upon their destination, a hidden cache that sparked a moment of hope amidst the exhaustion: two Land Rovers, cleverly concealed under sections of stitched-together foliage. The vehicles, equipped with two front seats and panel seating along the backs, stood ready to carry them forward.

It was as they were getting into the Land Rovers, however, that Molly spoke. "Is there a phone I can use?" she asked.

Santiago handed her his satellite phone without hesitation. "Be quick," he warned. "Council is always listening."

As Molly attempted to dial out, the group's collective frown deepened, Wally's most of all. His mind was still reeling from the incident on the boat. The beacon she'd pulled from her heel. He hadn't had time to bring it up yet. Perhaps now was that time.

However, the satellite phone remained stubbornly silent

against Molly's ear, no signal to be found. "It's being blocked," she concluded as she checked over the phone's settings in frustration.

"Why do you need a phone in the first place, Molly?" Allison's question cut straight to the point.

Molly hesitated, before deciding to go with the truth. "Because I'm working with Doc Parker," she confessed. "We figured out what you were up to pretty quickly back in Kirtland and made the joint decision that instead of stopping you, we'd assist you from the shadows. I've been reporting back to him since we arrived in Cuba. Parker, along with three US Navy submarines, are waiting just off the coast, ready to help us."

Allison cocked an eye at her. "You've been rather crafty, Ms. Hanson. Reporting back to Parker without our knowledge?"

The sudden thrum of approaching helicopters underscored the urgency of their discussion.

"Parker can help us," Molly insisted. "We need him."

"She's right," Noah declared. "We're gonna need them now more than ever. Where are they?"

"Just off the southern coast," Molly replied. "If we can get to them, we'll be able to escape."

Santiago, with his intimate knowledge of the local geography, stepped forward. "Santa Cruz del Sur is three hours from here by road," he declared, a plan formulating in his mind. "It's on the coast. Right where your friends are."

Allison turned to him. "Can you get us there?"

"Sure," Santiago responded with confidence. "Just follow me."

Without hesitation, Santiago led the charge to the lead

vehicle. Sarah took the driver's seat of the second one. The group then organized themselves with a sense of determined caution. Allison, securing Number Four with a firm grip, got into the back of the lead Rover. Marco, Renée, and Wally followed her, while Molly got in the passenger seat alongside Santiago. In the meantime, Noah took the passenger seat of the second Rover beside his wife as Jenny and Neil got into position behind them, everyone bracing for the journey ahead.

As they prepared to depart, they were filled with cautious optimism. The knowledge of the help waiting off the coast, mingled with the understanding of the risks they faced on the way to Santa Cruz del Sur, set a tone of silent determination among them as they embarked on the final, critical phase of their journey.

———

ABOARD THE USS *CHICAGO*, the crew worked feverishly to establish communication with Davis and his team. "Still nothing on the communications, sir," reported one of the operators.

"Keep trying," the captain commanded, his frustration obvious. The air was charged with the urgency of their mission as technical experts huddled over equipment, attempting to break through the silence that enveloped them.

It was in this moment that Doc Parker, leaning against the bulkhead, voiced a thought that had been gnawing at him. "You get a feeling something's coming?"

His question, more a reflection of his seasoned instincts

than mere speculation, added a layer of foreboding to the already heavy atmosphere.

"Sir?" one of the sonar technicians suddenly called out, his voice piercing the ominous quiet, drawing all eyes to him. "I'm getting a huge heat signature coming from the base."

Both Parker and the captain hurried over, their gazes fixed on the thermal imaging display. It showed an intense heat concentration at the heart of the Citadel, radiating outward in waves of red and orange. "It looks like something is powering up," the operator explained.

The captain turned to Parker. "Could it be what's blocking the transmissions?"

Doc Parker shook his head, his expression grave. "No," he replied. "This is something else."

FIFTY-FOUR

THE TWO LAND ROVERS EMERGED ONTO THE highway with a collective sense of relief. The subsequent journey to Santa Cruz del Sur, much to their surprise, unfolded with an unexpected ease, a very different experience than the harrowing events of the night. The persistent thrum of the helicopters that had been a constant presence along the river had gradually faded into the background, leaving a deceptive calm in its wake.

Despite the reduction in hostilities, the group remained on high alert, their weapons always within reach, their eyes scanning the lush jungle edges for any sign of pursuit. There existed a silent agreement between them that they were not yet out of danger. But as the sun climbed higher, bathing the highway in a warm, golden light, the only thing that emerged from the jungle was the day itself.

The band of gray road ahead of them stretched into the distance, a ribbon of hope cutting through the wilderness.

With each passing mile, the sense of vigilance remained, but it was tempered by the growing light of day.

They weren't far from Santa Cruz del Sur when the unnerving quiet was broken into by the sound of helicopter blades cutting through the air. This suspicion was confirmed when a fleet of choppers bearing the unmistakable mark of the Council buzzed overhead, all heading in the direction of the Citadel.

At first, everyone grabbed a gun, getting ready for a firefight. But soon, as the helicopters disappeared once more, it became obvious that they weren't actively looking for them and were merely returning to base.

A little while later, they caught sight of two Council military trucks through the trees, speeding along a dirt track parallel to the highway but in the opposite direction. They quickly passed it, the truck paying them no attention, more interested in getting out of there, by the looks of things.

"Why are they all heading home in such a hurry?" Sarah inquired, her gaze fixed on the retreating vehicles.

"I don't know," Jenny responded slowly, her eyes tracking the trucks' movement until the vehicles vanished into the jungle's embrace.

The sudden exodus of the Council's forces, both in the air and on the ground, added another layer of apprehension to their journey, leaving the group to wonder what the reasons were behind such a hurried retreat and what it might mean for their own precarious situation. Still, they pressed on, until finally, they reached Santa Cruz del Sur.

As the group's Land Rovers rolled into the heart of the town, the early morning sun was casting the picturesque town in warm hues of orange and gold. Colonial and

Caribbean-style houses, adorned in pastel shades, lined the streets, their shutters swinging open to welcome the gentle sea breeze. The locals were already starting their day, their voices blending with the distant calls of street vendors, creating a harmonious communal symphony.

Palm fronds swayed gracefully above, their leaves brushing against rustic balconies adorned with potted ferns and bougainvillea blooms. The scent of salty air intermingled with the earthy aroma of freshly harvested produce as the vehicles approached a bustling market square. Here, the town's heartbeat pulsed vibrantly.

Driving into this idyllic scene, the group couldn't help but feel the vast difference between the locals' mundane morning routines and their own uncertain situation.

Molly quickly spotted a payphone on the corner of the street and pointed it out to the others. Santiago, sensing the urgency, pulled the lead vehicle to the side of the road, allowing Molly to jump out and approach the phone box.

Inside the Rovers, the atmosphere was electric. As she pulled up behind the other vehicle, Sarah leaned over to Noah and whispered, "Do you think it's safe? What if we're being watched?"

Noah, his hand on his pistol, replied, "Stay vigilant. We can't be too careful."

Jenny, sitting in the back, exchanged wary glances with Neil. "This place gives me the creeps," she murmured.

Neil tightened his grip on his carbine. "Just keep an eye out, babe. We don't know who we can trust around here. Any one of them could be an agent of the Council."

They didn't escape the notice of the locals moving around the area. Some seemed to take a keen interest in the newcomers, prompting Marco to mutter to Renée, "These people are acting strange. Keep an eye on them."

Renée nodded. "Agreed. Something doesn't feel right."

As they all watched the surroundings with suspicion, the possibility of Council spies lurking among the locals weighed heavily on their minds. The sense of unease grew as they waited for Molly's report.

Inside the phone box, Molly frantically picked up the receiver and attempted to make a call, but her hopes were dashed when she discovered that the phone was dead. Frustrated, she left it and approached a local woman. Speaking to her in Spanish, she inquired about the phone's condition.

The woman shook her head and replied, "All the phones and the Internet are down. Even the radio."

"Everything is off? That doesn't seem normal."

The woman nodded gravely. "Yes, it's strange. It has never happened before."

Molly's heart sank at the realization that the entire town was cut off from communication.

Inside the back of the lead Rover, Wally began to notice unusual things as the group waited to continue their journey. He observed a street stall by the roadside that sold refreshments and newspapers. His attention became fixated on the water bottles stacked beside the cash register when something strange happened—the water began to bubble, as though it was boiling.

In the meantime, Number Four leaned in closer to Allison, his voice low. "You should have killed me back at the Citadel," he muttered. "It would have saved you all such pain. I mean, what is your plan now? You take me away from here and then what?"

Allison's response was straightforward. "He wants you alive," she explained, meaning Noah.

A hint of curiosity emerged in Number Four's voice as he probed further, "But what do *you* want, Allison?"

She turned to face him directly, her words laced with venom. "Isn't it obvious?" she said. "I want you dead."

At that moment, Molly returned to the lead vehicle, her expression filled with concern.

"The phones are all out. So's the Internet," she reported.

"Why's it getting so hot all of a sudden?" Santiago asked, his brow furrowed in confusion. "You feel it? Like the temperature is rising."

Right then, a fridge inside a fish stall began sparking, causing the fishmonger to cry out. Then, just as that happened, a man leaning against a metal post gazing at his phone began convulsing against it. The phone suddenly exploded in his hand, popping into a cloud of debris as the man continued to writhe.

Wally turned to them. "It can't be," he said.

"What can't be, Wally?" Marco asked.

Wally's thick eyebrows furrowed. "No, it can't. No."

"What can't?" Renée put to him.

Wally's voice trembled as he uttered one chilling word. "Microwaves."

The revelation sent a shiver down their spines. On the other side of the road, a metal fence began to glow red-hot, burning two men leaning against it and even setting a bird perched atop it on fire.

Back at the street stalls, the water continued to bubble, and suddenly, with a burst of sparks, the fridge exploded.

"Did you really think they'd let me get away?" Number

Four said to Allison in a voice filled with malice. "Don't you get it? They'd be willing to risk their own exposure in order to stop that."

Amidst the unfolding madness, an old man collapsed in the middle of the street, his cries of pain echoing through the air. The once tranquil town was now filled with the anguished sounds of people in distress, their skin itching, bodies wracked with pain.

"We need to get out of here," Wally urged the group. "Microwave radiation is absorbed by water, fats, and sugars, upon which it is converted into heat. Humans are full of water, fats, and sugars."

"You mean we're about to be cooked?" Marco asked.

"Exactly," Wally confirmed. "We need to find protection."

Allison turned to Number Four, who sat there with his eyes closed, seemingly accepting his fate. "You son of a bitch," she growled at him.

As panic engulfed the streets, people screamed and convulsed. A man clung to the roof of his car, his hand trapped as he was electrocuted by the microwaves conducting currents in the metal.

"We have to get out of the open," Wally instructed. "There!" He pointed at a large concrete apartment block in the distance.

Without hesitation, they abandoned the Rovers and began to run for cover. Panic and chaos reigned around them as people's flesh began to burn under the invisible assault of microwave radiation. The scramble for safety of the concrete building was frantic and desperate.

In the middle of the unfolding crisis, Number Four

picked his moment. In a sudden, violent jerk, he twisted, using his free arm to forcefully push against Allison's grip. The unexpected intensity of his action caused her to momentarily lose her balance, her fingers slipping from his skin, slick with sweat and the heat of the moment. This brief lapse was all he needed to wrench himself free, darting away like a cornered animal seeking its last chance at freedom. Or just to die alone somewhere.

Allison's instinct was to pursue, but Noah's firm hand on her shoulder halted her.

"We need to get into cover," he told her firmly when she turned to him.

But she wasn't going to leave it there. Resolved to get him dead or alive, Allison raised her pistol, the metal scorching against her skin due to the microwaves' omnipresence. Number Four was running straight down the road toward the sea. It shone in front of him like polished steel. He was dead no matter what. With a sharp crack, she fired, her aim true. As Number Four fell, the gravity of her action settled in. A big part of the Council was gone. But there was still so much more of it to pull down.

Allison discarded the overheated gun and joined the others, racing toward the apartment block's dubious sanctuary, the world ablaze. Amid screams and the surreal horror of people and objects ignited by the invisible threat, the group's desperate dash for cover underlined the direness of their situation, leaving them to confront the uncertain safety the apartment block promised against the microwave assault ravaging the town.

———

BACK ON THE USS *CHICAGO*, the crew's collective attention was fixed on the monitors displaying the alarming spread of microwave radiation from the base. Grim expressions adorned everyone's faces as they contemplated the situation.

Doc Parker stood before the captain, his voice steady yet filled with urgency. "It's radiation," he said. "Microwave radiation. And my people are out there in it with thousands of innocent victims. Are you just going to stand by, Captain?"

The captain's gaze had been focused elsewhere, distant and preoccupied, until the question was posed. Now his eyes locked onto Doc Parker with a sharp intensity. "What do you expect me to do?" he inquired.

With complete sincerity, Parker replied, "I expect you to hit that base with everything you have. You need to stop this. It's not just about our people anymore. It's about everyone in the vicinity of that damned machine."

The captain was visibly torn. "But firing at a nation's territory would be an act of war," he implored.

Parker's gaze remained unwavering as he presented his case. "You have no other choice. Thousands of people will die. Including our own people."

The captain, grappling with the weight of the decision set before him, asked the question that lingered in the room. "How do you know it's microwaves?"

Parker gestured toward the thermal images displayed on the screens. The heat signature had spread along the coastline, a damning piece of evidence. "Look at the evidence," he urged. "You can see that it's something serious just by the heat signature."

"But a giant microwave emitter? That's insane."

"Back at E & E," Parker went on, "we've been intercepting information on the Council for weeks. There are schematics for machines—killing machines. Things so evil you wouldn't cook them up in your wildest dreams. And one of those things is a giant microwave emitter capable of spreading electromagnetic radiation over large areas. Just like that."

He pointed at the video images showing smoke rising from parts of the coastline as the vegetation caught fire.

While the captain scrutinized the images, the shrink came out of Parker, his voice adopting a more composed and rational tone as he endeavored to engage the captain in reasoned dialogue. "Captain, you can see what's happening out there. This isn't just about military protocol; it's about preventing a massacre. We have the means to stop it. Can we really stand by and do nothing?" he pleaded.

The captain, torn between his duty and the dire circumstances, responded with a heavy heart, "Dr. Parker, I understand the stakes, but we can't simply disregard international law. There's a chain of command, rules of engagement to consider."

Parker's voice trembled with frustration as he continued to argue his case. "With all due respect, sir, those rules mean nothing if there are no survivors. This... this is genocide. We have a duty to do something. We're talking about a weapon that's indiscriminately killing everyone in its path. How can we justify inaction?"

———

THE BASEMENT'S air was thick, shadows cast by the flickering light of an old coal boiler in the corner stretched across the faces of Noah, his wife Sarah, and their companions, all nursing minor burns with grim determination. The space was claustrophobic, and the only sounds belonged to their low voices and the distant, muffled screams that seeped through the thick walls, a harsh reminder of the madness above.

Noah checked the doors and windows, ensuring they were sealed and covered against the invisible threat spreading across the town. "Stay away from anything metal," he advised, his voice steady but strained.

Sarah looked around, worry in her eyes. "Are we really safe down here?" she asked.

Wally, leaning against the cool concrete wall, nodded. "The density of this basement should shield us from the worst of the microwaves. We're certainly safer here than anywhere else above ground."

Despite his reassurance, a heavy silence settled over the group. Renée, gazing toward the sealed door, whispered, "Shouldn't we try to help those outside?"

The screams outside grew fainter, a haunting backdrop to their uncertain refuge. They knew they could not risk the exposure, the decision to stay put both a curse and a blessing. As they tended to each other's wounds, the reality of their situation weighed heavily upon them, each lost in their thoughts of the world outside, grappling with the knowledge of their narrow escape and the cost it had come at.

Allison stepped forward. "We should all..."

A sudden warmth in the air interrupted her and drew their attention to the old boiler, which was now radiating intense heat, its surface beginning to glow red. Wally, with a grave tone, alerted the group, "They're increasing the power."

———

ON THE SUBMARINE, the atmosphere was fraught, the crew poised in silent anticipation of their next orders.

"Look!" Parker pleaded with the captain, desperation sharpening his voice. "They're being burned alive out there. You have to do something."

The captain faced his communications officer, seeking any sliver of hope. "Anything, Ensign?"

"I'm afraid all communications are still being blocked, sir," the ensign replied. "There's no way to communicate with the Pentagon."

The captain bit his lip. The weight of the moment pressed down on him, the decision his alone to make in the silent void left by their isolation.

"This is your vessel, Captain. Without communication, this is your choice. I'm begging you. Make the right one," Parker implored, locking eyes with the captain, his plea hanging in the balance between desperation and hope.

After a moment heavy with the burden of command, the captain's resolve solidified. "Okay," he said, his voice firm with newfound determination. "Power up the cannon."

A murmur of approval rippled through the crew, a shared sense of purpose uniting them as they prepared to execute the command.

"Good man," Parker said, clapping the captain on the shoulder.

On the captain's order, mechanisms engaged, and with a smooth, hydraulic hiss, a large EMP cannon emerged from its concealed compartment on the dorsal fin of the USS *Chicago*, aligning itself with the distant silhouette of the Citadel.

"Cannon armed, Captain," the weapons officer informed him.

"Good," the captain said. "Now target whatever is making all that heat."

The targeting system locked on to the structure with unerring accuracy.

"The cannon is locked, Captain," the weapons officer bellowed.

With this final confirmation, the captain commanded, "Fire!"

The EMP cannon discharged a silent, invisible burst of electromagnetic energy. The pulse raced across the intervening space, a specter of disablement, until it collided with the rocky façade of the Cuban base.

The impact of the EMP was instantaneous. Within the base, the giant microwave emitter ceased its menacing hum. Screens flickered and died, lights dimmed into darkness, and the once-thrumming heart of the Council's operation fell silent, rendered inert by the cannon's pulse. The complex network of electronics that powered the emitter, and indeed the base itself, was effectively neutralized, leaving the structure of the Citadel a dormant giant amidst the crashing waves.

Back aboard the USS *Chicago*, the crew exhaled in collective relief. The successful deployment of the EMP cannon marked a pivotal moment in modern warfare. This had been what President Whitmore had shown Doc Parker and Molly underneath the Pentagon. This was the Chicago Project: America's own arsenal of EMP cannons.

"Let's see what effect that has," the captain finally said, breaking the silence. The crew leaned in, aware that the true repercussions of their daring move were yet to unfold.

FIFTY-FIVE

In the basement, the group of survivors began to notice a subtle change. The oppressive heat seemed to be waning, and the constant low-frequency hum of the deadly microwaves grew quieter. Tentative relief washed over them as they exchanged hopeful glances.

Noah and Sarah held each other close, their worried expressions gradually giving way to cautious optimism. Neil and Jenny shared a similar moment of silent relief, their fingers intertwined. Marco and Renée, the third couple in their group, shared a heartfelt embrace, their anxiety slowly ebbing away.

Santiago and Allison found themselves in each other's arms. Allison's voice quivered as she whispered, "Forgive me, Santiago."

Santiago responded in a gentle tone, "I always have, Allison. It is not me who cannot forgive, but Manuel. Imprisonment and the betrayal of his lover with his own brother have turned his heart to stone. It is he who harbors the inability to forgive, neither you nor me."

Molly and Wally, the two individuals who had been somewhat on the outskirts of the tightly-knit group, also shared a heartfelt hug. Despite their differences in age and backgrounds, they had formed a bond during their time of shared adversity.

As they pondered among themselves what might have caused the sudden cessation of the microwaves, Molly spoke up. "It must be Doc Parker," she announced. "He's the only one who could have intervened like this. The submarine he's on is armed with an EMP cannon. They must have used it to destroy the machine."

Allison admitted, "Maybe I was a little too hasty in scolding you earlier, Ms. Hanson. You may have saved us all."

With newfound hope and relief coursing through them, the group made their way up to the streets. What they found there was a scene of unimaginable devastation. Injured and lifeless bodies lay scattered everywhere, silent witnesses to the deadly onslaught of microwave radiation. In the wake of the attack, the once vibrant community was now marked by a terrible, all-consuming sense of despair and confusion. Bodies were scattered along the sidewalks, some motionless while others writhed in discomfort, their moans and groans a haunting soundtrack to the tragedy that had unfolded. The victims, overcome by the invisible assault, found themselves in a state of disarray, their expressions a mix of pain and bewilderment.

With heavy hearts, the group moved on, heading in the direction of the sea.

"Wait," Molly said, looking across at the Land Rovers still parked across the street. "The satellite phone."

She ran across to get it as the others continued onward. Arriving at the vehicle, she was relieved to discover the phone still working. It had spent the entire attack switched off and buried in the glovebox. Upon activating it, her relief deepened as its screen ignited, shining like a beacon.

While Molly tried to make contact with Doc Parker, Noah, his arm wrapped around Sarah and the two leaning heavily into each other, reached the lifeless form of Number Four. He was lying in the middle of the dusty street like discarded trash, a neat bullet hole between his shoulder blades. They gently turned him over and checked his pulse. "He's gone," Noah stated solemnly.

Allison came and stood beside them. "He's no more than a single cell," she observed with a cold detachment. "The rest of the monster is still very much alive."

Meanwhile, Molly managed to establish contact with Doc Parker. "Doc, it's Molly."

"Molly. Thank God. Is everyone okay?"

"Yes. We got Noah and the others. But we need help. We're in Santa Cruz del Sur. About eighty clicks west of the base."

"I know it. There's a marina. We'll send a boat."

"You need to send more than just a boat," Molly said, glancing around at all the casualties littering the street. "You need to send medical teams. These people need our help."

Doc Parker sighed down the line. "Molly. You must understand the difficulties in—"

"Doc!" she snapped. "These people need help."

He sighed again, this time with resignation. "Okay. I'll send what I can."

As the call ended, a sense of urgency enveloped the group. They knew help was on its way, but the gravity of the situation weighed heavily on their shoulders. They were survivors of an unprecedented attack, and now they bore witness to its aftermath.

Within hours, the coastal horizon was broken by the sight of three US Navy submarines surfacing near the marina. The first rays of hope shone with the arrival of these steel giants, signaling an end to the immediate isolation and despair the town had been thrust into. From the submarines, small boats were deployed, cutting through the water toward the marina with a sense of purpose and determination.

The submarine crew members, aware of the nature of the attack, were well-prepared but not in hazmat suits. Understanding that microwaves dissipate and do not leave a lingering contaminant in the same way chemical or biological agents might, they approached with standard military precision and medical readiness rather than a full contamination protocol.

As the boats docked, teams of Navy medics and engineers disembarked with medical supplies, communication equipment, and the essentials for establishing temporary shelters and aid stations. The medics, trained for rapid assessment and triage in disaster scenarios, immediately set to work. They moved among the victims with efficiency and compassion, providing first aid, stabilizing injuries, and preparing the more seriously wounded for transport back to the submarines where advanced medical facilities could offer better care.

Noah, Allison, and the rest of the group stood at the end of the quay, their eyes fixed on the last of the boats as it docked. Onboard this final vessel was the hawk-eyed Doc Parker. Stepping onto the quay, he approached them, his expression a mix of relief and stoic aloofness.

Standing before them, he began, "First and foremost, I want to tell you how relieved I am at seeing you all here, safe and sound. Noah," he added with a nod.

Noah nodded back.

"However," Parker went on, his gaze meeting Allison's, "we must address some decisions that were made. I understand the pressure you were under, but trust among us is paramount. Allison, Neil, Sarah, Wally"—he turned to them all—"your mission to rescue Noah should have included me from the start. Trust and teamwork are our bedrock. I shouldn't have had to send Molly to spy on my own people."

Parker now turned his attention on Molly. "As to Ms. Hanson's actions," he went on, "I hope you don't feel too betrayed. After all, her communication saved all of you today. So let's see it as an act of heroism. In our organization, trust is non-negotiable. We must stand united against those who seek to divide us."

"He's right," Allison said, stepping beside him. "I'm sorry, Doc. I should have brought you up to scratch from the get-go. I forgot the most important thing: that we're a team. That alone, we're vulnerable. Our enemies know this. They know our strength lies in unity. Let this experience reinforce our commitment to each other and our mission."

As the words resonated with the group, there were nods of understanding and agreement all around. Their expressions shifted from concern to determination. With a shared sense of purpose and unity, they prepared to board the boat, leaving behind the harrowing events of the past days, bound for safety and, hopefully, a brighter future.

FIFTY-SIX

THE TIRES OF THE DURANGO CRUNCHED ON THE gravel driveway, a sound that, after weeks of chaos, felt like a symphony of normalcy to Noah, Sarah, and Allison. The farmhouse stood as a beacon of peace, its familiar silhouette bathed in the golden hues of the setting sun, the shimmering waters of Temple Lake cradling it from behind.

Noah killed the engine, and for a moment, the trio sat in silence, each lost in their thoughts, allowing the reality of their return to sink in. The radiance of the sunset seemed to cast a healing glow over their radiation burns, now carefully wrapped in gauze, reminders of the ordeal they had just endured.

As they stepped out of the truck, the sound of the front door banging open broke their reverie. Norah charged out, her tiny legs propelling her with an energy that seemed to light up the entire world.

"Daddy! Mommy!" she squealed, her voice a balm to their weary souls.

Sarah barely had time to brace herself before Norah threw herself into her arms, followed by an equally enthusiastic hug for Noah. Allison watched, a warm smile spreading across her face as Norah turned to her, arms wide for an embrace that was no less fierce. "Aunty Allison!" she exclaimed.

"Have you been good for your sitters?" Sarah asked, smoothing back Norah's hair.

"Oh, she's been an angel, haven't you, Norah?" one of the sitters/bodyguards responded, her eyes twinkling with fondness for the child who had quickly stolen their hearts.

Norah's attention, however, was quickly drawn to the bandages peeking out from under their sleeves. "Why do you have those on?" she asked, her brow furrowing in concern.

Sarah and Noah exchanged a glance before Sarah refaced her daughter. "We forgot to put on sunscreen, and the sun was very hot," she explained, her voice light, though her heart ached at the fib. Protecting Norah from the harsh truth, for now, felt like the only kindness they could afford her.

Allison, ever the affectionate aunt, scooped Norah up into her arms, spinning her around as laughter filled the air.

A little later, as the sun dipped lower, painting the sky in streaks of orange and pink, the family and Allison found themselves gathered on the veranda, a scene of tranquil domesticity. They sat in comfortable silence, the kind that spoke of shared experiences and unspoken understandings. It was a moment of peace, hard-won and all the more precious for it.

Yet as the light faded and the first stars began to twinkle in the twilight sky, a shadow of foreboding crept into their midst. It was a silent acknowledgment that the world beyond their little farmhouse was still fraught with danger, and the peace they now enjoyed was but a fleeting reprieve.

Noah's gaze lingered on the horizon, where darkness began to swallow the last light of day. "We'll face whatever comes next," he said, more to himself than to the others. "Together."

Sarah reached for his hand, squeezing it tightly, a silent vow passing between them. Allison, sitting beside them, nodded in silent agreement. "That we will," she said.

Her presence beside them was a testament to the bond they had formed here in Kirtland, one that would see them through whatever storms lay ahead.

EPILOGUE

ONE WEEK LATER, THE CORRIDORS OF E & E BUZZED with the familiar hum of activity, but as Allison Peterson stepped through the doors for her first day back, the atmosphere shifted. Everyone stopped what they were doing and greeted her with a mix of congratulations and well-wishes.

Doc Parker awaited her in what was once again her office. With a solemn yet proud gesture, he handed the room over—a symbolic act signifying her regained control and leadership over E & E operations.

"Good to see you back where you belong, Allison," Parker said. "We've managed in your absence, but it's clear this place doesn't run the same without you."

Allison accepted her place behind the big mahogany desk, her expression composed yet grateful. "Thank you, Doc. I appreciate everything you've done to keep things on track while I've been away. Let's ensure a smooth transition."

The two of them didn't embrace; that wasn't their style. Instead, they shook hands, a mutual acknowledgment of respect passing between them. After that, Parker left.

Allison then got down to business, starting her computer and diving into the mundane grind that was daily life for the leader of E & E.

As the morning went on, more and more colleagues came into the office to welcome her back. However, as the day drew to a close, fewer and fewer came, and soon Allison was left alone to the sanctity of her newly reclaimed office.

About six p.m., her assistant informed her that she was going home. Now Allison was totally by herself.

She wasted no time in ensuring her complete privacy. Taking a small instrument disguised as a lipstick from her handbag, she activated an anti-surveillance device, a sophisticated piece of hardware designed to scramble any office cameras, rendering her next actions untraceable.

Seated behind her desk, she dialed a secure line on her encrypted cell phone. The call connected to one of the few people aware of her *true* allegiance.

"Number Six," she greeted, her voice adopting a tone of formality reserved for these covert communications.

"You were right after all, Number Eleven," came the reply from "Number Six," a voice cloaked in authority yet laced with an undercurrent of unease. "Number Four should have waited before going for Wolf."

"I told him as much," Allison responded. "Noah needs time to understand the potential of his role. Now Number Four is dead for having forgotten the virtue of patience."

"And you are sure that eventually Wolf will come over?"

Number Six pressed. "After all, he has caused us huge damage."

"The damage is all on Four," Allison affirmed. "I am confident that Noah will come over. Given time."

There was a brief silence. Then the conversation delved into the recent rescue operation that had thwarted their plans. "Have you discovered who it was that rescued Wolf and killed Four?" Number Six inquired, the question hanging between them like a sword of Damocles.

Using quantum cloaks, the assailants had rendered themselves nearly invisible, leaving the Council's surveillance with nothing but distorted shadows to analyze. Therefore, the Council were unaware who exactly had rescued Noah and the others. Meaning they were currently unaware that Allison, their newest member, was behind it; the Dragon Lady had been unable to risk Noah's death, no matter where her allegiances now stood.

"Yes, I've found out who it was," Allison replied, her voice steady. "Sarah Wolf, Neil Blessing, Wally Lawson, and Molly Hanson. Those at the Citadel were Sarah, Neil, and Molly. It was Wally and a Cuban contact of E & E's that the Citadel guards found at the shack."

Another silence lingered, one which made Allison nervous, Number Six clearly thinking things over.

Finally, he broke the silence. "Predictably," Number Six began. "Yet you ought to have anticipated this," he admonished, his words sharp as knives. "You were stationed at the Wolf residence, tasked with surveillance on the wife."

"I was taken by surprise," Allison retorted, her voice tinged with a defiant edge. "Sarah told me she was visiting her sister. I took her at her word and returned to my place."

"Convenient."

Without missing a beat, Allison responded, her frustration evident. "Are you insinuating something, Six?" she demanded over the phone.

A deliberate, heavy silence ensued, laden with contemplation. Eventually, Number Six resumed, "No accusation, Eleven. However, your assignment in Kirtland has barely commenced, and you've already overlooked two critical developments."

"Two?" Allison echoed, seeking clarification.

"Indeed. You missed both the wife's attempt to reach Wolf and the Americans' construction of their own EMP cannon."

Allison reddened. "In case you've failed to notice, I only came back to E & E this morning. Only today did I get security clearance to even know there was a meeting at the Pentagon at all. You'll have to excuse me for being uninformed about events that transpired during my detention by your people."

Number Six's tone darkened. "There's one thing you should never forget, Eleven," he snapped back. "You're one of us now. *We* are your people. Not E & E and not Noah Wolf. Not until *he* is one of us, too. So if you aspire to share in our future, you must fully embrace your role among us in the present."

The call ended. Allison Peterson, known to E & E as the Dragon Lady and now known to the Council as "Number Eleven," had laid the groundwork for a high-stakes game of chess—a game where Noah Wolf, E & E, and even the enigmatic Council were but pieces on a board she was determined to master.

As she sat there, she couldn't help thinking back to a night two weeks ago. On a platform in the middle of the Atlantic Ocean.

———

TWO WEEKS EARLIER, in the dimply lit confines of a room on the Council's platform, Allison Peterson had stood alone, her mind a whirlwind of strategy and anticipation. The room, stark and functional, served as the final staging ground for what was to be her most daring act yet—a meticulously orchestrated "rescue" that would cement her role within the intricate web of alliances and deceptions she navigated.

She began by covering herself in goose fat, the thick layer serving as a barrier against the biting cold of the Atlantic. This old method, though primitive, was effective and would help her survive her daring plunge. Next, she applied anti-shark repellent to her skin, the pungent smell filling the room, another layer of defense in the unpredictable waters below. These preparations, though physical, were as much a part of her mental conditioning, reinforcing her readiness for the ordeal she was about to face.

As she worked, Allison's mind raced. *This charade, necessary as it is, complicates everything,* she thought. Her feelings for Noah, complex and fraught with the tension of their intertwined destinies, added a layer of personal stakes to the operation. *To save him, to guide him, even if it means deceiving him... It's all for a greater purpose.*

The necessity of the act was clear to her: It was a means to an end, a way to remain embedded within the Council's machinations while protecting Noah and steering him toward his potential role in the larger scheme.

The heavy door creaked open, and Gruber, the giant tasked with executing the next phase of the plan, stepped in. His towering presence filled the room, his expression unreadable yet tinged with the gravity of what was to come.

"Eleven." Gruber's voice was low, "Wolf and the other one are climbing the platform."

Allison met his gaze, her determination steeling. "Then we begin," she replied, her voice steady.

"And you're sure it will work?" Gruber asked her.

Allison stared at him, her resolution unwavering. "Like I told your superiors, it is the best way to gain total control. E & E and Noah Wolf are all that stand in the Council's way. Gaining control of them both will leave it clear for the final act."

Gruber's nod was barely perceptible, a silent acknowledgment of the stakes at hand. As they exited the room, two soldiers, clad in the dark, unassuming gear of the Council's forces, fell into step behind them. The quartet moved with a purposeful stride, their footsteps reverberating off the metal corridors that led to the platform's edge.

Reaching an outer door, they paused, the silence between them thick with anticipation. Gruber lifted a finger to his ear, his attention focused on the incoming communication through his earpiece. His stance stiffened, a signal that the message received was both urgent and final. "Wolf and the other one are leaving now," Gruber relayed in a low grumble, turning to face Allison, the two soldiers looming ominously behind her. "Are you ready?"

Allison nodded once.

With a swift motion, Gruber thrust the door open to the fury of the storm. Rain and wind assaulted them instantly, the Atlantic's tumultuous waves a vast, churning expanse below. Without hesitation, the soldiers grasped Allison's arms, their grip firm as they propelled her forward, out into the tempest.

They dragged her to the platform's edge, where Gruber took over, his hand closing around her throat with a menacing firmness. Lifting her up, he held her out over the water, the icy depths writhing below her dangling feet.

Behind them, a figure emerged from the shadows— Noah Wolf, his expression one of shock, his eyes locked on Allison.

As she hung precariously over the churning waters, Allison met Noah's gaze. Fixing her eyes back on Gruber, she told him, "He's watching. Do it now!"

Gruber obliged, dropping her into the relentless Atlantic.

———

BACK IN HER OFFICE, Allison was reflecting on the orchestrated rescue. Lying in the submarine, her thoughts had been a mix of relief and calculation. The plan had unfolded as intended, but the implications of her actions were far-reaching. Her success in deceiving Noah, while ensuring her own survival, had solidified her position but also deepened the web of lies she navigated.

Allison's reflection was not just on the success of the immediate operation but on the broader horizon ahead. The path she had chosen was fraught with danger and duplicity, a tightrope walk between opposing forces. Yet within her, a resolve hardened, fueled by the knowledge that her actions, however morally ambiguous, were aimed at a greater good.

Her thoughts returned to Noah, the pivotal figure in the unfolding drama. *Noah, if only you understood the necessity of my actions. One day, perhaps, you will.* With that thought, Allison steeled herself for the challenges ahead, her role as both protector and manipulator more critical than ever.

**Don't miss IN THE GRIP OF DARKNESS. The
riveting sequel in the Noah Wolf Thriller series.**

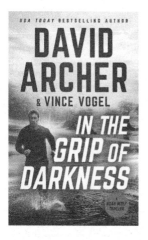

Scan the QR code below to purchase IN THE GRIP OF
DARKNESS.
Or go to: righthouse.com/in-the-grip-of-darkness

(Or scan the QR code below.)

DON'T MISS ANYTHING!

If you want to stay up to date on all new releases in this series, with this author, or with any of our new deals, you can do so by joining our newsletters below.

In addition, you will immediately gain access to our entire *Right House VIP Library,* which currently includes *THE WAY OF THE WOLF*—a prequel in the Noah Wolf series.

righthouse.com/email

(Easy to unsubscribe. No spam. Ever.)

ALSO BY DAVID ARCHER

Up to date books can be found at:

www.righthouse.com/david-archer

ROGUE THRILLERS

Gates of Hell (Book 1)

PETER BLACK THRILLERS

Burden of the Assassin (Book 1)

The Man Without A Face (Book 2)

Unpunished Deeds (Book 3)

Hunter Killer (Book 4)

Silent Shadows (Book 5)

The Last Run (Book 6)

Dark Corners (Book 7)

Ghost Operative (Book 8)

ALEX MASON THRILLERS

Origins (Prequel - Free)

Odin (Book 1)

Ice Cold Spy (Book 2)

Mason's Law (Book 3)

Assets and Liabilities (Book 4)

Russian Roulette (Book 5)

Executive Order (Book 6)

Dead Man Talking (Book 7)

All The King's Men (Book 8)

Flashpoint (Book 9)

Brotherhood of the Goat (Book 10)

Dead Hot (Book 11)

Blood on Megiddo (Book 12)

Son of Hell (Book 13)

NOAH WOLF THRILLERS

Way of the Wolf (Prequel - Free)

Code Name Camelot (Book 1)

Lone Wolf (Book 2)

In Sheep's Clothing (Book 3)

Hit for Hire (Book 4)

The Wolf's Bite (Book 5)

Black Sheep (Book 6)

Balance of Power (Book 7)

Time to Hunt (Book 8)

Red Square (Book 9)

Highest Order (Book 10)

Edge of Anarchy (Book 11)

Unknown Evil (Book 12)

Black Harvest (Book 13)

World Order (Book 14)

Caged Animal (Book 15)

Deep Allegiance (Book 16)

Pack Leader (Book 17)

High Treason (Book 18)

A Wolf Among Men (Book 19)

Rogue Intelligence (Book 20)

Alpha (Book 21)

Rogue Wolf (Book 22)

Shadows of Allegiance (Book 23)

SAM PRICHARD MYSTERIES

Fallback (Prequel - Free)

The Grave Man (Book 1)

Death Sung Softly (Book 2)

Love and War (Book 3)

Framed (Book 4)

The Kill List (Book 5)

Drifter: Part One (Book 6)

Drifter: Part Two (Book 7)

Drifter: Part Three (Book 8)

The Last Song (Book 9)

Ghost (Book 10)

Hidden Agenda (Book 11)

SAM AND INDIE MYSTERIES

Aces and Eights (Book 1)

Fact or Fiction (Book 2)

Close to Home (Book 3)

Brave New World (Book 4)

Innocent Conspiracy (Book 5)

Unfinished Business (Book 6)

Live Bait (Book 7)

Alter Ego (Book 8)

More Than It Seems (Book 9)

Moving On (Book 10)

Worst Nightmare (Book 11)

Chasing Ghosts (Book 12)

Serial Superstition (Book 13)

CHANCE REDDICK THRILLERS

Innocent Injustice (Book 1)

Angel of Justice (Book 2)

High Stakes Hunting (Book 3)

Personal Asset (Book 4)

CASSIE MCGRAW MYSTERIES

What Lies Beneath (Book 1)

Can't Fight Fate (Book 2)

One Last Game (Book 3)

Never Really Gone (Book 4)

ABOUT US

Right House is an independent publisher created by authors for readers. We specialize in Action, Thriller, Mystery, and Crime novels.

If you enjoyed this novel, then there is a good chance you will like what else we have to offer! Please stay up to date by using any of the links below.

Join our mailing lists to stay up to date -->
righthouse.com/email
Visit our website --> righthouse.com
Contact us --> contact@righthouse.com

facebook.com/righthousebooks
x.com/righthousebooks
instagram.com/righthousebooks